MW01133899

A Warden's Worry

By
Randall Probert

A Warden's Worry
by Randall Probert

Copyright © 2005 Randall Probert

www.randallprobertbooks.net
email: randentr@megalink.net

Second Edition 2018

Art and Photography credits:

Front cover illustration by
Ed Palmer, Andover, Maine

The Warden's Worry Streamer fly,
pictured on the front and back of the cover,
provided by Alvin Theriault, Patten, Maine

Author's photo, page 271, by Patricia Gott

ISBN: 978-1722692308

Printed in the United States of America

Published by
Randall Enterprises
P.O. Box 862
Bethel, Maine 04217

Acknowledgements

I first met Phyllis Goff in the spring of 1978, while she and a friend from Virginia were fishing the East Branch of Howe Brook. From that encounter, through the years, Phyllis has shared many stories about life in the village. She showed me many old photographs of the village and scenes around St. Croix Lake. She gave me keys to her house there at the village and said, "Here— use the house, don't let it go to waste." I did use it, for vacations as well as a place to get out of the weather. I can still recall the many foggy nights that I spent on the porch steps or in a lawn chair behind the white birch trees, listening and watching for illegal hunting.

Thank you, Phyllis, for your friendship, your generosity and your help with this book.

I would also like to thank Roy Russell, Micky Dumain, Gerry Lewis and Stanley Pierce for all of your stories about life at the village and there are too many others to list here. Parnell's cabin on the knoll was actually Stan Pierce's cabin.

Dan Glidden's story about the tree-climbing hunters was actually true, except the names were changed to protect the innocent. Thank you, Dan, for letting me use your story.

And special thanks to Johie Farrar for your help with typing, the many rewrites and your patience with misspelled words and my terrible handwriting. And thank you, Amy Henley, for your help editing this for a second edition. And I want to thank Laura Ashton for formatting this for printing.

More Books by Randall Probert

A Warden's Worry

Preface

A *warden's worry* is traditionally known as a fly or streamer used in the sometimes complicated art of fishing. I say complicated, because fishing, at one time, used to be enjoyable, with the expectancy of eating a fat orange-bellied trout or silvery salmon for supper, or with eggs and toast at breakfast. There wasn't the worry of accidentally violating one of the special regulations that have invaded our waters like a plague. No longer can an enthusiast simply take a pole and a can of worms and head for a favorite and secret fishing hole, but now one must be well versed in the blue ribbon fish regulations—many difficult to understand terms, their meanings as applied to fishing and to know and understand the location of lines of demarcation. That sounds a bit like a military term, but it now applies to fishing.

I have sort of wandered from my original point. A warden's worry in this book will be about a game warden's most ardent adversary, a poacher—a wily, cunning and sometimes desperate individual who enjoys immensely playing a joke on the local game warden or a close friend.

The story is not about any particular individual. Parnell Purchase is fictional as are many of his escapades. So, too, is Parnell's closest friend, John Corriveau. But many of the characters in this book are real people and they are portrayed in the book as they are in real life.

Howe Brook Village did exist at one time and I have tried to capture some of the village's history and the character of that quaint little spot in Maine's history.

Chapter 1

Peace had finally been declared in Korea after a long series of lengthy negotiations. And then only after the newly elected President, Dwight D. Eisenhower, threatened to unleash nuclear bombs on North Korea and China if some agreement wasn't settled at the peace talks. Finally, both sides agreed upon the former line of demarcation at the 38th parallel. But all was not quiet. The allies had stopped all movements, but the North was still causing problems along the parallel—enough so that allied troops had to form a defensive line along the parallel, with orders not to shoot unless a North Korean had crossed the line and was firing at the allied troops.

It was Captain Peasley's job to protect a portion along this parallel. He and his squadron of forty men. The North Koreans would take pot-shots everyday across the line, occasionally hitting an allied solider. Captain Peasley had requested night duty. There was something about the darkness and the eerie quiet that he found exciting.

It was early July 1953. There was no moon, total darkness. He was sweating from the high temperature and humid air. His senses on full alert. He would rather be thinking about his girl, Alana Wilcox. But those thoughts he had to push out of his mind and concentrate on his responsibilities here. His life and his men's life depended on it.

During his third year in college, he had enrolled in the ROTC program and had intended at that time to make a career in the Army. He and Alana would be married after his tour in South Korea. But now, eighteen months later, he had had enough of Army life, and too much senseless killing. Too many close friends dead. Their screams of agony still echoing in his head. And too much human deprivation and suffering. He was tired of war and had had all he wanted of it. All he wanted now was to get home, marry Alana and buy the fishing boat that he had been dreaming about.

"Bill, you stay here. I'm going to work my way up the line and check on the others," Peasley said as he picked up his rifle and started inching his way along the barricade.

"Okay, Captain, you coming back?" Bill whispered.

"Maybe later. Keep your head down and don't fall asleep."

There was a little sporadic shooting from the other side but nothing serious. The North Koreans were firing blindly into the darkness trying to unnerve the Americans.

Captain Peasley didn't return that night to Private Olson's position. He stopped and talked with each man along the line, making sure each man was alert and offering encouragement. He spent a few minutes with each and then took up a position beyond the last man.

Parnell Peasley arrived in South Korea during the winter of 1951, a second lieutenant, shortly after finishing his basic training. Before adjusting to his new surroundings and the war, his entire squadron was ordered out on patrol near Inchon. Colonel Phillips had received information that the North Koreans were preparing for a new offensive and were actively transporting supplies each day.

Captain Newall had sent Thomas and Jones out on point and they had been ambushed by a North Korean scouting party. In the ensuing battle all but one of the scouting parties had died and the survivor had escaped and was heading back, probably to his company commander. Captain Newall had been fatally wounded and Private Siems had received a belly wound.

Sergeant Claimore said, "Lieutenant, we should retreat before that bastard brings his entire company down on top of us!"

Parnell just stood there thinking. He hated to run back with his tail between his legs.

"Lieutenant, did you hear me?"

"Yes, Sergeant, I heard. And we're not retreating." He looked around at his men. "Bauber, did you ever shoot any gators at night in the swamps of Louisiana?"

"Sah, that's illegal" Bauber replied.

"That's not what I asked."

"Yes, Sah, a few." He was more surprised by the question than any one else.

"Hawkens, where are you from?" Parnell asked

"Black Hills of South Dakota, sir. Standing Rock Indian Reservation."

"What's your Indian name?" Parnell asked

"Don't Eat Dog. My grandfather gave it to me, sir."

"Claimore, we're going to set up an ambush right here."

"Ambush, sir?" Sergeant Claimore asked questioningly.

"Yes, Sergeant. We're going to show them how Crazy Horse defeated Custer."

"Yes, sir."

"Sergeant, I want two of your best sharp shooters on top of that bluff. I want three of the men with BARs up by that point." And he pointed. "They'll close the door behind Charlie when he follows us through in the ravine. The rest, Sergeant, I want spread out and dug in along here. And I mean dug in. So an eagle flying overhead can't see you. Am I clear on that, Sergeant?"

"Yes, sir. What will you be doing, sir?" Claimore asked.

"Bauber, Hawkens and I will be the rabbit. We'll let Charlie chase us down this ravine. When Charlie passes the BARs I want them to close the back doors. You'll be dug in here and we'll block their front. I want everyone dug in, in ten minutes."

"Lieutenant, what happens if Charlie shows up with some heavy stuff?"

"As long as they don't have tanks, our surprise with hand grenades should be enough."

"Bauber, Hawkens, you're with me. Come on." Parnell said almost cheerfully. Parnell took the lead.

"Why Don't Eat Dog?" Parnell asked.

"When I was born we were at our summer rendezvous camp. One of the younger men was chasing a dog through the camp and my grandfather stepped out just as the dog was caught and my grandfather hollered, 'Don't Eat Dog.' The young man had intended to eat him. That became my tribal name."

They all were a little apprehensive about stumbling onto the enemy. But twenty minutes later Charlie was spotted. Coming towards them.

"Okay, we'll hold them here. Only briefly. When the shooting starts, Bauber, you run back about fifty yards and give us cover fire. Then Hawkens will go back and join you and you two will cover for me. We'll leap frog like this back to the ambush sight. We'll make them think that there is only the three of us."

They didn't have long to wait. As soon as the shooting began, Bauber retreated fifty yards and provided cover fire for Hawkens and then Lieutenant Peasley. This was working well. When they had retreated back to the ambush site, Sergeant Claimore had his men so well entrenched that Parnell didn't even know he had reached the sight until the BARs started firing. Then all hell broke loose.

The skirmish was over almost before it got started. Parnell didn't lose anyone and only had a few minor wounds. The North Koreans lost thirty-one dead, fourteen badly wounded and six prisoners.

When writing his report, Lt. Peasley was brief and stayed more with the overall view of the incident. But Sergeant Claimore was more thorough, giving credit for the success of the battle fully to Lieutenant Peasley. Colonel Phillips awarded the Silver Star to Lieutenant Peasley and the Bronze Star to Privates Bauber and Hawkens. And Lieutenant Peasley was promoted to Captain.

Before leaving Korea he would be wounded again, in the left shoulder, and receive the Purple Heart. And once this night was over, Captain Peasley would be rotated back to the States.

In the meantime, Parnell had a great deal of time to seriously think about his fate to be. One thing was for sure, he never wanted to experience another war where politicians disregarded human life so totally. He had literally seen hundreds upon hundreds of dead bodies. A few had become close friends.

It was decided he would resign his commission and return home, to Boothbay Harbor, Maine, and the only girl he had ever loved, Alana.

* * * *

A week later Captain Peasley flew into Camp Pendleton, California, and then to Fort Dix, New Jersey. There he would stay for another two weeks while he undertook readjustment classes in public relations. Sometimes it wasn't so easy turning off the killing instinct that is acquired while fighting the dirty, bloody battles of war.

Parnell had not said anything to Alana about his decision to return home to the life he knew best and forget all about the military. Only that he had been rotated back to the States. He wanted to surprise her by suddenly showing up at her doorstep.

The day finally arrived when he signed his discharge papers, adorned civilian clothes and boarded a Greyhound bus for Portland, Maine.

Chapter 2

Parnell transferred to a local bus in Portland for the final ride to Boothbay. It was late in the evening when the bus pulled to a stop next to the post office. As he had expected, no one was there to greet him. Why should there be? No one knew he was coming home. He shouldered his duffel bag and picked up his suitcase. It was only a short walk to Alana's parents' home.

As he was approaching the house, he noticed an unfamiliar vehicle sitting in the driveway. But then why not, he had been away for more than two years. Alana walked out onto the porch followed by a man about his age. Alana didn't recognize him until she and this other fellow were at the driver's door. Parnell was standing by the rear bumper.

There was a long embarrassing moment. Parnell's face started to show signs of rage. Alana became very nervous and Burt didn't know what to do. Only that he would like to have crawled into a hole and out of sight.

Finally Alana broke the silence, "I'm sorry, Parnell, you had to find out this way. If only I had known when you were coming home." There, now it was his fault for coming home and trying to surprise her. She continued, "It wouldn't have worked anyhow, Parnell. Can you see that? I can't be married to the Army. You have no idea how much I have suffered while you were in Korea."

Parnell just stood there, heartbroken, as his life ebbed away before him. He was speechless. There was absolutely nothing he could say or wanted to say at that precise moment. He picked up his gear and walked off. He went to the local tavern and dropped his gear inside the door and sat down at the bar.

He started drinking beer but soon changed to straight whiskey. Beer wasn't strong enough to make him as anesthetized as he wanted to be. He drank not as a man wanting to quench a thirst, but someone with a deep-rooted problem.

His last drink he spilled on his shirt and dropped the glass on the floor as he lay his head on the bar.

"Hello, Richard? This is Harry down at the Water Front Tavern. Your brother Parnell is here, passed out on the bar. I have to close in thirty minutes. Can you come get him?"

"You said Parnell? Harry? Okay, Harry, I'll be right down."

A few minutes later Richard was at the tavern; he put his arms under Parnell's and lifted him to his feet. "Come on, Captain Parnell, you have had enough for one night. Thanks, Harry," as he helped his brother out to his car. "You must have found out about Alana and Burt." No reply. "Come on, solider boy, let's go home to Mother."

* * * *

Parnell woke up the next morning thirsty, with a headache and rolling thunder in his stomach and a heart shot all to hell. He stumbled downstairs to the kitchen. "Hi, Ma. I had wanted my homecoming to be more than this. Sorry."

"Parnell, we all knew Alana had taken up with someone else. I just couldn't bring myself to tell you."

"How long are you home for, Parnell?" Richard asked.

"For good. I quit the Army. I'm not going back."

"Why in heavens name? What happened to you, son? When you left here you were going to make the Army your life."

"I changed my mind, that's all. I – I – I saw too much senseless killing. Lost too many friends."

Parnell's sister Becky arrived at lunchtime. She hugged her brother and kissed and hugged him again. "Tim couldn't come, Parnell; he had to work."

"That's okay."

"What will you do now?" Becky asked.

"I saved a lot of my military pay and I think I'd like to buy a fishing boat like Dad."

"Yeah, and that killed him when he was still a young man," his mother answered.

"Well, that's what I want to do," he replied.

* * * *

That evening after supper, Parnell went back to the Water Front Tavern. After several drinks he met up with a high school buddy, Sam Chase. They had a few drinks and then Sam asked, "What are you doing tomorrow, ole buddy, now that you're not soldiering anymore?"

"Not much of anything."

"How about you and me go to the race track at Union. The horses, they start running tomorrow. It's an entertaining way to spent what could be a rather boring day. Might make some money on the horses too. What d'ya say?"

Parnell didn't return home that night. After the barkeep threw he and Sam out, he slept it off on the grass lawn next to the library. When he awoke the next morning Sam was there with his car. "Come on, ole buddy, you make a pretty good drunk for a solider boy."

"I ain't no solider boy. Not anymore."

"Okay, okay—you want to eat before we get on the way, or pick up something on the road?"

"I don't feel much like eating right now. Let's eat later," Parnell said as he rubbed his stubbly chin.

During the ride to the Union Fair Grounds, Parnell's mind was blank. He was more zombie than life. Even though his eyes were open, he could only see total blackness.

At the racetrack they each ate a steamed hotdog and washed it down with a beer. Then they moved to one of the ticket windows. Parnell put twenty dollars on the number five horse. "Why did you bet on the five-horse? I told you the three-horse was a sure winner," Sam said.

"I don't know—guess I just liked the number five." Sam made his bet on number three and they found seats in the grandstand.

The number five horse won the first race with number three trailing by a head. Sam looked at Parnell almost disgustedly, then he grinned and said, "At least one of us won"

Parnell was not so lucky after that. In fact before the end of the day he had lost all of his money. And now he was really hungry. Sam had only slightly better luck. He had enough money left to purchase a sandwich for both of them and the rest bought enough gasoline to get them back to Boothbay Harbor.

* * * *

During the next two months each week was much like the first. Except in different towns—Bangor, Scarborough, Lewiston, Farmington, and the last race of the year was at Fryeburg where he and Sam were arrested for public intoxication and for fighting.

Parnell had lost all of his dignity and character that he had had as Captain Peasley. Those days were gone and would never return.

By the middle of October, Parnell had lost all of his money. Even his savings that was going to buy his fishing boat. He was penniless, no job and most days he was in a drunken stupor. "Parnell," his mother said, "I want you out of my house today. Look at yourself—you have become a drunken bum. Penniless and dirty."

Parnell left without argument. He put his clothes in his duffel bag and closed the kitchen door behind him without saying anything. He walked down to the fishing wharfs. Besides the military, the only other thing he knew how to do well was lobstering and fishing. He found Rusty busy at work repairing his boat.

Rusty looked up from his work and was surprised to see Parnell standing there. "Hello, Parnell. You going somewhere?"

"Looking for work, actually. You going out soon?"

"Tomorrow, if I can complete the repairs to this capstan winch. I need a good hand. Someone who has been out there before. Someone I can trust. Joel is going out, but Davy quit."

"I'd like the job, Rusty," Parnell almost pleaded.

"You're a good man in a boat, Parnell. But I have one strict rule: you stay sober and no booze on the boat."

"I won't let you down."

"I hope not. You can store your gear on board and give me a hand with this capstan. If you need a place to stay tonight, you can stay on board."

* * * *

Parnell awoke early the next morning aboard the fishing boat. He had been true to his word. He had stayed away from any liquor. Rusty arrived early also, probably to check on Parnell more than anything. "After breakfast we'll load our supplies and motor over to the processing plant for a ton of ice.

"Parnell, you know the way out to sea as well as I. You take the wheel; I'm going below for a while. Joel is a good deck hand, but he couldn't navigate his way around a traffic circle."

"Where exactly are we going?" Parnell asked

"Cape Sable off Nova Scotia, and then East to Sable Island. Reports have it that cod and haddock fishing is good this year just beyond the island. We'll stay out until the holds are filled. Then back to Boothbay. Unload, and lay over just long enough to resupply and back to Sable Island. We'll do that all winter until the lobsters start in the spring."

The first day of fishing was productive. The nets were full each time they were pulled in. It was a messy, smelly job, cleaning the fish, but once cleaned they were laid out in ice and frozen. Each fish meant money in their pockets.

With each new day there was less and less alcohol in his system. He was back to his usual self. But instead of thinking of Alana and the hurt she had caused him, Parnell was again thinking of the war and all those young men who died trying to defend Old Glory... and the thousands of North Koreans and Chinese soldiers who died so senselessly. He was sure of one thing now—he would never return to the military. But he was a commissioned officer and in time of war, he could be reinstated. He would have to do something about that, but what? He was thinking as he stood against the railing watching a cloud shadow the full moon.

* * * *

Rusty and his crew returned soon with their holds full of cod and haddock, resupplied and back to sea again. The fishing was good and no one wanted a break, just now.

Every ten days that fall they returned with a boatload of fish. At Christmas, Rusty returned in time for Christmas dinner and then back to sea that evening. Parnell and Joel stayed aboard the boat and resupplied her.

The last half of the winter wasn't as productive as the first, but Rusty and his crew did okay. When the winter fishing was over, Joel left the fishing wharfs to enlist into the Army. He had had enough of handling smelly fish and going to sleep each night smelling like a fish. Parnell—he stayed aboard the fishing boat and spent the spring repairing lobster traps, nets and cutting fish bait for lobstering.

"Parnell, sit down a minute." Rusty said as he mended an old net. "You were good to your word, Parnell. All winter you went without drinking. I really didn't think that you could stay off the booze. You going to fish for the rest of your life, or what?"

Parnell picked up a lobster trap and was looking at it. "I don't know for sure. When I was in Korea that's all I wanted. My own boat—but then Alana was part of the plan also. I just don't know now."

"Why in the hell did you ever quit the military? You had it made there. You were on easy street."

"I saw too much senseless killing. Too many young men in my company died for nothing."

Nothing more was said about the military. But that conversation put ideas or perhaps more like questions in Parnell's head. Did he really want to fish for the rest of his life? If not, Then what am I going to do?

* * * *

A month went by and all of the traps and nets had been repaired, and enough fish bait cut to last the summer. The price for wholesale lobsters was low just going into the season. But that was the usual trend. For the first five days, Rusty and Parnell set out the lobster traps and tended on the sixth and seventh. They continued that schedule, five days setting or moving traps, two days tending.

The catch was good but the wholesale price kept dropping a few cents each week. Rusty didn't like the way this trend was looking. "If the prices continue to drop, Parnell, we'll have to pull our traps and quit for the summer. I can't lobster at a loss each week."

Every night Rusty went home to his family but Parnell refused to return to his mother's house. He had made a fool of himself and she had hurt his feelings. No, it would be best to stay away, so he did. He slept every night on board the fishing boat.

By the first of August, the wholesale price on lobster had dropped so low that many other fishermen were already pulling their traps for the season. "We might as well pull also, Parnell. We can't continue to fish at these prices."

It took them two weeks to pull all the traps. What lobsters they did have in the traps were released. When the work was all done, Rusty said, "Parnell, we had a good winter. I'm going to haul the boat out and take it over to Harry's to have her refitted, and the engine rebuilt. You'll need to find another place to sleep for a while."

"Maybe I'll go up to the blueberry fields for a while. The air is good and there surely won't be any smelly fish around."

"Good luck, Parnell. We'll leave for the winter fishing

grounds first of October. Take my advice and stay away from the booze. You don't handle it so well."

"See you in the fall, Rusty."

* * * *

Parnell boarded a bus in Boothbay for Cherryfield. There would be many stops along the way. He had seen an advertisement in the newspaper about blueberry growers in Hancock County needing rakers. Seven cents a pound and lodging would be provided at the fields. That sounded like exactly what he was looking for. The fields would be a welcome relief from rough seas and smelly fish. The bus left the terminal in Boothbay at 9:00 a.m. and six hours later he was in Cherryfield, Maine.

There he found another, older school bus with a handwritten sign on it, Blueberry Workers. When the bus left the terminal, it was loaded. Of course it was a much smaller bus than the Greyhound. It was a ten-minute ride to the fields or barrens, as the foreman, Nelson Rupert, was calling them.

Lodging at the barrens consisted of old World War II Army tents. But at least they were on wooden platforms. The meals were communal, cooked over an open fire pit. Parnell found an empty tent in the back, away from the crowds and next to the tree line. He hoped he wouldn't have to share. As he unpacked his gear, he was reminded of his earlier visit at Fort Dix, New Jersey, during basic training. As hard as he tried to forget his former Army life, there were times when those memories would slip back into his conscious mind. Yeah, if he had stayed in he probably would have been promoted to the rank of major by now. But there was little sense of thinking about probabilities.

Everyone was awakened the next morning at daylight. After a quick breakfast of black coffee and oatmeal, everyone walked the center road that separated the field; boxes and crates were stacked at the center of the road. The field was divided into square sections with string. Each person was assigned a section and told not to leave it until it had been thoroughly raked. And there would be an inspector to check.

Parnell didn't have to work too long before he realized that this wasn't going to be as easy as he had first thought. It was a backbreaking job and at seven cents a pound he would have to work like a dog in order to make any money at all. And he did work hard or fast. Whichever. By lunchtime he had already cleaned two sections and had started on a third. The foreman hollered over, "Hey, Parnell, you have a hundred and six pounds already."

Parnell began to laugh. "All that for seven dollars and forty-two cents."

Lunch break was as short or as long as you wanted. Parnell finished his sandwich and water and went right back to work. By evening he had a total of two hundred and fifteen pounds. About fifteen dollars and change. "Well, it's better than working in a canning factory."

For supper that night—and every night—the workers had beans and bread and watermelon for dessert. He slept well that night. He was exhausted. The camp was quiet that night. Everyone was tired.

Parnell worked hard each day trying to rake more than the day before. By the end of Friday he had raked just over eleven hundred pounds for the week. Seventy-eight dollars and change. That night many of the workers went into town for booze or to spend their money foolishly. Parnell lay on his cot, with the tent flap open looking at the stars and thinking about his life so far, and what he wanted out of his life. "Raking blueberries surely isn't it and neither is life on a fishing boat." He laughed a cynical laugh then and said, "Maybe Alana did me a favor after all."

He rolled over and tried to go to sleep. But sleep was impossible. One, there was too much noise in the camp, and two, he was still thinking about what he wanted to do in life.

By morning he had decided that life in a tent and blueberries wasn't what he wanted. But neither did he know what direction he should turn. He packed his gear and without saying good-bye to anyone, he left the barrens.

He walked to town and found the train station. That would be as likely a place as any to find where his destiny should go. He didn't know why but he wanted to go north, although he had never been north of Bangor. He stood back from the ticket counter studying the schedules posted on the wall. One town stood out above all else. Howe Brook Village. He didn't know exactly where that was but he would find out.

"One ticket to Howe Brook, please?" Parnell asked.

"That'll be twenty-three fifty," the ticket agent said. He began to fill out the ticket. "Your name, please."

"Parnell," —just then Parnell saw a sign on the counter in front of him that read Purchase Your Ticket Early; he started to read out loud and said—"Purchase."

The ticket agent interrupted him and said, "Mr. Purchase."

"Yes, Parnell Purchase."

"Mr. Purchase, your train leaves the North Gate in twenty minutes," the agent said.

"Thank you," Parnell replied.

Twenty minutes later, Parnell was seated in the coach car smiling radiantly to himself. "Parnell Purchase, I like that." No one else in the car could possibly understand why he was smiling so happily. There was no more Parnell Peasley, Captain Peasley. He would never again be recalled to fight in another bloody war.

"Excuse me, sir, your ticket please," the ticket conductor asked.

Parnell gave him his ticket and the conductor punched a hole in it and handed it back. "Thank you, Mr. Purchase, have a nice trip."

"Yes, thank you."

Chapter 3

As the train started to slow on the approach to the Bangor terminal, the conductor came back to speak to Parnell. "Mr. Purchase, if you are going on to Howe Brook Village, you'll have to switch trains here; you go into the terminal and look for the B&A North Gate. That will take you to Howe Brook."

"Thank you. Where exactly is Howe Brook?"

The conductor turned back around with a puzzled look on his face, "I don't know. I have never been there. All I know is what your ticket tells me."

"Thanks," Parnell replied.

He found the B&A Terminal and the North Gate was already open. "You're just in time," the ticket agent said. "Your train is leaving in five minutes."

"Thank you," and Parnell boarded the northbound train and found an empty seat away from the other passengers.

The ticket conductor was coming up the aisle checking tickets. "Your ticket, sir."

Parnell handed him his ticket, "Where exactly is this Howe Brook Village?"

"It is in the County—Aroostook County. On the shore of St. Croix Lake about twenty miles north of Oakfield or about one-hundred-and-twenty miles north of Bangor. Why may I ask are you going there if you don't even know where it is?"

Parnell smiled and said, "The adventure."

"Thank you, Mr. Purchase. Have a nice adventure."

The train made many stops along the way. It seemed that just as the train reached its maximum speed it would start to decelerate as it approached another stop. But he was in no particular hurry. He had no idea what to expect at Howe Brook Village, what he was going to do once he arrived, or how long he would stay. This was a new adventure for him and a totally new life—Mr. Parnell Purchase.

* * * *

At six-thirty that evening, the train started to decelerate as they were approaching Howe Brook Village. The ticket conductor said, "Mr. Purchase, this is your stop."

But this was nothing more than a stop over in the middle of the woods. He didn't even know but perhaps he should stay aboard and buy a round trip ticket back to Bangor. But, "Well, I've come this far; might as well see the town."

"Good luck to you, Mr. Purchase," the conductor said.

Parnell stepped off the B&A coach car and stood on the platform for a few minutes taking in the scenery and breathing the fir- and spruce-scented air. It was the sweetest smelling air he had ever breathed. The air was clear but hot. There were several log houses across the tracks that he could see, and the station house seemed to be part hotel and a general store in back. There was a sawmill, but that was quiet, everybody probably at home eating supper.

He picked up his duffel bag and walked off the platform and headed towards the lake. There was no breeze and the water surface was like glass. "Maybe I'll stay awhile." Parnell could feel roots here. *Why?* He didn't even know. But he could surely feel the character of Howe Brook Village in the air.

He walked back to the station house and crossed the tracks and walked down what had to be called Main Street. There was a schoolhouse. It looked like a one-room schoolhouse at that. Painted red. A rather spacious livery stable that seemed a little out of place until he looked around again and saw very few automobiles. Behind the livery stable was a field or pasture and several workhorses were feeding. Adjacent to the pasture was a hay field. Part of the field had been mowed recently and new grass was beginning to grow back. The smell of hay lingered in the air around the field. Parnell sat down under a maple tree at the edge of the mowed field. He could just see the lake over the treetops. The little village was quiet. So quiet he lay back and was soon asleep.

The night air was warm and the only sounds were those of nature—loons on the lake, an owl overhead and something chasing mice in the hayfield. But Parnell was not aware of any of this as he slept beneath the maple tree.

At precisely seven o'clock the next morning the mill's steam whistle blasted its signal that the day's work was commencing. Parnell awoke with a start. His heart beat rapidly until he awoke enough to understand what the noise was all about. He rubbed sleep from his eyes, stood and stretched, and then lifting his duffel bag to his shoulder walked back to Main Street crossing the Little Canada Brook. He stopped to splash cold water on his face and wash his hands. He was hungry and decided to have breakfast at the station house.

As he walked along Main Street towards the station house he could just faintly hear the rumbling sound of a train on the tracks. Before he got to the station house the southbound from Ashland pulled into the village and passengers were getting off. There, the engineer switched to a sidetrack to pick up more freight cars loaded with sawed lumber. This was all interesting, but Parnell was hungry.

The cook-waiter took his order and said, "I'll be about ten minutes, Mr. Purchase." He smiled. People already knew who he was.

"I don't suppose you'd have today's newspaper?"

"On the counter. They just came in with the train."

That surprised him. Today's paper available way out here from nowhere this early in the day. He scanned through the headlines, but found little interest in what was happening around the world.

As he waited for his breakfast, he began to think of his financial situation. All he had with him was the money he had earned while raking blueberries. He had money in the Maine Savings Bank in Boothbay and he probably could have some transferred to a local bank up here someplace. He had deposited most of his earnings from the fishing boat, totaling twenty-seven-hundred dollars. He would make do with what he had and if the need be, he could get a job here at the village.

When he had finished his breakfast he asked the cook-waiter, "What's your name? You obviously know mine."

"Henry, where can I leave my duffel bag, I'd like to walk around some."

"You can leave it on the platform outside. No one will bother it. You staying long?"

"I don't know. Have to be somewhere. Thanks."

Parnell left his duffel bag on the platform and started strolling through the village. One thing he noticed right off, none of the vehicles he had seen so far had a license plate. But then again, one wouldn't be required in the woods. As long as it never left the woods. *But surely these people must get out to town sometimes?*

He crossed the bridge over the Little Canada Brook and decided to see where it went. On the left side of the tracks beyond the hayfield where he had spent the night was another small clearing and a vegetable garden in the middle. He heard a screen door slap close at a nearby cabin.

Just then he heard someone holler, "Hey you! What you want? What you doing around my cabin?" He stepped out of the bushes then and confronted Parnell.

Parnell was astonished. He wasn't sneaking around. This guy who stepped out of the bushes was wearing a green and gray flannel shirt, sleeves rolled up. Gray pants and leather boots. But what was most peculiar was the black knit hat he was wearing. The hat wasn't odd, except one usually didn't wear a knitted wool hat in the summer. "My name is Parnell Purchase and I'm not sneaking around your cabin."

This guy walked up to Parnell, looking him over closely. "You're new around here. You the law? No, I guess not. Pardon me. I mistook you for another." His attitude changed then. He extended his hand to shake Parnell's. "I'm John—John Corriveau. This is my cabin." He pointed through the bushes, "And that was my garden you were looking at."

"Hello, John, I'm Parnell—Parnell Purchase. And I ain't the law."

"Where are you from, Parnell?"

"I came in from Bangor yesterday," he answered.

"Maybe you are hiding from something. I asked where you from, not where you have been."

"Boothbay—Boothbay Harbor." This guy was very astute.

"What brings you to Howe Brook?" John asked, as he picked his teeth with a wooden match.

"I was tired of smelling stinking fish and breaking my back raking blueberries."

"Now that we know who each other is—come in and have coffee, and my wife, Stormi, just finished making donuts." Before he could decline, John was pulling him by his arm, but Parnell noticed he was still looking around like maybe he was looking for someone.

"Stormi, we got company. How about coffee and some of your fresh donuts," John hollered from outside the cabin.

"Well, John Henri, I ain't looking to bring 'em out there, you two will have to come in."

John introduced Parnell to his wife. Stormi certainly was an unusual name, and perhaps it was only a nickname.

"These donuts are very good, Mrs. Corriveau," Parnell said as he finished eating the first one.

"Thank you, but just call me Stormi. Mrs. sounds so formal. We're all family in here."

"Where are you going, Parnell?" Stormi asked.

"I was just walking around. Seeing what there is to see."

"You tourist or looking for work?" John asked.

"I'm no tourist. I may decide to stay for a while." He couldn't help but notice, it seemed as if both John and Stormi were a bit nervous.

"This road," John pointed to the one that Parnell had been walking on, "only goes as far as the roll dam on Smith Brook Deadwater. From there, there's only a footpath to the Kennedy Tote Road that'll take you out to Symrna Center. Or you can go to Cut Pond and Shorey Siding on the tracks."

"What is a roll dam?" Parnell asked.

"Small wooden dam used to hold back the spring freshet of water so the river drivers will have a reservoir for driving logs downstream. There's a roll dam at the outlet of this lake, too," John said.

"You probably haven't seen too much of the lake yet." More statement than question. Stormi looked at her husband and knew what he was thinking. "How 'bout you and me taking a little canoe ride. I show you Howe Brook from the lake."

"I would like that," Parnell replied. "I left my duffel bag on the platform at the station house. Will it be okay there?"

"No problem."

When they both had had their fill of coffee and donuts they walked outside and Stormi hollered after them, "Now, John Henri, mind you, don't get that young fella into any kind of trouble. 'Cause if you do, you know the Lord will bring His wrath down on the both of us."

Parnell turned to look at John. "Oh, don't pay attention to her. She always is saying something about the Lord or the church to me. She one of those real religious women." Parnell followed him down to the shore where a green canvas canoe was pulled up on shore and turned over to keep the rain out.

"You ever done much canoeing before, Parnell?"

"Some. I did most of my boating on the ocean in a fishing boat."

John steadied the canoe as Parnell climbed in and then he

seated himself in the stern and pushed away from the dock. The lake wasn't calm, just a gentle ripple. But John kept the canoe close to shore, following the shadows towards the outlet. John had a nervous habit of looking behind him and through the trees that lined the shore. "You in the service?"

"The Army, in Korea. I didn't like it much."

"I was in the Army, too. WWII, wounded twice at Normandy. Took a bullet in my left lung and a piece of shrapnel in my left shoulder. I thought they'd send me home. But instead, after I recovered they sent me back to the front in France. I get a nice pension now."

They paddled past the sawmill and village. Couldn't see much of either, really. "We'll paddle around the shore to the other side. I have another canoe there I'd like you to bring back." John waited a minute before continuing. "I was over here yesterday doing me some fishing and got turned around and ended up behind Emerson Ridge and crossing Smith Brook just up from the lake. I should have stayed on right side of Tracey Brook."

Parnell thought it strange that John could get so turned around in his own backyard, so-to-say. But he wasn't going to call him a liar. They paddled beyond Howe Brook, the brook itself, before John started to swing the canoe towards the other shore. Parnell was convinced he was trying to keep out of sight of something. *But what and why?*

John pointed the canoe up the mouth of Tracey Brook. "This brook is real good fishing in the spring. Now everything has gone back to deep water." *Then why did he come fishing here yesterday if he knows the fish have gone back to deep water in the lake?*

Parnell was beginning to suspect that there was more to his trip than John was telling.

They had paddled in from the lake about three hundred yards and there was a high knoll on the left. "Those camps there," John pointed with his paddle, "were once sporting camps. Not used anymore. Good den for porcupine."

There was a small tributary that ran out from behind the knoll and Parnell was surprised when John turned the canoe into this. "This is as far as we need to go," John said.

"Just exactly what are we doing here, John?" He just looked at him and didn't say anything. They got out and John tied the canoe to a small cedar tree.

"This way." Parnell started following, hoping John wasn't going to include him in some dastardly deed. They had only walked a hundred feet or so along a well-used game trail when they came to a spring freshet coming out of the brook side of the knoll.

John sat down and motioned for Parnell to do the same, then he removed two cigars from his shirt pocket and gave one to Parnell and lit the other. He put the cigar between his teeth and removed his knit hat and wiped the sweat from his forehead. Parnell was not hot or sweating. Why was John?

"What are we doing here, John?" He only pursed his lips and put his finger up to his lips, meaning for Parnell to be quiet. So he waited. He was glad for the cigar. The no-see-ums were out and his arms were already burning.

John put his cigar in the water and Parnell did also. On the other side of the freshet John removed some fir boughs and ferns, and there, lying in the little cavity, were four deer legs. "I shot this spike horn yesterday."

"What do you fish with, a rifle?" John knew what Parnell meant.

"Nah, that's illegal. We'll carry these back to the canoe." They had to make two trips each.

"Help me turn the canoe, then you get in and paddle back to my cabin."

"What are you going to do?" Parnell asked.

"I have to get the other canoe. I dragged it further up the brook and cached it. You go ahead, I'll be right along."

Parnell did as he was told. Not liking it at all. The current was taking him back to the lake. He paddled also, to get out of

31

there as fast as he could. But as he neared the lake, someone in uniform stepped out and caught his canoe by the bow.

"Holy shit! Who in the hell are you! And where did you come from?" All in one breath.

The uniform started laughing. Then after a while he said, "Excuse me, I am Ian Randall, Game Warden, and you, sir, are definitely in possession of illegal deer—or parts—and you are under my arrest."

Parnell just sat there dumbfounded. He didn't know if he wanted to cry or laugh. Or who he was madder at, the warden or John for getting him included in his scheme. The warden had pulled Parnell and canoe out of the current in the brook and onto the shore of the lake.

"Who are you? I have never seen you around here before," the warden asked.

"Parnell—Parnell Purchase. I am new here. I arrived yesterday."

"Okay, Mr. Purchase, you understand that you are in possession of a deer or parts thereof in closed season and that is why you are under arrest."

"Okay, now what happens?" Parnell asked.

"Well, I take you to jail." Ian looked at Parnell and it was easy to see that he was angry.

"You stay right here, I'll get my canoe."

Parnell watched as the warden disappeared into the woods and then reemerge pulling his canoe behind him.

"You get in with me and I'll tie yours to the stern of mine. Now, I expect you to help paddle, but any funny business and I'll swat you behind the head with my paddle and put the cuffs on. Okay?"

"Okay," Parnell grunted.

* * * *

John Henri heard Parnell holler in surprise and he stopped dragging his canoe and listened. He recognized that other voice—Ian Randall. He had been half expecting him to appear. He waited until he was sure Ian and Parnell were well across the lake before he finished dragging his canoe and load down the brook to the lake. Then he waited until they were out of sight up the inlet of Smith Brook, and then he waited for darkness before he pushed off in his canoe for home.

The sun was beginning to set as Parnell and the warden started up Smith Brook. Parnell sat silent. "If we're lucky we'll catch the ten o'clock freight train southbound out of Mapleton. That is if it stops tonight at Weeksboro Siding. If not, we'll sleep out tonight and catch the morning freight south."

It was dark by the time they got to the railroad bridge over Smith Brook. Ian pulled his canoe ashore, turned it over and tied it off. He pulled out a pack and put it on his back. "This way; we'll have to walk about a half mile."

There wasn't much at Weeksboro. A side track and a little cordwood piled up. The ten o'clock southbound didn't stop that night. Hell, it never even slowed. "We camp out tonight. Find some wood, I'll get some birch bark and kindling." There was plenty of wood lying around and soon Ian had a nice fire going.

"Are you hungry?"

"Yeah."

"Well, there is no sense in letting all this meat go to waste." The warden pulled a hindquarter out of his pack and sliced off several thin strips of meat. He wrapped the strips around the end of a stick and roasted it over the fire. It wasn't long before the meat was cooked. The warden emptied his water jug into a blackened tea pail and set that on the coals to boil. And surprisingly enough, he had two metal cups. He put a tea bag in each and filled them with boiling water. He handed Parnell one cup.

So far there had been little conversation. Parnell was still fuming about John getting him involved. Ian, from experience, wanted Parnell to *relax* from the experience and then he might learn a little more of substance through conversation.

33

"There's more hot water," Ian said. "You said earlier that you only arrived at the village yesterday."

"Yeah"

"Where are you from?"

"I came up from Bangor."

"Just visiting or do you have work here?"

"I'm not sure.

"How did you happen to be out there today? I mean right at the mouth of Tracy Brook?" Parnell asked.

"I saw your canoe leave the lake and turn into the brook. Fishing can be pretty good up the brook at times. Only brook fishing closed yesterday. And besides, fish usually are in deeper water when the weather turns warm like this. I didn't know who you were, but I figured you were up to no good."

"You didn't just happen to be here today, did you?" Parnell asked.

"Nope—been here three days now. That's why I'm all out of food. And now out of tea bags also." Ian drank more of his tea and put more wood on the fire. "Who was in the canoe with you when you went up the brook?" Parnell didn't answer.

Ian continued, "The way I see it, I don't think you shot that deer. You didn't have a rifle with you. And I didn't hear any shooting—today. Heard some yesterday, while I was at Levesque City. Two shots about thirty minutes apart. By the time I had concluded my business there, I didn't get on St. Croix Lake until—well, it was just in time to see you turn up Tracy. I don't figure you shot this deer, but I'll make a deal with you. You tell me who was in that canoe with you and I'll see the judge goes easy on you. I think I know, and that's the old reprobate that I really want."

Parnell thought to himself, *That's the old reprobate that I want too*. Then he began thinking of the consequences if he should tell. In the end he decided to keep John out of it. For now anyhow. He'd settle scores later.

"No deal."

"I didn't honestly think that you would." They both sat silent in the warm glow of the firelight. The wind was blowing a slight breeze. It kept the mosquitoes away. Owls hooted; crickets chirped. Those were the only sounds.

Parnell was beginning to drift back in his thoughts to the war and the bloody carnage. To get himself away from those thoughts he said, "What is this Levesque City? I have never heard of a city with that name. And where is it?"

"It's a lumber camp owned and operated by J.P. Levesque. About five miles east of here. There are no roads that'll connect Howe Brook Village to Levesque City, only foot trails from the roll dam on Smith Brook Deadwater."

"How do you get around in the woods when there are no roads?" Parnell asked.

"Either by canoe or foot. I have canoes cached all through these woods. If you ever find yourself anywhere near the city, it would be worth your time to stop. For fifty cents the cook will feed you. And it'll be the best food you have ever eaten."

"Do you have a family, Ian?"

"Wife, son and daughter."

"What does your wife think about you being away from home so much?"

"She doesn't. She complains every time we're together. She says I sleep more in the woods than I do in her bed. She's right of course. The maddest she ever got was when I missed our first wedding anniversary. That really got her going. Me too. I had to leave home then and go back in the woods; she kicked me out of her bed. She said, 'And you can sleep on the couch and pretend it's the ground and there is a spruce tree overhead.' Then she slammed her bedroom door." Ian started laughing. "Then, she— she was two years getting over that. I just don't understand it."

Parnell observed that Ian obviously enjoyed his job. And in the future he would conduct his affairs, hopefully, so he wouldn't have to worry about the local warden on his trail ever again.

They both were silent then and soon they were asleep.

35

* * * *

Just before daylight the next morning the train went through Weeksboro and when the engineer saw the warden sleeping on the ground by a burnt out fire he blew his air horn. Both Ian and Parnell woke with a start, Ian cursing in French and Parnell trying to calm his nerves.

Ian shaved with cold water and no lather. Parnell left the stubble on his chin. "We'll have to hike it to Shorey Siding now. I don't think the train will be stopping here anytime soon." Ian said and he started walking, between the rails.

"What makes you think they'll stop at Shorey?"

"There's a work crew there. I'll talk to the foreman and he'll put out a flag for the engineer to stop."

It was only two miles to Shorey Siding and they would have two hours to wait for the South Bound coming out of Ashland. "Just remember, Parnell, you are in my custody. No shenanigans or I'll cuff you."

"I give you my word." The last thing Parnell needed now was more trouble.

The train was late. But it was the Ashland to Houlton train, and they would not have to switch trains in Oakfield. But by the time they walked from the train station in Houlton to the courthouse, court had adjourned for the day.

Ian looked at Parnell and said, "Well, I have no choice now but to deliver you to jail. Tomorrow morning one of the deputies will escort you to arraignment."

Parnell didn't say anything.

* * * *

Ian left Parnell in the custody of the Aroostook County Sheriff and then walked over to the district attorney's office to write out his report.

Parnell was given supper and locked in a holding cell until the morrow. He slept quite well that night, in spite of his problems. He was tired.

The next morning he asked one of the deputies, "Excuse me, Deputy, is there a chance I could have a razor so I can shave before you take me over to the courthouse?"

He had cleaned up the best he could, but his clothes still smelled of wood smoke. Deputy Kirby escorted Parnell to the courthouse early. The public defender wanted to speak with the accused before arraignment. Once inside the courthouse, Deputy Kirby removed the handcuffs. Kirby left him in a small anteroom across the hall from the courtroom.

In a few minutes the door opened and a man only a little older than Parnell stepped in and closed the door behind him. "Good morning, ah—Mr. Purchase. I'm Julian Werner, Public Defender. I read over Warden Randall's reports. He apparently caught you with four deer quarters in your canoe, is that correct?"

"Yes."

"But you didn't shoot the deer, correct?"

"Correct."

"And you wouldn't tell the warden who did?"

"Correct."

"I'll plead you not guilty and that'll give me time to prepare your case."

"Prepare what? He caught me red handed, as it were. I'm not leaving here today only to have to return. No, I'll get it over with today. I'm guilty and there's no worming my way out of it."

"Well, if that is what you prefer—"

"It is."

"Okay." The deputy came in and escorted Parnell to the front row seats in the courtroom. The room was slowly filling.

The door to the judge's chamber opened and a tall, gray-haired, older man dressed in a black robe walked in. The plainclothes deputy said, "All rise for the Honorable George T. Archibold."

The judge motioned with his hand for the audience to be seated. There were several cases ahead of Parnell, and Judge

Archibold seemed to be in a joyous mood. "Let's see, Mr. Parnell Purchase. That's an unusual name, Mr. Purchase."

"Yes, sir."

"You have been charged with illegal possession of deer or parts of deer in closed season. This is a class D crime and you are entitled to a jury trial. How say you, Mr. Purchase?"

"Guilty, Your Honor."

"Knowing Warden Ian Randall, I'd say that was a smart decision." The judge wrote something on the report and said, "The fine for illegal possession of a deer is usually fifty dollars, but you were asked to cooperate with the warden and you chose not to. I'm going to set a penalty of seventy-five dollars. Are you prepared to take care of it today?"

" No, Your Honor, I am not."

" Is there someone who could get you the money?"

"No, sir, there is not."

"Well, then you can work the fine off five dollars a day in jail. That'll be fifteen days. And to help pay for your room and board, you'll work eight hours each day for the county."

Parnell was escorted back to jail to begin his fifteen days. That seemed like an awful long time, but he understood the judge's reasoning.

Work would begin the next morning. For the rest of that day and night, Parnell had nothing to do but to lie on his back and relive the experience. He vowed to get even with John Corriveau.

He had come to the realization that John must have suspected that the game warden was in the vicinity; that would explain why he had taken him on a round-about route around the lake and why he had appeared so nervous, and that old Corriveau had set him up to take the blame just in case the warden was near. He wasn't as angry as he would have thought. Some of that anger was diluted by dreams of revenge. He would find a way to get even.

Not all the inmates had to work. Only a few. Mostly he cleaned streets, either sweeping the sand or picking up trash. He didn't mind. It was a good deal better than being locked in his cell all day and night.

The day came when Parnell was released. He said goodbye and walked over to the train station.

"I'd like a ticket to Howe Brook, please."

"I can get you to Oakfield, but not to Howe Brook. Beaver plugged the culvert at White Lake and washed the road out. It'll be a week before it can be repaired."

"Okay, as far as Oakfield, then. I'll walk the rest of the way."

"Ah—Mr. Purchase, that's twenty miles from Oakfield. That's seventy cents, please."

Luck was with him for once, the train departed for Oakfield only moments after he was seated in the coach car. It was a short ride to Oakfield.

Before leaving town, he stopped at a small local store and bought some cheese and cold meat for the trip. He knew he'd have to sleep out that night and he wasn't going to go hungry.

He got on the rails at Smyrna Mills and started following the track back to Howe Brook. Two miles out of Smyrna Mills he found the wash out. There was a small brook that passed underneath the rail bed and a beaver had plugged the culvert and the water had loosened the gravel in the bed. Finally, as the water rose behind the beaver dam, the water-soaked gravel gave way and left the rails hanging, a space of eighty-yards. "Hey, where you going?" one of the workers hollered.

"Howe Brook."

"That's another sixteen miles from here."

"Yeah, I know. You boys all local?"

"Yup, we all from town here. I was born in Howe Brook actually. Names Roy Russell. My dad, Hadley, worked for the railroad camp way back. And he and Mom lived at Howe Brook. Well, you have a nice walk, young fella, I've done it a few times, myself," Roy said.

It was a peaceful walk along the tracks and it felt good to stretch his legs. He walked until about dusk and got as far as Weeksboro. He kindled a fire where he and Ian had spent the night. He leaned back against the same log listening to the evening sounds and eating some cheese and cold meat.

He was pondering on how to get back at Corriveau, without much luck. He just didn't know what he could do. But one thing was in his favor—time. He was mad enough to beat his face in, but he would rather come up with a scheme that would embarrass the old reprobate. He'd sleep on it.

At about midnight, Parnell woke up with a marvelous idea. It was so good he began laughing. He made sure the fire was out and he struck out for Howe Brook again; this time he was almost running, not strolling like he had been doing earlier. If this was going to have the effect that he wanted, it had to be done in the dark. It was a mile and a half to John's cabin. There were no lights about and all was still. He walked very quietly down to the dock where he had seen, a few days ago, a fish pole with a bare hook. He took all of the line off the reel and very carefully coiled the line so not to knot it. He then crept up until he was underneath John and Stormi's bedroom window.

"Good, the window is up," he said to himself. He anchored the hook in the screen about three inches from the corner. He walked backwards being careful not to trip on anything, bailing out the line. He had about twenty feet between him and the window. He pulled the line as tight as he could, without pulling the hook out of the screen. Next he wet his fingers and pulled on the line, letting the line slide between his wet fingers. The sound was unholy. He did it a couple of more times and then he stopped and let the line go slack and took cover behind some bushes.

From inside the cabin he heard John saying, "What in all holy tarnation was that! Did you hear, Stormi?"

"Yes, probably just an old bear or raccoon. Come back to bed, John Henri."

Parnell had to bite down on his arm to keep from laughing, "The night ain't over with yet, ole buddy."

Parnell waited patiently in the corner of the bushes for the Corriveaus to just be going off to sleep again. He pulled the line tight and slid his fingers along the line for a long duration this time, followed with a short pull. Then he let the line go slack and found cover further away from the cabin this time.

There was more conversation inside. "Holy Mother of Christ! What in the hell is that?" John exclaimed.

"John Henri! You stop that cussing right now. You probably brought this—whatever it is—down on us because of your wicked ways," Stormi exclaimed.

Again, Parnell had a difficult time holding back his laughter. There was a light out on the porch. John was shining it all around looking for whatever it was that was making that unholy sound. He switched the light off and sat down on the step and waited. He laid his shotgun across his knees and wiped the sweat from his forehead.

There was no movement, no sound, so John stood up and went back inside. Parnell waited for about a quarter of an hour and crept back to the bushes and picked up the line and this time he slid his fingers along the line very gently, so the noise from the screen was just audible. Just one pull.

"John! Ignore it. Maybe it'll go away. Whatever it is," Stormi said.

John sat back down on the edge of the bed and looked out the window. There was nothing out there. He wiped the sweat from his face again.

Parnell waited until he could hear John snoring. Then he pulled the line through his fingers again. A long drawn out pull and then several rapid short pulls. Then he ran back to the tracks.

"Jesus! Stormi! There it is again. Holy Mother of Christ, whatever that is has come to get me!"

"John Henri! I told you to stop that cursing, now you get out of my bed! Go on, get! You go sleep in the other room. I won't share my bed with any man who's going to curse like that."

John dressed and left the bedroom and closed the door. He

picked up his shotgun and light and went outside. He walked around the cabin, shining the bushes or anywhere, where this thing could hide. He walked out onto the ledges and shined his light out into the lake. Nothing there. Actually he wasn't sure he wanted to see whatever it was that was making that ungodly noise. He was sure whatever it was, God had sent it to punish him for his evil doings. He went back on the porch and sat down in a chair.

It wasn't long before things quieted down and Parnell stealthy crept up and unhooked the fishhook from the window screen and coiled the line in his hand. To further the events of this night, Parnell tied the line to a small stone just above the hook and threw it as far as he could out into the lake. Then he broke off a crotched limb and wedged that between the boards on the dock and leaned the fish pole in the crotch.

But the night wasn't over yet. He crossed the driveway where the ground dropped down low into a wet area. Then he started screaming a high-pitched wail and running through the swamp beating the bushes with his hands as he ran. He kept screaming like a banshee until John fired two shots from his shotgun. Parnell heard the pellets going through the trees above him. "He's using buckshot." He found his way back to the tracks and hiked back to Weeksboro, laughing with every step. He would wait until midday before making an appearance at the cabin.

Parnell laughed again, "Those fifteen days in jail was worth this night of entertainment." He laughed so much his sides were hurting.

He rested, but he didn't sleep much. The rays from the sun started to shine just as he leaned back against the log. He was so comfortable there, he stayed and simply lounged in the sweet smelling air until about mid-morning when a pickup truck that was specially rigged to run on the rails, stopped. Two men got out. "Any problems here?" the driver asked.

"No, I was just resting before I finished the hike to Howe

Brook," Parnell answered.

"Where are you coming from?" The driver asked.

"From Oakfield. I spent the night here."

"I'm Ansel Snow and this is Micky Dumain. I'm the engineer on the southbound through here in the mornings and Micky is a project engineer. We're on our way to the wash out at White Lake."

Parnell shook hands with each man. "Hello, I'm Parnell Purchase."

"Well, we have got to be on our way. Nice meeting you, Mr. Purchase."

"Same here," Parnell moved as they were driving off.

It was time. He walked the mile and a half to John's cabin in quick order. He reminded himself that he was supposed to be angry. He walked up the steps of the porch and John was just coming outside. The two men stood there eye-balling each other. John's Adam's apple nervously bobbed up and down.

Parnell finally broke the silence. "You crazy old man! You set me up on purpose." Parnell was tapping John on his chest with his finger. "You knew that warden was around and you set me up with your deer so I'd get caught red-handed. I ought to punch your lights out."

Before John could answer, Parnell continued, "Come on, I'll paddle you around the lake so you can get a good look at the village. But you skirted around the shoreline for two reasons— you didn't want to be seen crossing the middle of the lake and you were scanning the shoreline looking for Ian Randall."

"Well, you and the warden on a first name basis now?" John asked.

"Why not? I had to spend a lot of time with him, thanks to you." Parnell hoped he hadn't carried his supposed anger too far. He actually liked the old reprobate.

"Look, Parnell, to make up for what I did to you, I have another log cabin on the knoll across from the station house. It's yours for as long as you want it. It's all furnished and a root cellar off to the east side dug into the bank. There is traps in the shed. There's an old 12-gauge shotgun—it's all yours." How could he be angry with John now, unless there were strings attached? "Besides all that, I got us winter meat. You—me. While you entertained the warden, I brought back four quarters and the loins of a yearling moose. Some is hanging in root cellar and Stormi has been doing canning ever since."

"You knew the warden was about, didn't you?"

"I did. The moose. Now we have winter meat and I don't have to worry no more about that old warden. I trade one small deer any day for nice moose. Besides, the fine on moose is a lot more than deer.

"How did you get here?" John asked.

"I got out of jail yesterday morning and I walked from Oakfield. Spent the night at Weeksboro. Beaver have the roadbed washed out at White Lake. I talked with Ansel Snow and Micky Dumain this morning at Weeksboro, they were going to inspect the work at White Lake." That should have settled any curiosity, if John had thought Parnell had been responsible for keeping him awake last night.

"Well, maybe it is a good trade off. I'll hold you to the cabin deal, but no more games."

A beaver slapped the water with his tail out in the lake and John jumped and started to curse and then thought better of it. He gritted his teeth and knotted his fists. Parnell knew what the real problem was, and he wanted to laugh.

Stormi came out on the porch and said "Parnell, you must be hungry; come in and I'll fix you a nice breakfast of steak and eggs."

John poured them each a cup of hot coffee and then he happened to remember, "Stormi, were you fishing off the dock yesterday?"

"No, why do you ask?" she replied.

"Well the fish pole that's always down there—the line was throwed out and the pole set in a crotch stick." She stood there with eggs in her hands looking at John and John looking back. They didn't have to say anything for Parnell to understand what they were thinking. The banshee. He started to laugh and choked on a mouth full of coffee.

Parnell was thinking then whether or not he'd ever tell John and Stormi who *the banshee* was. But he bet one thing for sure, that from now until they died, the doors to their cabin would be locked at night.

Stormi set a plate of steak and eggs on the table in front of Parnell. "That steak smells awfully good!"

Both Stormi and John began to laugh. "Well—it should, young fella, you paid for it!" Stormi said.

Parnell sliced off a piece and ate it. "It is delicious. I take it this is the moose."

John rocked back in his chair and smiled. When Parnell had finished eating, John said, "Come on, Parnell, I'll show you to your new home."

As Parnell was getting up from the table to follow John, Stormi said, "Now, John Henri, you remember your promise."

"Yeah, woman, I remember. Come on, Parnell."

"Thank you, Stormi, for breakfast," Parnell said.

"What about my duffel bag that I left on the station house platform?" Parnell asked.

Stormi came out of the bedroom with his duffel bag. "I went up and fetched it right after you and John left in the canoe."

"Thank you again, Stormi."

On their way up to Parnell's new home, John explained to Parnell about the promise without saying anything, actually, about the unholy banshee. "We had—some problems last night and I started cursing and swearing—Stormi, she kicked me out of bed and bedroom. This morning I had to promise to attend church functions for a month to make amends for me cussing. Only way I could get back in my own bed. She awful woman— awful pious and expects me to be pious too. I don't like sleeping sitting up in other room. So I pious, me."

"I didn't know there was a church here, John."

"Ain't none, services and functions are held at the school house. Preacher, he come down on morning train from Masardis and back on evening train."

"What is the function this evening?" Parnell asked.

"Church supper. Everyone brings dish to eat. Then all sing songs. You being a jailbird now, maybe you come. Be good for you to get a little piousing, you." They both laughed.

The door to the cabin wasn't locked. As John had said, it was furnished. Nothing fancy, but comfortable. One large main room and two separate bedrooms. An old 12-gauge shotgun hung over the front door on racks attached to the wall. John showed him where the outhouse was and the root cellar. This door had a lock on it, and John gave him the key. There were three moose quarters and one deer hanging and many canning jars filled with a variety of vegetables and meat. In the far corner was a pile of sawdust with huge ice blocks buried in the sawdust. Parnell understood then why the temperature was so cool in the root cellar while it was so warm outside.

"Well you probably want to settle in and relax a little before the festivities tonight, so I'll leave you here and go home."

Parnell couldn't believe his good fortune. Perhaps there was something after all in the saying that something good will happen after something bad has occurred. He sure got the best end of this deal, even considering the fifteen days in jail.

Two hours later he woke up. He started looking around to see what there was. In the shed attached to the cabin there was firewood and kindling, but not enough for winter. There were old leg-hold traps on the wall. A roll of telephone wire, two crock-pots, an assortment of hand tools, old paint cans and a chopping block with a razor sharp axe stuck in the top. Inside the cabin there were plenty of dishes and cookware, and what Parnell liked the most were the five cast-iron fry pans hanging neatly on the wall. The wood cook stove looked to be in excellent condition and there was a heavy wood heater.

For the first time in a long time he was feeling tranquil and at peace. He honestly believed he had found his place in this world. This would be home. He sat at the table and wrote his mother a letter explaining how he felt about his new place in life and not to worry. He also told her that he hadn't had any booze since she kicked him out of her house.

When he finished the letter he walked down to the station house. There had to be outgoing mail. Mr. McBride was also the postal clerk. "You caught me just in time, Mr. Purchase. I was just closing up. The church supper starts in a few minutes. Are you going to the supper?"

"Yes, I am. Guess we can walk over together."

The one room schoolhouse was almost too small to accommodate almost the entire village. Everyone had already heard about the new resident from down Bangor way, a Mr. Purchase, and wanted to meet him. "Hello there, you must be Mr. Purchase, I'm Phyllis Goff. My husband and I have the red house down the shoreline from here."

There seemed to be plenty of food and the aromas were delicious. The railroad track truck stopped out front and Ansel Snow and Micky Dumain came in behind Parnell and Henry McBride. Everyone finally found an empty chair after all the introductions were made, and Ansel Snow led the group in prayer.

John Corriveau was anything but happy. Stormi insisted that he sit with her and not his sometimes-troubling friends. When the supper was finally over and some had already left, John looked over where Parnell was in deep conversation with loyal friends. John started to cross the room and join his friends but Stormi stopped him. "John Henri, would you get me another cup of tea please." John took her cup. "Oh, you're so sweet."

John was muttering to himself on his way to the kitchen, "Oh, what a wicked woman. Any man alive would have cussed if attack by that damned banshee, me. And I have whole month of this. Oh, woman, you'll get yours someday." But until his probationary month was over he would have to behave himself.

Ansel and Micky were saying goodbye. "Thanks, folks, it's always a pleasure to stop here and visit," Micky said.

"Come again," Roy replied.

Parnell, McBride and some of the other menfolk were leaving. And John knew why. McBride had been making some rhubarb wine and undoubtedly he was taking his friends to sample it.

"John Henri, will you help me dry these dishes?" Stormi asked. Oh, she was an evil woman.

* * * *

Parnell and John were sitting on his porch watching several deer feeding along the shoreline across the lake. "At the church supper the other night, Ansel was saying that the Hafford Farm in Ashland is going to need some potato pickers. I thought I'd take a train up tomorrow. Are you interested, John?"

"I've done before, a lot of hard work. Me back probably couldn't take it so well. I'm older than you."

"Well, hard work or not, I need some money to see me through the winter. There are some things I need to buy."

The next morning Parnell bought his train ticket ($1.25) for Ashland and Ansel asked him, "Hey, Parnell, you want to ride in the engine?"

"Yeah, there won't be any problem, will there?"

"You bought a ticket, didn't you?"

"Yeah,"

"Well it doesn't assign you to any particular seat, does it?"

The ride was quite an adventure. There were other smaller villages along the tracks.

"Sidings, actually. Some winters, crews work the woods behind the sidings and pile up their wood close to the tracks."

There was Pride, Hawkins and Griswold Sidings. There was a moose in the tracks up ahead.

"Aren't you going to stop for that moose?" Parnell asked.

"If I jammed on the brakes now, by the time free travel in each car caught up with us we might derail. Besides, there is no way we could stop in that short of a distance." Before the train reached the moose it had left the tracks.

There were deer everywhere. "You should see them at night coming down this stretch."

"Someone with a rifle up front on this engine could have all the deer he wanted."

"That has actually happened. Not on my run though. I wouldn't let the guy do it. There was this guy, he worked for the railroad also, one night he sat up front with his rifle, shooting deer. But he made a bad mistake at Griswold Siding. The old cabin close to the tracks back there?"

"Yeah."

"That belongs to ole Bill. Well one night Bill was out along the tracks, probably getting himself a deer too—well, anyhow, his light wasn't so good and this guy up front thought Bill's light was deer eyes. He shot Bill in the leg. After that, the railroad had a policy of no guns."

It was an interesting and an informative ride in the engine with Ansel. He said goodbye and found his way to the Hafford Farm. Here, like the blueberry barrens, Parnell found Army tents for living quarters for the workers. Only five dollars a day was deducted from his pay, to pay for the lodging and food. If he could pick one hundred barrels a day, that would be fifty dollars a day. It sounded like good money, but the work was even harder than raking blueberries.

By the end of that first day Parnell thought his back was broken and he was covered with dirt from head to toe. Again, he kept pretty much to himself, preferring a tent by himself. Instead of going into town like a lot of the workers, Parnell went back to the fields and picked cull potatoes for himself. Any potato left behind the workers could have.

By the end of the first week Parnell had earned over two hundred dollars and a backpack of potatoes. The crews didn't work on Sunday because of their religious beliefs. So he hopped the late train south, a freight train that didn't ordinarily stop at Howe Brook in evenings, but during potato harvest the railroad made an exception.

As fast and as hard as he worked, there were kids on either side of him that picked as many barrels as he did. *And I'm not that old.* He learned that in the County during potato harvest, the schools closed their doors so the students could work in the fields and earn money to buy school clothes and such. When he thought about it, he decided that was an excellent way to teach kids how to be responsible.

He had to buy more clothes at McBride's Store and he washed out his old ones. There was enough for him to do around his own cabin that he didn't have time to visit with the Corriveaus. He wondered if John was still keeping watch for the banshee. He laughed out loud.

It rained a lot during the next week and the fields were muddy, but anyone who wanted to work could. Parnell worked each day either picking or driving tractor pulling a digger. Apparently the usual driver didn't like working in the rain. Mr. Hafford noticed how Parnell pitched in, and soon he was taken out of the picking crew and assigned to one of the diggers for the remainder of the harvest.

By the end of the harvest Parnell had accumulated fifteen hundred dollars. Before going back to Howe Brook, he took the train to Presque Isle and bought some winter clothes, boots, mittens, snowshoes and a .35 Marlin lever-action rifle and two boxes of cartridges and a box of number-six birdshot for his shotgun. Now he figured he was all set for winter and he still had thirteen hundred dollars left.

He also bought Stormi some flannel pajamas and a wool shirt for John. In spite of the mean trick they had played on him, he owed them both a lot. They were as close to family as anyone could be.

* * * *

Parnell went to visit the Corriveaus early Sunday morning, before church. It had been more than a month now since the night of the banshee and he assumed John's religious probation period was over. But Stormi would undoubtedly go to church. He gave them each a present that morning. "My word what is all this, Parnell?" Stormi asked.

"Just a little appreciation for all you two have done for me." Anyone would have thought by the way Stormi was carrying on that she had been given a mink coat. John sat and watched his wife, happy for her—she was feeling so happy. He took his old shirt off and tried on the new wool shirt. It was perfect.

"Are you busy today, Parnell?" John asked.

"No, the harvest is over and I won't have to travel out, now."

"Good, I have a chore for us. Stormi is going to church and she wants us to get her a bear so she can render the fat into lard for cooking."

"Bear fat!" Parnell asked. He was skeptical.

"Yes, it renders down to pure white lard; the best there is for cooking."

"Do you know where there is a bear?" Parnell asked. "How do we hunt them, like deer?"

"You could, but probably you would never see a bear that way. Got to make bear come to you."

"How?"

"With food. Mimi at the restaurant has been saving food scraps for me. We, you and me, will have to pick it up and take to the woods."

"Okay, where?"

"I'll show you."

They took two pack baskets and lined the inside with a plastic red-checkered tablecloth. But the shoulder strap on one basket was torn. "I have a pack basket. While you are at the restaurant, I'll go up to the cabin and get it."

"Okay, I meet you there."

Parnell put his new .35 Marlin rifle in his pack and put the pack on his back and walked down to the restaurant to meet John. Mimi had set aside a lot of pork and beef scraps and fruit pies that had gone to waste. There was enough to fill both pack baskets.

John had noticed Parnell's rifle sticking out of the top of his basket, but didn't say anything about it. He assumed that Parnell being from the city might feel a bit more secure if he took a weapon while setting out bear bait. And he didn't have any objections.

"Where are we going with this, John?"

"Oh, not far. Some of the woods crews have been seeing a big boar crossing the road up along East Branch of Howe Brook. Be shorter walk to take road behind your cabin. Save a few minutes walking."

John walked as if there was a real urgency to set the bait out. Parnell wondered why, but soon forgot about it. "One of the company's wood cruisers knowed about his bear, too. And all he want is the tail."

"Why just the tail?" Parnell inquired.

"State pays thirty-five dollars bounty. There are too many bear, too much damage to cabins and farmers. I want bounty too, but Stormi wants fat."

"What about bear meat?"

"No good. If we get small bear, meat okay."

"You said company woods cruiser. What company?"

"Griswold Heirs own the woods and village, but taken care of by P&C, Prentsis and Carlisle. This cruiser he real bad poacher."

"Where does he live?"

"Oxbow. McDougal—Alfons McDougal. You see him around station house some. Only speak French. I don't know if he can speak English or not."

"McDougal. That's not a French name. It's Irish. What's an

Irishman doing speaking French?"

"He come from Allagash."

As if that was supposed to explain everything. When John saw the puzzled look on Parnell's face he explained. "Everyone in Allagash is Irish. And everyone speak French, not the English. Allagash was settled by the Irish. Come over from Madawaska and New Brunswick."

"But why do they speak French?"

"I don't know. They just do."

Not far above where the East Branch joins the Howe Brook there was some drying mud in the road. John stopped to check for animal tracks. There were deer, moose, and one large bear track. "This must be the bear that the boys are talking about. We'll see if we find his tracks up the road again."

They found more mud in the road after about a half-mile of walking and this time the bear was following the road. They stayed on the road for another mile but didn't see the tracks again and there were three more muddy areas. John began looking for a likely spot. "You take that side, Parnell, and I'll take the brook side. Look for a small clearing. Preferably on a knoll."

Parnell went off the graveled road only a short distance when he saw movement about thirty yards ahead. He removed his pack and took the rifle out. He inched along not making a sound. There was a slight breeze hitting him in the face. That was good. The bear wouldn't be able to wind him. He saw the movement again and stopped. He could see the bear and he was eating something. When the bear picked his head up Parnell took a fine bead just behind the head and fired. The bear went down, but its legs were still thrashing. Parnell waited and soon the bear was still.

John came running out from the brook and hollered, "Hey, Parnell! That you that shot?"

"Yeah, I got the bear," Parnell hollered back.

John was running now. "Jesus! Jesus! Holy Mother of Christ! What have you done?"

Parnell was somewhat taken back. "I thought you wanted a dead bear, for lard."

"Yes! But holy-cow Parnell, today is Sunday. The game warden doesn't take kindly to Sunday hunting. If he is anywhere around today he will have surely heard that shot. But one shot only is difficult job finding bearing—where it came from. It is a nice bear."

"It was eating something. Whatever it was, it fell on top of it," Parnell said.

"We can't very well haul it back in daylight. I know we could borrow a truck. But not in daylight."

"Why don't we skin it and cut the fat off and carry it back in our pack-baskets?"

"We could do that. It just might work," John was smiling now. "The lard plus the bounty. Not bad for a Sunday afternoon. If'n we don't get caught." They rolled the bear over on his back and John began skinning. He was very meticulous, fleshing the hide as he went. He cut the tail off and put it in his pocket. When the skin was off they stretched it out under the bear and began slicing off the fat. When they finished, they had filled one basket completely with the fat.

"Roll that hide up and put it in your basket. If'n there's room left, we'll take the head, otherwise we'll leave it here."

Parnell neatly rolled the hide up and it filled his pack basket. "Cut the ears off and throw them out in the bushes."

Parnell did, "Why cut the ears off and throw 'em?"

"That's bait this bear is lying on and I have a feeling it was probably put here by McDougal. Sometimes an old bear like this one has rubbed his tail off. Then you can turn both ears in and collect the bounty also. I don't want McDougal collecting no bounty on the bear you killed. Won't he be riled when he sees this?" And John began to laugh.

Parnell was intrigued with the skill that John removed the hide and fleshed it at the same time, and the way he sliced off the fat without making a huge mess. "Is McDougal going to know who got his bear?"

"Well, once we collect the bounty everyone is going to know. What's going to make him madder than anything is the fact that you shot it over his bait."

They helped each other with their pack baskets. They were heavy. Back on the graveled road, Parnell asked, "Where does this road go?"

"Goes up to Tie Camp Brook. There are a few crew camps next to the brook. When the camps were built there were some nice meaty spruce and pine trees there.

"Next spring I'll take you fishing up there. Where Tie Camp puts into Boom Branch Deadwater. Some of the best fishing that I have ever seen."

"Do we have to walk all the way?" Parnell asked.

"We might get someone to drop us off, but we'd have to walk back. Probably camp out one night."

About a mile down the road from where Parnell shot the bear, Parnell stopped, listening. "Hear that, John?"

"No. I don't hear nothing."

"A vehicle is coming up the road. Not going very fast."

"Come, we better get in woods and see." In a few minutes the old pickup came into view. John flattened out on the ground behind some small fir trees and indicated for Parnell to do the same. He mouthed the name silently, *McDougal*. As soon as McDougal was out of sight around the bend in the road, John said, "Come on, we get back to village now."

They started walking, almost running. Parnell was younger in years by a wide margin, but he had all he could do to keep up with John's pace, "Who was the other fellow with McDougal?"

"One of his cronies. Lives at the village off and on, Lester Tramlin. Oh, ain't he going to be mad." Then John began to laugh.

"Come on, Parnell, we got to hurry and get to your cabin. He'll know that I got his bear and it won't take him long to figure out who I'm with. He'll go to my cabin first, and Stormi, she'll just tell him that I'm with you someplace. That'll give us time to get things setup."

They were on the road now that went by Parnell's cabin, and five minutes later they heard the pickup heading for the village. "Good, we got time. We put these baskets in root cellar and then we clean up, wash face and hands and put on clean shirts. You get fire going in the stove. I'll make coffee and get cribbage board out. Make it look like we been here for a while drinking coffee and playing cribbage."

The fire was going and the coffee was hot. John had just enough time to pour two cups when McDougal drove in and parked behind the cabin. Parnell started to get up. "No, sit down. We play cribbage, make him come in." Parnell was just dealing the cards when McDougal and Tramlin walked around the corner of the cabin.

They could surely see the smoke in the chimney but they still didn't know if there was anyone inside. McDougal pushed the screen door in quietly and then looked through the window in the door. John waved his arm and motioned for them to come in.

"How about a cup of coffee?" Parnell asked. McDougal didn't answer. It was easy to tell that he was confused. He didn't have any idea that he'd find these two here drinking coffee and playing cards.

"What brings you two gentlemen here today? Come in and sit down," John said.

Parnell noticed that McDougal kept watching his hands. John kept his hands in his lap so neither of them could see. He was playing with him.

"Oh, we're just out riding around and stopped to say hi."

"Would you like something to eat," Parnell got up and walked over to a cupboard door. "We just finished a couple of sandwiches."

"That's okay, we're not really hungry. You boys haven't seen the game warden about today, have you?" Tramlin asked.

"Heard earlier that he might be over at Lévesque City. There's a rats nest of poachers over there." John said without cracking a smile. Now he put both hands on the table. Still playing with them.

It was obvious they didn't find what they were looking for. "Well we had better be on our way," Tramlin said as he went back outside and McDougal close behind him.

"Well, boys," John hollered after them, "Come again. We'll have to get together more often. Don't be strangers now."

As they drove off the knoll and out of earshot, both John and Parnell broke-up laughing. "Do you suppose they suspect anything?"

"That's why they were here. They know, all right, but they can't prove it. They'll know, once you register that bear tomorrow and collect the bounty," John said.

"How about the rest of the coffee?" Parnell emptied the pot in John's cup.

"You got anything strong?"

"Yes, yes I do. Been saving this for a special occasion." Parnell went into his bedroom and came back out with a new bottle of whisky. He broke the seal and poured some into each coffee cup.

John raised his cup and said, "To—to tomorrow. Boy that was a tongue-twister."

Parnell raised his too and said, "Tomorrow."

Between the whisky and the excitement of shooting McDougal's bear and getting away with it, they ignored the cribbage board. Before long they even had a drink to the local game warden. "And here's to ole Ian Randall, we got one over on you too."

"Well, you know Stormi don't like me none drinking. Let alone on Sunday. She's sure going to raise her hackles some. But she'll calm down when I tell her about the bear fat.

"Now, Parnell, we have to play tomorrow very careful. Crews leave here for the woods about 4:00 a.m. You'll have to leave here about 2:00 a.m. So's you can walk down Main Street with your pack basket and hide, so none sees you. We're going to do this thing right." John stood and took his knit hat off and wiped the sweat from his forehead. "Wow, she's hot in here." With that said, he left without saying anything else.

When John walked past the station house, McDougal and Tramlin were sitting on the platform. "Good day to you gents." They didn't reply.

* * * *

Before going to bed that night Parnell set the old wind-up alarm clock for 1:30 am and decided to sleep in his clothes so he wouldn't have to turn on a light in the morning. He hated the sound of the old clock. Tick, tick, tick.

1:30 a.m. came and the clock made so much noise he was sure the entire village must have heard it also. He got right up and went out to the root cellar and strapped on his pack basket and started walking down Main Street to John's cabin. There were no lights on yet in the whole village. His heart was racing and he'd be glad when this day was over. John met Parnell on his porch. "Where's your rifle?"

"Left it at the cabin, didn't think we would need it," Parnell whispered.

"That's okay, I'll grab my .35 and a hand full of shells. About you knife?"

"Don't have it."

"You feeling alright? How you can skin a bear without your knife? You never go anywhere without." That's one point Parnell would never forget.

John gave Parnell his .35 and he took his favorite rifle, a .38-55 Winchester. Now they could leave. "Where're we going now?"

"We going to get in my canoe, and very quietly paddle to the other side the lake."

As Parnell seated himself in the bow, John said, "Don't

load your rifle 'til daylight. If ole Ian is about, we don't want to be arrested for night jacking." John guided the canoe slow and silently across Smith brook inlet and then to a hidden trail by Emerson Ridge.

John handed Parnell his rifle and pack, "I'll get the canoe." He pulled it up and out of sight of the lake. "We'll wait here for daylight. Then we go over the ridge to a swamp and shoot bear." John peered through the bushes watching the lake. "Good place to see if warden follow."

Daylight broke and still they waited. John never took his eyes off the lake. He knew Ian and his reputation, and he didn't want to tangle with him unnecessarily. Not today anyhow.

Two hours had passed since daylight and there was no movement on the lake. "Looks like we go now." And John led the way up Emerson Ridge, and down the other side, and sure enough, out into a black muck swamp. They both were covered with the black muck, as John groaned, "Okay, we stop here and shoot bear. Fire one shot into air."

Parnell loaded his rifle and fired one shot into the air. "Okay, now we wait a little before shoot again." While they waited, John pulled the hide out of Parnell's pack and rolled it around in the black muck. Then he rolled it back up again and placed it back into the pack. "Okay, shoot two more times, about ten seconds apart."

Parnell did as he was instructed. "Now what?"

"We wait one hour right here. Like we were skinning bear. Then we go back to the canoe to make this look real."

"I wish I had had you in Korea."

"You sounding like you were an officer."

"Captain, actually."

"Well I'll be damned. I never would have guessed. Then what you doing here if you are officer and gentleman?"

"Trying to outsmart ole McDougal, without getting caught by Ian Randall."

"You see much action?"

"Yeah, too much. I was in frontline infantry. Best two men I had were Bauber from Louisiana, and an Indian from the Black Hills, Don't Eat Dog."

"You mean his name was Don't Eat Dog!"

"Yes, and he was proud of it." Parnell told John the story behind the name.

After an hour John said, "Well, we covered with black muck, shot and skin bear. Now we go to station house and tag. Then we get bounty." Parnell followed John back to the canoe. This time John was anything but quiet. As they paddled back across the lake towards the village, John began to sing a little French song. Parnell had no idea what he was saying.

Ian Randall was sitting in a chair on the platform as John and Parnell walked up the steps. He got up and walked over to the steps. "Well, Mr. Purchase, I bet you have been hunting this morning."

"Yes, sir. Got me a big bear too."

"Did you shoot it, or John?"

"I did," Parnell replied.

"I'd like to see your rifle." Parnell handed Ian his rifle and Ian opened the action and an empty cartridge was ejected. He opened the action on John's rifle and ejected a live round. "Well, you look as if you've been hunting."

Parnell removed the pack basket and removed the hide and unrolled it. "Look how big this is!" It was obvious Parnell was excited. *Maybe he did shoot it,* Ian thought.

"What happened to the head? Seems a big bear like this you'd want the head."

John was about to answer, but Parnell cut him short. "There wasn't enough of his head left to bother with. My first shot just blew his lower jaw off. He took off running but he must have been stunned, 'cause he couldn't go very fast. My next shot missed completely and my third shot hit him right in the ear and blew his skull to pieces." John was somewhat surprised. He had created a monster.

"Why didn't you bring out the whole bear?"

"Just look at us. We're all covered with mud, and there was no way we could have dragged him through the swamp."

"I suppose that if I asked you to show me the rest of the carcass, you could."

"No, sir, I'm afraid I couldn't." Ian was smiling now. But so too was John.

"We were in so much muck that when John rolled the carcass off the hide—it sank in that black awful stuff. We had no choice actually; we could take you back where we shot it and skun it, but there won't be any carcass."

"Where exactly is this swamp?"

Parnell turned to John then, "Swamp is behind Emerson Ridge in T7-R4."

"If I might ask you a question, Ian."

"Go ahead."

"I don't suppose you'd tell me how come you happen to be here just as we bring this bear in to collect bounty."

"No problem. Lunch and a cup of coffee." Now he was grinning, and John didn't like that.

"Gentlemen, have a good day." There wasn't much more he could do. But what irritated him most was that John Corriveau knew it also. When Parnell had shot the bear on Sunday over McDougal's bait, Ian had been at Boom Branch, where Tie Camp Brook puts it. He had gotten word that two workers from the Tie Camp crew were using gill nets across Tie Camp Brook. Tie Camp being a natural spawning ground for brook trout. He had sat there for two days and no one had appeared. He had heard Parnell's shot and knew it was close. He took a compass reading and had come out on the graveled road by the East Branch, but had seen no one. That is until McDougal and Tramlin had driven by, then turned around and drove by again in the direction of Howe Brook. He was sure that McDougal and Tramlin were the ones using the gill net.

He had camped all night where McDougal had turned around

to see if he or anyone else would return. He knew something had died close by. Deer, moose, bear? He wasn't sure. In the morning after daylight he had decided to walk to the village, just to see who was around.

After Ian had left and there was no one else to overhear, "You learn well. You almost convinced me. Hope you never turn against me. Ian—he wasn't hungry. I don't know how but he knows when and where that bear was shot. Mark my words, he'll be our worst nightmare until he gets us. And he will get us; he ain't happy, no siree."

They collected their thirty-five dollar bounty. "Just in case Ian didn't leave, we should render that fat now at your cabin. Don't want to get caught with that in the open after that line you gave the warden. He'd walk us out of here and lock us up for the winter.

"You should nail that hide to the wall of your wood shed and stretch it, for a bear rug. Get some hemlock bark and rub the bark over the fleshy side every day. This will tan the hide and soften it. It'll make a great bedroom rug, so you won't have to step on a cold floor when you get up."

* * * *

When the story circulated about John and Parnell getting a bear across the lake, and getting covered with black muck from the swamp, McDougal and Tramlin didn't champion their cause any further.

The following weekend Ian Randall found the gill net strung across Tie Camp Brook near Boom Branch. He hoped, no he'd give his left arm, if John Corriveau came back to tend it. But John and Stormi had taken the train out to Oakfield to visit her ailing sister.

The gill net was about ten feet long and probably extended to the brook bed. Ian could see a few fish caught in the net, but he knew if he disturbed it, then whoever set it probably would shy away. So he waited patiently, knowing, this time, he would catch the culprits. The fine would be so big he'd have to walk them out of there to ensure their appearance in court.

About midnight Saturday it began to rain. Only a mist at first, but by 3:00 a.m. it poured. He was vigilant, though; he waited.

Sunday turned off hot and humid for the first of October. Unusual weather. At 1:00 p.m. he could hear a pickup with a loud exhaust coming up the East Branch road towards Tie Camp. He was getting excited and his legs began to shake with anticipation. Then he had to pee. The pickup came to a stop and he heard two doors close. He waited what seemed like an eternity. Finally he could hear someone stumbling through the bushes. They were talking French. He knew it had to be McDougal. He was right. They soon came into view. But they too were being cautious. They dropped out of sight and waited to see if they were being followed before they approached the net.

When McDougal thought it was safe he motioned to Tramlin. He came up behind with a burlap bag. McDougal picked the net up and untied his end and then pulled sharply and the other end broke free. "Hey, look at all those fish!" Tramlin exclaimed as he began to fill the burlap bag.

When McDougal had finished cleaning the net he rolled it up and tucked it under a bush. Tramlin said, "We have over two hundred."

Ian stood up behind them. Neither of the two had seen him yet. "Well, hello boys." Ian said rather friendly. "This is Sunday so you can't be bird hunting. Nope, no shotguns." Tramlin stepped in front of the burlap trying to conceal it. "My this is a beautiful day." He rubbed the stubble of whiskers.

McDougal was smart enough to understand from that gesture that Ian had been there waiting for them, at least two days.

"Why don't we hike back to the crew camps and we can talk this over. You two carry that bag of trout. Now before you get any stupid ideas; if you think because there is two of you and only one of me, let me dissolve any intentions you might have of giving me any trouble. Because if you do, I'll drop the both of you right here. Is that understood?" Tramlin reluctantly nodded his head. "How about you, McDougal? I know you understand English, even if you can't speak it."

McDougal said, "Okay."

The two plowed their way through the bushes, Ian following close behind. They were met in the camp yard by McDougal's boss, Lucien Shelly. "What's going on here, Ian?"

"I caught these two gill netting. This burlap is full of trout. I'm going to walk them out to jail."

McDougal and Tamlin suddenly had a sick expression on their face. "That's a mighty long walk. Which way you going, Ian?" Lucien asked.

"They'll have to go to Houlton so I'll hike 'em down to Shorey Siding where we can board the train."

"Tell you what, Ian. You release them to my custody and I'll make sure they're in court Thursday. I need them both for the next two days. We're laying out a new road."

"On one condition. You give me a ride, with that bag of fish, to the station house so I can catch this afternoon's train."

On the way to the station house, "Would you have actually walked those two losers all the way to Shore Siding? You might have been able to catch the 6 o'clock southbound. You could have had a hot meal and a roof over your head," Lucien said.

"With characters like those two, it would be best to get them out of familiar territory, their domain, as quick as possible. At the village they might be tempted to show off for their friends. Then there might have been real problems. When a man has hot food in his belly and a night's sleep, he can be uncontrollable. By walking them to Shorey and waiting all night for the morning train they would have been tired and too worn out to cause too much problem. Besides, out here in the woods they're on my turf."

"How much of a fine is ole Archibold apt to give 'em?"

"Probably twenty dollars plus a dollar for each fish. That'll hurt them."

"I'm glad I don't have to worry about you on my trail. You be careful of those two, Ian."

"Aw they're just like school yard bullies, needing to be taken down a peg. Thanks for the ride, Lucien."

Ian carried the burlap bag of trout into the general store. "Hey, Henry, do you have a cooler I could put this bag full of trout in so they don't spoil?"

"Sure thing. I have just the place in my cellar."

"Thanks, Henry. Train probably has been through already?"

"Yeah, it was early today. Forty minutes ago."

Ian sat at a table in the restaurant and ordered the special, boiled ham. Before he had finished ordering Parnell came in. "Do you mind if I sit at your table?"

"Sit. You aren't indignant because you had to do fifteen days in jail?"

"Not at all. Why should I be? It was my own fault."

"There's a lot of folks who would have held a grudge."

"As I said, my own fault. I'll have the special also." Henry took his order and left.

"You look as if you have stayed out for a few days. Chasing anyone I know?"

"Oh I think you know them alright. Alfons McDougal and Lester Tramlin. They don't seem to be too fond about you or Corriveau. Where is John, anyhow?"

"He and Stormi went out to Oakfield." He purposely stayed away about any more mention of McDougal and Tramlin.

"How long have you been out here this trip?"

"Week from Friday."

"What about your family? Won't they be worried?"

"Yeah, my wife is apt to divorce me this time. Good thing she's not the jealous type."

"Why don't you stay home more?"

Ian almost choked on his coffee as he began to laugh. "Yeah, and let you yahoos have the run of the woods. There wouldn't be a deer or moose left in the country." Ian changed the subject then. "You seem like a pretty likeable fellow with a good sense of direction about you. What ever possessed you to come to Howe Brook to live?"

"I got tired of the civilized world. I saw too much senseless killing in Korea."

"You running away from anything? The law?"

"Nope. I like it here and it doesn't take much money to live here."

"Not as long as you live on moose and deer meat." They both laughed.

"Where are you staying tonight?"

"I got a room in the hotel. It'll be quite a change from sleeping on the ground."

Their boiled dinners came and they ate in silence.

* * * *

Parnell was up early the next morning and went down to the station house for breakfast. "Good morning, Henry, is Ian up yet?"

"He's gone."

"What do you mean? The train hasn't arrived yet."

"He must have gotten up during the night and left. When I went to wake him he had already left. He left that burlap bag full of trout. He'll be back."

Parnell scratched his head. Where in the hell has he taken off to now? It was the first day of partridge hunting, maybe he went out to get himself a few birds. After breakfast Parnell went bird hunting also. By mid-day he had three. "That's enough for today."

On his way back from the roll dam on Smith Brook he stopped to see if John and Stormi were back yet.

Stormi saw him crossing the tracks. "John Henri, Parnell is coming up the driveway."

John met him on the porch. Parnell held up the three birds. "Should be enough for lunch," Parnell said.

While they were cleaning the partridge Stormi started frying up some potato. "I had supper with the warden last night." No comment. "He was in here all last week. He caught McDougal and Tramlin. But he wouldn't say what they were doing illegal."

"You're getting pretty chummy with the warden, aren't you?"

"Can't hurt to stay on the good side of him."

"Maybe, but he'll still arrest you. Just be careful he doesn't try to pump you for information about what goes on out here."

"He has already tried. Didn't do him much good. This partridge is delicious, Stormi."

"That's cause I fried them in bear fat. That reminds me, John, when you and Parnell have finished eating, why don't you take your pack basket and go back with Parnell and bring back some more bear fat and canned venison."

On the way to Parnell's cabin, John asked, "Are you going to trap this fall?"

"I haven't given it a thought."

"The season starts on the fifteen. If you are, then you should boil your traps and hang them up in the fresh air. You'll have to take my name tags off and put your own on."

"I have never trapped before. Will you help me get started?" Parnell asked.

There was no hesitation. "Nope. That you'll have to learn as you go. I'll show you where to hunt, where to fish, hell I'd even share my wife before I would share my trapping secrets. No hard feelings. That's just how it is."

After John left with the bear fat and venison, he built a fire outside and put a large tub of water on the coals, to boil. In the meantime he started scraping the rust off the jaws and springs. It had been a few years since these traps had been used.

* * * *

67

The traps cleaned and boiled and hanging on the shed wall, Parnell spent each evening perusing the many books and magazines John and Stormi had left, looking for anything to do with trapping. The only thing that he could find had to do with bait and lure. The best lure was beaver castor mixed with fat. The bait was any meat, as long as it wasn't rotten.

Parnell went partridge hunting every day. The breast he canned and the wings and carcasses he stored in the root cellar and would use that for bait.

The fifteenth arrived and Parnell shouldered his pack basket of traps, bait, and axe. He decided to run a trap line along the railroad north towards Pride Siding or as far as his traps would take him.

Trapping was new to him and he was slow preparing each set. The traps were off the roadbed in the woods and each set was marked with two rocks. By the time the sun was starting to set he had only gotten as far as the falls on the St. Croix River. But he didn't have enough traps left to string a line all the way to Prides.

He was tired that night and went to sleep sitting in his overstuffed chair. He didn't awaken until the next morning when the southbound train went through the village. He ate breakfast, shouldered his pack and struck out to check his traps. None of the traps had even been touched until he checked the last one he had set yesterday. He had a nice fox.

He put the fox in his pack basket and moved on, setting more traps. He only had five left and those were set by 2:00 p.m. He returned to his cabin, and while his supper was cooking, he skinned the fox on his kitchen table. He put the hide on a stretcher to dry and he ate supper, cleaned up and went to bed.

He checked his trap line every day. And each day he would have a piece of fur: fox, raccoon, fisher or pine martin. He had set for mink and otter but as yet none of those traps had been disturbed. Cold weather was setting in and he found that his traps were freezing to the wet soil and the animals were stealing the bait.

He got up one morning to eight inches of new snow. Today would be a good day to pull all his traps. He had done fairly well for a newcomer. He had four red fox, three raccoons, five pine martins, one fisher, and one otter. No mink. He hadn't seen his friend John at all during the trapping season, and he hadn't seen or heard of the game warden being around since the morning when he had left early. Henry McBride had told him later that the warden had returned later that same day and picked up his burlap bag of trout and had taken the train to Oakfield. But no one had seen or heard from him since then.

* * * *

For Thanksgiving everybody gathered for dinner at the stationhouse—combination train station, hotel-restaurant, and general store. Tables from the one-room schoolhouse were brought up and everybody brought something for the celebration. Parnell brought a bushel of peeled, washed potatoes. Some brought pies, some brought vegetables, someone brought a bottle of wine, P&C donated four big turkeys, Stormi made two blueberry pies.

McDougal was with his own family in Oxbow, but Lester Tramlin was at the celebration with his family and taking his share of ribbing after being caught by Ian Randall. Parnell shied away from any conversation with the man.

Ansel Snow arrived with his wife and she had made a pumpkin pie. During dinner Ansel asked Parnell, "Parnell, my wife is going back on the late train but I'm going to stay over to hunt tomorrow. There's no room in the hotel, that's why my wife is returning this evening. If you have an extra bed, I'd appreciate it."

"John, do you want to hunt tomorrow with Ansel and me?" Parnell asked.

"I would like to, but I still have traps out that I need to pick up before the snow gets any deeper. Maybe you could shoot me a nice spike horn," They all laughed.

That night in Parnell's cabin, Ansel asked, "Where are we going to hunt tomorrow?"

"I have been seeing a lot of deer where Beaver Brook crosses the tracks."

They were both awake early the next morning; Parnell fried up a large breakfast of moose steak, and eggs and leftover potato fried in bear fat. It was still dark when Parnell shut his cabin door. Daylight would bristle forth in the cold air soon. The snow was still fluffy and steam rose into the air with every breath.

Just beyond the village they found where many deer of all sizes had come onto the roadbed from along Howe Brook. "Maybe we should have been out here last night," Parnell said.

The deer didn't leave the tracks until Beaver Brook. Then they turned east up along the brook. "They're probably going to yard before the snow gets any deeper," Ansel said. Ansel crossed the brook and Parnell followed the deer tracks. If Parnell jumped the deer and they crossed the brook Ansel would already be there. They were only out of sight of each other by fifty or sixty yards. Ansel soon found where a single deer had recently crossed to his side of the brook. Probably spooked by Parnell. The track was fresh and he decided to follow it.

The deer took him into a cedar thicket. The top canopy was thick and heavy and there was little snow that had filtered to the ground. Ansel was just moving his way along. He could see about one hundred and twenty feet ahead of him. He stopped and listened. There was movement directly ahead of him. But he couldn't make out what it was. He didn't think the deer knew he was being followed yet. Ansel moved at the same time as the deer. Hoping to mask his own noise. The deer stopped and so did Ansel. This time he could see the hindquarters. The deer was looking ahead. Ansel whistled softly and the deer turned his head looking over his back, directly at Ansel. All Ansel saw were the antlers. A heavy wide set. Ansel pulled his rifle to his shoulder and took a fine bead just under the deer's chin.

To Parnell, Ansel's .30-06 sounded like a .105 howitzer.

There was just the single shot. The deer Parnell had been following separated. One bunch went off to his right and there were two still following the brook.

Ansel saw the deer drop, but he waited. Ready to shoot again if he had to. The deer wasn't moving. He walked up slowly, ready to shoot again. He started counting points while he was eight to ten feet away. Fourteen in all. He started dressing the deer. "Guess I'll make the afternoon train after all."

Parnell now could see movement directly ahead of him. He dropped to his knees. The deer took another step and Parnell could see his antlers. He aimed at the neck and fired. After the recoil, he still had his rifle held tight against his shoulder and looking down the barrel, the deer was still standing there looking back at him. He fired again and the deer went down. Parnell didn't hesitate. He walked right up. Holding his rifle ready to shoot again if he had to. He swallowed real hard. There were two dead deer. "I'll be damned. I didn't think I saw horns that second shot."

When Parnell had fired his first shot Ansel had both hands inside of the deer's ribcage cutting away the lungs and windpipe. The first shot surprised him; it was close. He jumped and stuck himself with his knife. The deer was too big to drag out alone. He crossed the brook and hadn't gone far at all when he came across Parnell bending over two deer.

"I wondered what all the shooting was about."

"Pure accident," Parnell said as he stood up, blood up to both elbows.

"You all finished?" Ansel asked.

"Yeah," Parnell wiped his hands in snow and then on his pant leg.

"Didn't take you long. We have a real job ahead of us now. How many points is your buck?"

"Six. Yours?"

"Fourteen. We'd better leave these right here and hike back to the village and see if we can borrow a sled."

"John has one specially made for dragging out deer. I was going to give him the doe anyhow."

* * * *

John heard them talking and met them on the porch. "We need your help, John, and your sled."

"Sure—sure thing. Come in and have some coffee. Stormi, get us some coffee."

"We have a doe for you, John, if you want to put your tag on it." Parnell said as he sipped his coffee. "We have two nice bucks too."

"How much of a drag is it?"

"About two hundred feet off the tracks at Beaver Brook," Ansel replied. "We didn't know if you'd be back yet or not. Did you get all of your traps pulled?"

"Yeah, just in time, I'd say."

Stormi had been baking bread when Parnell and Ansel arrived. "You boys want some hot bread with your coffee?"

They ate their bread and when the coffee was gone they started back up the tracks dragging John's deer sled.

Nearly four hundred and fifty pounds of deer doesn't drag easy. Not even with a sled and over snow. The snow made it easier but by the time the three had the deer at the station house to tag, they were worn out and the sun had set.

"I can just hear the northbound train," Ansel said, "making a lot of noise coming up the grade from Shorey. Just in time too. I think I'll wait right here on the platform. I'm too tired to move."

John and Parnell took their deer and hung them in Parnell's woodshed. "I'll come up tomorrow afternoon and we'll pull the hides off. They sure are going to be good eating."

"Do you want any help dragging that sled back, John?"

"I ain't that old."

"Okay, see you tomorrow."

Parnell fixed himself a sandwich and then went to bed. He was exhausted.

* * * *

Parnell slept late the next morning. For breakfast—just coffee. He looked outside at a gray overcast sky. For the remainder of the morning he worked with his fur. Those that were dry he took off the stretchers. He combed and preened the fur until the hairs glistened with their own natural shine. He was proud of how his pelts were looking. He hoped to get top dollar. He would do better next year.

For lunch he fixed the deer heart with onions and boiled potato. He was just finishing the last of it when John walked in. "Boy! It's getting cold outside. We'd better get those hides off before they freeze solid."

"I'll put a new pot of coffee on to boil while we're skinning," Parnell said.

"I haven't seen Ian since he caught McDougal. Has he been around at all?"

"I heard he was working someone at the Friel crew camp north of Frost Adams Ridge. Then I guess he had to look into a fatal hunting accident near the Farrar Crew Camps west of Route 11 at Weeks Brook in T7-R6. He's been too busy to be bothering us. Good thing, too, I guess."

Parnell told John the story of accidentally shooting the doe. "Purely accidental it was."

"Maybe, but I doubt very much if Ian would have looked at it like that."

"Where does he live, John?"

"Knowles Corner."

"Have you ever seen or met his family?"

"Nope. I'm told though, she's a good looker."

"She must be quite a woman to put up with her husband gone so much. I think he lives more out here in the woods than he does at his own home."

"He likes the game that's all," John said.

"What game?"

"Poachers poach to see if they can outsmart the warden and the warden sees if he can outsmart the poacher. All in the game. That's all it is. But I doubt if Ian would ever admit to anyone that it is just a game.

"Oh, before I forget it, the fur buyer from Presque Isle is coming tomorrow on the late afternoon train. Have your fur ready by then and down at the station house. He pays in cash too. How was your catch for your first time at it?"

"I got fourteen pieces. How did you do, John?"

"Not much better, I was feeling poorly last month."

"What was wrong with you?"

"Not sure. Didn't have no spunk. Each evening I was exhausted."

"You should have said something yesterday before helping us drag the deer down here."

"I was actually feeling more better yesterday. But after supper I felt exhausted. Stormi, she's worried although she tries not to show she is.

"We're skinning these just in time; the buyer will pay five dollars a hide. We'll let these deer hang for a few days before we start canning. Stormi wants me to bring back two jars of moose meat and cabbage."

When the deer were skun, Parnell filled his pack basket with moose meat and cabbage. "Do you want me to carry this pack back for you?"

"I can carry it myself, but thanks."

* * * *

Parnell received two hundred and fifty five dollars for his fur. He had hoped for more but he was satisfied with that. John had trapped mostly for otter and mink and he received more than twice what Parnell was paid.

Three days later began the beaver trapping season. The weather had been unseasonably cold and the ice was safe enough to be on. "We'll have to trap beaver together, Parnell. You don't have any beaver traps, and out in the deep woods like this it is safer to team up together. One day the ice will be safe and the next you could step right through. When we sell the hides, we split fifty-fifty."

"How much are beaver hides worth? More than the hides we just sold, I hope," Parnell said.

"Depending on the demand, but I've seen 'em go as high as a dollar an inch and a super large beaver will stretch upwards of seventy inches. Then of course there's the castor. Sometimes we get as much as five dollars a pound. There's an ice chisel in the wood shed. Sharpen that tonight and your axe. Tomorrow bring a lunch. After tomorrow, we eat beaver. Bring a pot to boil coffee in too. I hate tea."

Parnell was up at daylight the next morning. The thermometer said it was -10°F. He pulled on a sweater over his sweatshirt and then his wool jacket.

"Where are we going, John?"

"Tracy Brook. There's always beaver there and in the smaller feeder brooks too." They didn't put their snowshoes on until they had crossed the lake. It was brutal out in the open. Parnell thought he would freeze for sure. But once they had their snowshoes on and breaking trail going up Tracy Brook, he soon forgot about being cold, as sweat dripped from his face.

The first colony was on the small stream on the left where John had shot the deer that had gotten Parnell arrested. "I don't think I'll ever forget this spot." John didn't understand what he was referring to.

"You cut us a hole in the ice about two-feet square and I'll cut us some wood." John picked up his axe and cut a four inch fir tree, cut the limbs off and cut it about six feet long. Then he found some small popple.

Parnell had finished his hole. There was only six inches of ice. John tested the stream bed to see whether it was hard or soft. "Good, gravel bottom."

He showed Parnell how to make a chair for the trap and

how high above the chair to nail the bait (popple). When the pole and trap were in the water, John wired a cross stick to the pole. "So we don't lose the trap down the hole."

Then John showed him how to set a blind set against the bank and this time the trap was on bottom.

"A surefire way to catch beaver is to make a little trough in the top of the dam to let out some water. Beaver are always checking the dam for leaks. Set trap firmly in the trough and you'll have yourself a beaver."

John started putting on his snowshoes and Parnell asked, "If it is such a sure-fire way of catching beaver, why aren't we doing it?"

"That, oh, that's an illegal set. I expect the warden will be around in a day or so checking. I do use the trough set some, but I don't leave it overnight. I either build fire and wait, or I come back same day. Not now, though. Wait until ice gets more thick."

"In January we can trap bobcat too. They follow brooks looking for carcasses. When we get a beaver we make special blind for the cat. The cat can't resist the smell of castor. Fifteen dollar bounty too. Turn-in tail like bear."

By the end of that first day they had set up colonies on Tracy, Roll Dam Brook, Ikes, Lewis, and Pierce Brooks. "We come back tomorrow and tend. We'll have some beaver."

John hadn't said anything but Parnell knew he was tired. The pace had really slowed. But then again, he was tired, too. Stormi had supper ready when they got back. A boiled dinner with canned moose meat. There was little conversation during supper. They were hungry and tired.

When they had finished eating, Parnell excused himself, "I'm so tired, if I don't leave now I'll fall asleep at this table." John was almost asleep already. He didn't get up when Parnell left. "See you tomorrow, John." He didn't answer.

There were a couple of inches of new snow the next morning and the cold held on. At first both John and Parnell still showed signs of tiredness, but by the time they were halfway across the lake their pace had picked up. There was nothing in the traps at the first colony. "Don't get discouraged. It might take a few days but we'll get them," John said as he was leaving that first flowage.

They had three flowages on Roll Dam Brook to tend. They had a large beaver at each of the three flowages. "You build us a fire and I'll start skinning."

By the time Parnell had a good fire blazing John had the first beaver skun. "Cut off the hind legs and roast them over the fire."

Parnell watched with fascination as John pulled the hind legs off. The hides were not fleshed. They would have to do that later. The three beaver were skun before Parnell had finished roasting the meat. "This would be a likely spot to catch ole Mr. Bobcat. There's plenty of blood on the ice and snow to attract him." John built a cubby at the base of a spruce tree. He wired one carcass to the tree and set the trap just inside the cubby. The cubby was built with dry sticks standing up to form a Tipi over the carcass and trap. Then he smeared some castor on the bark of the spruce tree for lure.

"The meat is done," and he handed one leg to John. "Wish I had thought to bring some salt."

"Did you make any coffee?"

"Yeah, I set your cup over there out of the way."

Parnell took a bite. He was only a little skeptical. But after that first bite he devoured the rest.

"I've slowed down a lot this year, Parnell. My age is begging to catch up with me."

"How old are you, John?"

"How old do you think?"

"Well, you have the experience and the wisdom of someone over a hundred." John choked on his coffee. "But you don't look a day over fifty-five."

"Sixty-five, to be exact. Maybe it is time to slow down some."

Parnell didn't like the way John was talking. Did he know something that he was not saying?

Lunch was over and the bobcat trap was set. It was time to move on. They cut through the woods to Ikes Brook instead of following the brook back. They saved valuable time. There they caught a super large, or super blanket, beaver.

"You skin this one, Parnell, don't worry about getting it clean. We'll do that when we flesh it."

Parnell was a fast learner. He wasn't as quick as John, but he would learn to be.

They had one on Lewis Brook and another on Pierce Brook. That made them six for the day. "That'll figure up to good wages for the day." Under an overhanging fir tree next to the bank, Parnell made another trap cubby like he had watched John do.

"Now it's time to go home, but our work isn't done yet. We still have to flesh these and stretch them on boards."

They worked late into the night fleshing and stretching the hides. Finally at 10 p.m., the last one was nailed to the drying board. They set the boards out in the woodshed where it was cold. "When the hides freeze, the flesh side turns white. The fur buyers like to see that. We'll take tomorrow off. Stormi said she heard on the radio that it is supposed to snow tomorrow. Bobcat will be moving tonight. Wouldn't surprise me none if we might'n have one next tend." John said as he wiped his face with his shirtsleeve.

Parnell dragged himself home and had to restart the fires in both stoves. Then he had to sit up for a while until there were enough coals to bank the fire for the night.

It was two days before the weather cleared. The wind was still blowing out of the north but the temperature was more seasonable, about 10 degrees Fahrenheit. That day they had two large male bobcats and no beaver. "These aren't worth as much as two beaver but not a bad day's wage."

For the next two days they set up flowages on Smith Brook and Weeksboro tributary. There was more snow and the snowshoeing was slower and more tiring; Parnell broke trail. He looked behind him; steam from John's head was rising through his knit cap.

* * * *

At Christmas the whole village got together again to celebrate. It was the most enjoyable Christmas that Parnell could ever remember. The entire village was actually one big family, not merely friends or acquaintances. When the meal was over and everything was picked up and cleaned, they sang Christmas carols. Later there was eggnog. The adults had theirs with a bit of brandy and the children had a scoop of ice cream with theirs.

The day after Christmas, John said, "Tomorrow morning Stormi and I are taking the train into Oakfield. Stormi insists that I go and see Doctor Stevens in Smyrna Mills. I know what he'll tell me, 'You're not as young as you used to be, John. You have to slow down.' But I promised Stormi I'd make the trip out. So for the next couple of days you'll have to tend traps on your own."

The next day Parnell crossed the lake before daylight. The snow on the ice was wind driven and packed hard enough so he didn't need his snowshoes until he left the lake. The snow was now up to his knees but it was still dry and fluffy.

He had eight more beaver before he left Tracy Brook for home. He wasn't as fast as John had been skinning the beaver but he enjoyed himself immensely. He roasted beaver meat for lunch, with bread and coffee. He pulled the bobcat traps and questioned whether or not to pull the beaver traps. He did pull the traps on the two flowages further away.

The next day he remained at home and fleshed the hides and nailed them to the drying boards. They had fourteen large beaver now, and two large bobcats.

The next day he tended the traps on Smith Brook and Weeksboro Tributary. He had four more super large beaver. After skinning them he set two more bobcat cubbies before striking it for home.

On his way back he stopped at the Corriveau cabin and started a fire in the wood heater. Then he went home and fleshed and stretched those four beaver.

The Corriveaus didn't return the next day like John had anticipated, and Parnell began to worry if there was something really wrong with John. He kept the fire going in their cabin. The Corriveaus finally returned home Friday afternoon, five days later.

Parnell was out tending traps again up Tracy, and this time he pulled all the traps. He had three more blanket size beaver. As he was crossing the lake he noticed lights on at the Corriveau cabin. He took a detour before going home.

"Thank you, Parnell, for keeping the heater going. It was so nice to come home to a warm cabin," Stormi said.

"How has the trapping been?"

"Good. I have three today and I pulled all the traps up Tracy. Before that, I got eight one day and four the next and I set two more bobcat cubbies down on Smith."

"Sounds as if you have been busy. That's good. I guess my trapping days are over. For the rest of this winter at least. Dr. Stevens said my blood pressure was too high."

"Very high, he said," Stormi added.

"That's why we were out longer than we had intended. He had me do some stress tests. Running and stepping to measure how high my pressure would go. He said no overexerting myself. That, he meant no snowshoeing, trapping, or shoveling snow or carrying firewood. But that ain't the worst of it! No siree, not by a damned sight. He wants me to starve myself to death."

"Now, John Henri, it won't be that terrible."

"No? Listen to this, Parnell. No fat. Only lean meat, no starch, that means no potatoes. No pie or cakes or brownies because of the lard (fat). No real butter, only two cups of coffee a day. He called it a bland diet. Bland! I'll say. There is one good thing, though. He wants me to drink liquor everyday. Says it'll thin my blood."

"John Henri, he said not more than two drinks a day."

"You'll have to do all the setting and tending, but he did say I could flesh and put hides on the boards."

Parnell made three more trips to Smith before he finally pulled his traps. He had gotten three more beaver and one extremely large bobcat.

"Last fall I saw some beaver workings where the East Branch puts into the main brook. I'll catch a ride up with the crew in the morning."

"Beautiful up there, Parnell. That lower deadwater never makes good ice. Too many springs to freeze too solid. You be careful or you'll become fish bait."

"I'll watch my step."

When the crew stopped to let Parnell off, it was still dark. The snow was so cold that it actually squeaked with each footstep. He strapped on his snowshoes in the road and then crawled his way over the snow bank. He hadn't traveled very far up the brook when he came to his first flowage. It was a short dam and a small house. "Probably just a pair."

He set two traps and moved on. There wasn't much snow on the deadwater. The snow had melted and then had frozen again. A short ways up the deadwater, he found what was left of a dead deer. He didn't know if bobcats had killed it or not, but there were cat tracks everywhere.

He found a well used trail and set a blind set in the cat trail. Trying to stay out of the trail while he set the trap and wired it to a tree. "Sure wish I had me a snare."

A little further up the deadwater and he found a large concentration of deer. He saw many and judging from all the tracks and trails, he figured there had to be more than two hundred.

Just beyond where he had seen the deer crossing the deadwater, he found another dead deer. This had recently been killed. There were cat tracks but no designated trails yet. He cut off a hindquarter and wired that to a tree and made a cubby set, brushing out his tracks when he had finished.

He found an active beaver house and feed bed and set up three pole and chair sets, around the feed bed.

He continued on towards the upper end of the deadwater and when he arrived at the top end, he suddenly stopped in his tracks. There were snowshoe tracks going off the brook heading westerly. There was no way the new tracks could have been his even if he had somehow gotten turned around, they were simply going in the wrong direction. They had to have been made by someone else. But who? He couldn't remember ever seeing where another set of snowshoe tracks had come onto the ice.

He was more than a little bit curious. He put his snowshoes on again and started to follow. The trail was taking him into some excellent deer wintering habitat. The snowshoe tracks kept going in the same direction. Westerly, never varying. He continued a little further and the tracks suddenly stopped. They disappeared. There was a well used deer trail in front of him traveling perpendicular to the direction he had been traveling, but there were only deer tracks in this trail and nothing beyond it or going in the opposite direction. He was puzzled, but there had to be a reasonable explanation.

He looked again at the deer tracks in the trail. They were fresh. He took his snowshoes off and stepped into the trail. The snow was packed hard in the trail and he wasn't leaving much of any track, but he could see his boot prints. He started following the deer. Not knowing what he was going to find. He could hear equipment running in the direction he was going.

He had only walked a little further when the deer trail forked. The freshest tracks went to the left. He was inclined to go in that direction but something in the other trail caught his attention. He backed up one step and bent over for a closer look. It was a boot heel print. The deer tracks must have obscured the boot tracks. What was this fellow up to? He was some cunning son of a devil.

Parnell was more curious now than before. He continued following, being very careful not to leave any more sign of his intrusions than he had to. In some places the boot prints were readily visible and at times he couldn't see them at all. The trail was beginning to veer around to the backside of a fir-covered knoll. Parnell kept following, but at a very slow pace. And then he saw him. He stopped dead in his tracks and stared at the aberration half buried in the snow just behind the top of a knoll looking straight ahead where the equipment noise was earlier, looking through a pair of binoculars, was Ian Randall.

Well, it was obvious now what he was doing. He was on the scent of some illegal hunting. Probably one of the crew. "Good luck to you," he whispered. Parnell backed up carefully. Trying not to make a sound or any sudden movement that would catch Ian's attention. When he thought it was safe, Parnell turned around and walked back to the deadwater. He traveled the entire length of the deadwater and not aware he had done so until he stopped to put on his snowshoes. His mind was back there with Ian Randall. What drove him to such extremes to catch someone? Was it an inner need of right versus wrong? Or was it simply part of the game?

He didn't go straight home. He went first to visit the Corriveaus and brought in enough firewood to last for a few days. He told John about his experience today, of tracking the game warden and finding him half buried in snow watching someone through binoculars. "You had better be careful of him, Parnell. We ruffled his feathers last summer with that bear you shot. He's not likely to forget.

"I'll walk with you back to your cabin. Stormi wants some potatoes and vegetables. Besides I haven't been outside these walls today. Legs getting stiff."

While John was in the root cellar he cut off a choice piece of steak from his deer. "There ain't no fat on that piece of meat. If Stormi complains too loud I'll come back here and fry it."

Before leaving Parnell's cabin, "Oh, Parnell, I almost forgot. There's going to be an important meeting at noon on Sunday at the station house. Everyone in the village is asked to attend. Adults that is."

"What's it all about, John?"

"I don't know, only that it is important."

Parnell didn't return to the deadwater to check his traps. He worked around his cabin, banking the outside with snow. Sorting through everything in the sheds and throwing out old food that had spoiled. He and John played a lot of cribbage, and while Parnell drank coffee, Stormi did allow John one cup of coffee and one drink of whisky, and his second drink of the day was usually enjoyed after supper.

Everyone was anticipating Sunday and what could possibly be so important. Parnell made another tend up on the deadwater before Sunday. But his mind was not on trapping. It was Sunday, and what would transpire. He didn't have any beaver, but he did catch two more large male bobcats.

That night while he and John were skinning the cats. "What do you think Sunday is all about, John?"

"I don't know. Everyone in the village is talking about it and worrying what's going to happen. No one has heard nothing." He took his knit hat off and wiped the sweat from his forehead. Parnell watched what John was doing and didn't think it was that warm. But then John never removed his hat except when he went to bed.

* * * *

Sunday arrived and every adult in the village was waiting anxiously at the station house. A special train from Oakfield arrived pulling only the B&A company car. Everybody found a seat. P&C's manager, Kyle Wentworth, "I wish I didn't have to be here today to bring you this news. The saw mill will be closing. It'll operate until this winter inventory is gone. And then the mill will be taken down. Levesque Lumber has been clearing a right of way for a new road into this country since last September. It is coming in from Route 11 just below the upper McManus Farm in T8-R5. By spring breakup, the new road will be complete as far as the St. Croix River at the St. Croix Siding. When the spring runoff drops, then a bridge will be put across the river. Then the following year the road will be continued to intersect with the Horseback Road that crosses the East Branch of Howe Brook, then there'll be a drivable road from Route 11 into Howe Brook Village.

"The mill will be closed because, one, we have just about cut off all the high grade spruce and pine and Levesque wants the wood for his saw mill in Masardis."

"What about the village?"

"The company buildings—hotel, station house, etc.—will come down. P&C will honor all of your leases. No one will be thrown out of their homes. Times are changing fast outside of Howe Brook. Levesque has employed some new equipment called skidders. It is a four-wheel-drive tractor that can wallow through deep snow and mud. A crew of three should be able to out produce the horse and crawler crews at least five to one.

"The Levesque mill wants fir as well as spruce trees. Most of the wood will be going out of here by rail, but there'll be trucks hauling all winter also. I'll stop for now and turn the floor over to Micky Dumain. I'll take questions later."

"Kyle has already said the station house will be coming down. That's because B&A will be terminating the passenger service here at Howe Brook. We will still be operating a passenger service, just won't be stopping here any longer. We'll maintain a siding here but as of September 30th there'll no longer be a passenger service here at the village."

"When will the village be torn down?"

"By September first, all the company buildings will all be torn down. We'll start probably by the first of August."

"What about those of us who have jobs at the mill or in one of the crews?" Lester Tramlin asked.

"Levesque has already said that he would hire anyone who wants a job with J.P. Levesque. Either in his mill or in one of the crews; that was a guarantee."

"But what about the way of life that we have had here at

Howe Brook?"

"When P&C built this mill and village, there was no permanency guaranteed. Times have changed."

There was nothing more that could be said. Kyle Wentworth and Micky Dumain left. Slowly, one by one, the villagers got up and returned to their homes without any social talk with neighbors. They were all sick to their stomachs. As Parnell was leaving he looked at John and Stormi. Stormi was crying and there were tears in John's eyes. He went back to his own cabin on the knoll and sat in his rocker staring at the floor. There were no words to describe how or what he was feeling. There were tears in Parnell's eyes too.

* * * *

After breakfast the next morning, Parnell walked down to see the Corriveaus. He was worried about what they might do after the bad news of yesterday. "Good morning, Parnell," Stormi said. "The cold weather has seemed to have broken."

"Yeah, but no good deed ever goes unpunished." Stormi just looked at him. She wasn't sure what he was trying to say.

John had been out in the outhouse and now he came through the door. "Some of the beaver hides will have to come off the boards today, and all the bobcat. But first, a cup of coffee.

"Have you decided yet what you'll do, Parnell?"

"I finally decided on my way here this morning. I'm staying. How about you and Stormi?"

"I want to stay— Stormi wants to go out to Oakfield to that new senior citizen living complex. But we won't have to do anything until September.

"These beaver hides are the best that I have ever seen," John commented as he pulled nails from the edges of the hides.

"I like these bobcats even though they aren't worth as much as the beaver."

"Things are really going to change around here," John said. "It'll be real sad."

"John, do you know what a skidder is?"

"Nope, I never even heard the word before. I don't understand how Levesque expects a tractor, four wheel drive or not, to work through deep snow and mud. Hell, crawlers even get stuck at times."

They finished with the beaver and bobcat hides and Parnell said goodbye and went back to his own cabin. He stoked the fire, made a pot of coffee and found a good book to read and sat down in his rocker. Before he had read two pages his chin had dropped to his chest and he was snoring.

"John Henri, go for your walk and get out of my hair for a while," Stormi raved.

There was only one place to go, Parnell's. He didn't bother to knock. He kicked the snow from his boots and opened the door. Parnell woke up with a start and his book fell to the floor. "How long has that coffee pot been boiling?"

"Oh, since the temperature reached 212 degrees Fahrenheit. You want to try a cup?"

Parnell poured two cups and dug out a bottle of ginger brandy and added a jigger full for flavor. While Parnell was doing that, John found the cribbage board and set it up. For the rest of the afternoon they played cribbage and drank brandy-flavored coffee until the coffee got too rugged, then Parnell filled their cups with just brandy.

The mill crew was done work for the day and John decided it was time to go home. After the bad news from the day before, Stormi didn't say anything to John about being away for so long, or that he had been drinking.

The next day Parnell caught a ride with the crew to the East Branch Bridge and followed his snowshoe trail to the deadwater. He had three beaver; two super blankets and one blanket. He skun those and cut off two hind legs that he put in his coat pocket for lunch later.

He wanted to follow the brook up to Boom Branch and look for beaver. From the lower deadwater to Boom Branch it was impossible to stay on the brook; he had to break trail along side of it.

He was tiring and needed a rest. There was a fir blow-down and he sat on the exposed trunk. It was just enough to accommodate him quite well. The blow-down moved. It must have just settled some, he thought. But it moved again and not down. Again and again. The whole tree was moving.

Parnell tried to stand up but he couldn't because of the tree moving. Then an ugly bear stuck its head out through the snow under the tree, between Parnell's legs. "Hey, Damn!" The bear stood up and knocked Parnell over backwards in the snow. The bear didn't run off. He stopped. He had his nose pointed in the air sniffing. He could smell the two beaver legs Parnell had in his coat pocket. He threw one leg at the bear. The bear pulled it out of the snow and ate it.

Instead of gulping like Parnell thought a hungry bear would; especially after not eating for five months, he very gently bit off small pieces and chewed it before swallowing. The first leg now gone the bear started sniffing the air again. There goes lunch. Parnell threw the second beaver leg. The bear took a long time devouring this leg. When it was gone the bear sniffed the air again. The scent was gone and so too was the bear. The bear left a two-foot wide path behind him. Parnell's heart was still racing. He picked himself up out of the snow and brushed himself off. "Wow, that was as close as I ever want to come to a live bear. Hope we don't cross trails again."

He wasn't as tired as he had been earlier though. He resumed his trek to Boom Branch. This was a very picturesque flowage. He walked the entire length of the dead water and didn't find any sign of beaver. There were several deer tracks and trails at the mouth of Tie Camp Brook.

Discouraged, he followed his trail back to the Lower Deadwater. He detoured around the fir blow-down where he had awakened the bear. He doubted if the bear would come back after having been so rudely disturbed, but he wasn't taking any more chances with another encounter with that fella.

His stomach was growling. He found one of the carcasses he had discarded earlier, built a fire and had lunch. He wondered if the bear would find these carcasses. Probably not. He would be looking for another blow-down to crawl under.

* * * *

The ice was getting thick and Parnell wasn't having as much fun as he would if John was out in the cold with him. He tended his traps on the lower deadwater once more and pulled everything. He had just one beaver. A blanket.

"The fur buyer will be here tomorrow, Parnell. We can take everything off the boards."

"Is it the same buyer that was here last fall?"

"Yes, coming in on the afternoon train."

They hand brushed each piece of fur. The hair glistened with their own natural oil, even the bobcat. When they were all done, John said, "You might as well have these drying boards and the fleshing beam and knife. I doubt if I'll ever have use for them again." Parnell figured then that he had made up his mind to leave the village. Hopefully not till summer. He wanted to ask John if he had decided against it. Right now the mere mention of having to leave would cause too much sorrow.

The next day Parnell and John carried their hides up to the stationhouse and had a cup of coffee in the restaurant while they waited for the afternoon train. "The train is beginning its approach. It's starting to slow." Parnell listened but he couldn't hear anything.

The train only stopped long enough for the fur buyer to disembark. No one was going south and the train left.

"Is this your fur outside?" The buyer asked when he saw John and Parnell at a table in the restaurant.

"They are."

"Well let's look at 'em. Then I'm hungry." He handled each piece sorting them by size. Then he looked at the bobcat and ran his fingers through the hair. "You two take good care of your fur. I've looked at some before and there'd be dirty, boot tracks on the flesh side and the hair would be all-full of snarls. You have six bobcats. I'll give a total of three hundred dollars for the cats. The beaver—the super blankets, I'll give you seventy dollars apiece and fifty-five for the blankets. Let's see that would be eighteen hundred-twenty for the beaver and three hundred for the cats. Total of twenty-one-twenty!"

"What about the castor?" John inquired.

"Don't want castor this year. There's been a work stoppage in France and Italy and the perfume is not selling this year. Maybe next year; just keep 'em dry."

"That's a good amount for winter's work. Just wished I could have been in the woods more with you. But for a flatlander, you did okay." They both laughed.

"Come up for a drink. I still have some of that brandy left."

"Thanks, but no. I promised Stormi I'd come home as soon as we sold the fur. We got thousand-sixty each. That's better 'n working in that mill. Good night, Parnell."

Parnell was figuring that if he worked a little harder at fall trapping, then between that and beaver trapping he should be able to make enough money to sustain his staying on at the village.

For the remainder of that winter Parnell cut ice for his root cellar, Mr. McBride's general store, the hotel and restaurant, and any family that wanted ice. He simply needed something to occupy his time. Then he threw out all the old sawdust from his root cellar and replaced it with new sawdust from the mill.

Until after spring breakup there wasn't a whole lot he could do, except walk. He almost wore his snowshoes out that first spring. When the snow was gone he walked the road—to Tie Camp, Roll Dam on the Smith Brook Deadwater, Levesque City and up the tracks to St. Croix Siding where the new bridge was going to be built.

On his way back he stopped at the falls on the river. The

water was high and making a loud noise surging over the ledges. He sat with his back against a spruce tree wishing he had lived here a hundred years ago as an Indian.

* * * *

Spring finally did arrive with warm sunshine. The ice was gone from the lake and the only snow left was in cool, shady spots. Everyone had the windows and doors open in their homes, airing out the old musty, damp air. The mill was still operating but there were only enough logs for another month of operation. Then the mill crew would start tearing down the building and loading the machinery onto railcars.

One cloudy afternoon in the middle of May, "Stormi, you and me let's go fishing."

"That sounds like a wonderful idea. Remember though, John Henri, you can't overexert yourself, so no long hikes."

"I thought we would canoe over to Tracy and fish from the bank. You know, where it's grassy. And you can look up and see the old sporting camp."

"Oh, I know where you mean. Okay." While John loaded the canoe, Stormi put up a quick lunch.

As John paddled towards the mouth of Tracy Brook, he kept scanning the shores as if he expected to see something. "Beautiful day ain't it, Stormi."

"Oh, John Henri, I think I'll miss this more than anything when we leave the village."

"Stormi, throw the anchor over here. We'll fish here for a bit." Stormi literally threw the anchor, instead of easing it over the side. They each baited their hook and threw it over the edge of the canoe. "Stormi, throw me a sandwich. I'm hungry."

Stormi caught one about ten inches and John caught two about eight inches apiece. "Let's go up the brook and try here again later. Pull the anchor in, Stormi."

Stormi started paddling to help John in the swift current. Once they were around the bend, John put ashore on a sandy beach and pulled the canoe up out of the water. "We better each take a creel, Stormi, just in case we get separated."

They fished side by each for a while and the fishing was slow. Stormi had caught a couple and then she moved upstream a short ways. John caught a couple short ones and he put those in Stormi's creel. Then he picked out two that were about nine inches each and he put those in Stormi's creel also. Stormi was having better luck upstream. She had two twelve-inch trout.

"Aren't they nice fish, John Henri?" She was excited. "Did you bring my creel with you?"

John handed her the creel and baited his hook again. "Stormi, you probably would have better fishing in that dead pool right below those rips. I'm going upstream a short ways. Don't worry, I'll be within talking distance."

Stormi moved up and before her worm hit the water in the pool at the base of the rips a fourteen-inch squaretail broke water for the worm. Stormi set the hook like an old pro. John was having pretty good fishing also. He caught one, just one, in each pool. The trout were hungry. He kept a mental count of how many he had.

He started thinking about all the trout he had taken out of this brook over the years. And the deer and moose he had shot on this side of the lake. One more trout and he would have his limit. He changed to another pool and got one about eight-inches. "That's enough." Just then he felt a sharp twinge in his chest. And then the pain disappeared as fast as it had come on. He ignored it and picked up his creel and started back to see how Stormi was doing.

She was still fishing. "Let's start back, Stormi."

He waited while she picked up her creel. He really didn't want this day to end, because it would probably be the last day ever of seeing Tracy Brook or this side of the lake. Or fishing for that matter.

They were seated in the canoe and John was letting the water current swing the bow around, pointing downstream. "This has been a great day, Stormi."

"It sure has."

As they canoed out into the lake another canoe was tucked along shore behind the point. It was gray and green. There was only one canoe around that color. "Hello, Ian," John said. "Just a perfect day isn't it."

"Can't complain. How was the fishing?"

Stormi beamed right out, "Fantastic! I caught a trout with almost every cast."

Without asking, John handed Ian his creel. "Just my limit, Ian."

Ian counted twelve. "Just right. But I must say I'm surprised, John. I thought you'd fish until they stopped biting."

"I did." They all laughed.

"I'd like to see your license, John and yours also, Stormi."

John passed Ian both their licenses. "I heard the company is closing the mill and B&A is stopping the passenger service to the village. It won't be the same around here. What will you folks do?"

"We'll be moving out to the settlement before September. The only person staying is Parnell."

Ian handed their fishing licenses back and said, "Have a good day, folks," and he started to push off.

"Hey!" Stormi said. "Aren't you going to check my creel too?"

"Okay, if you insist." Stormi handed Ian her creel and she was smiling radiantly.

The first trout he pulled out was the fourteen-incher. "Did you get this one in the lake, Stormi?"

"Nope. Right below that first set of rips. Right where you told me to fish, John Henri." She was still beaming with joy.

Ian pulled out several more. There were three short ones he set to one side and he continued emptying her creel. The legal length trout he put in one pile and those that were too short, he put in another. Just then John remembered he had put two short ones into her creel when she wasn't looking. So much for his mental counting.

"Stormi, you have four short trout." She wasn't filled with radiant joy any longer. She wasn't even smiling. "But that isn't your worst problem."

"What do you mean Ian?"

"The legal limit is twelve. You have, counting these four short ones, twenty."

"Oh my, I was having so much fun I never bothered to count."

"Stormi!" John exclaimed. "I'm married to a poaching wife! Well it's a good thing we'll be leaving the village. When the good folks in Howe Brook learn about my poaching wife— Well, I'll be laughed right out of the village. Stormi, I never would have dreamed that you would be a poacher. Never in all my days! Ian, you might as well take her to jail this day. Save me the embarrassment."

Ian sat his canoe and didn't know what to think. He was beginning to feel sorry for Stormi.

"Stormi, how could you do something like this to me? If'n it were me with too many fish—well Mr. Warden here would haul me off to jail." Now Ian was really feeling bad.

"I tell you what I'll do, Stormi. I'll write you a citation for eight fish over the limit and forget about the short ones."

"Oh thank you, Ian."

"You said you'd be leaving before September. I'll make your court appearance September fifteenth. That way you won't have to make a special trip out of here."

"Oh thank you, Ian, and I'm awfully sorry."

"How much will the fine be?" John asked.

"It usually is twenty dollars for the offense and one dollar for each fish."

"Twenty-eight dollars, Stormi. Plus travel to Houlton and back," John said.

Ian took the eight illegal trout leaving Stormi with just her legal limit of twelve. "Have a nice day, folks," Ian said as he pushed their canoe away from his.

As they paddled away, Ian sat in his canoe, smiling. He wanted to laugh—he had known how Stormi had treated John after some of his earlier poaching capers and how she had punished him, when she caught him cursing. He had heard in the village about the night of the screaming banshee and John's cursing and how Stormi had punished him for a month. He would never be sure if John had set her up on purpose or not. "He's a clever ole reprobate. I'll miss him when they leave."

"I'm sorry, John Henri. I'll never punish you again," She said, sobbing.

"I'll forgive you, Stormi. But no more poaching."

"Okay, John Henri."

John Henri Corriveau sat in the stern of his canoe, shoulders set square with his course and wearing a satisfied grin. He should have done this years ago.

* * * *

Since most of the wood crews would be replaced with the rubber-tired skidders, there would be no more stabling the work horses at the village any longer. There were a few shipped out by rail each week, most of them going north to Ashland. But there was one carload that was shipped to Houlton.

The hayfield where Parnell had slept his first night in the village was now lusciously green with new grass and clover. Every time Parnell walked by the field, memories of that day and night flooded his conscious mind. And there was a nice spikehorn deer that seemed to live right there in the field. The spikehorn's coat was reddish-brown.

One day while eating lunch at the restaurant, Parnell overheard two strangers talking about the spike horn. After the strangers left, Parnell asked McBride, "Henry, who were those two strangers?"

"They are camped at Cut Pond just east of Shorey Siding. They're from Ludlow, I think, Jimmy Hoggan and Steve

Lawrence. They're good boys to stay clear of. The game warden has been after them for a long time. I don't know what they're doing up here. This is the second time this month. They are up to no-good, if you ask me."

Parnell was wondering if that spikehorn might be in danger. They probably have a mess of trout cached somewhere that they'll pick up and take back.

Whenever Parnell visited John and Stormi, he noticed how attentive Stormi was towards John. She no longer nagged at him or promised to punish him for cursing. And John, out of respect for Stormi, never told Parnell about Stormi's encounter with the warden. That would be a secret he would take to his grave.

A month went by and again Parnell saw the same two strangers at the restaurant while he was eating lunch. This time they were talking about shooting the spikehorn and having it for the July 4th celebration at Cut Pond. Apparently Hoggan and Lawrence had a camp full of cronies coming in then.

Parnell was more interested now than ever. Here were two from outside the village planning to take, illegally, one of their deer. He heard Hoggan saying to Lawrence, "We ought to come back tomorrow night, after the lights go out in the village and shoot that deer."

"Yeah, we could cut the legs off and the saddles and put them in our pack baskets and be on our way before the village knew where the shot came from," Lawrence added.

They left. Parnell had another cup of coffee, thinking, *Tomorrow night yeah. Well you boys are going to get the surprise of your lives.* He paid for his lunch and extra coffee. He didn't say anything to Henry about his plans. Although he guessed that Henry knew what Lawrence and Hoggan were up to.

Parnell returned to his cabin. He went out to the woodshed and took the coil of telephone wire off its peg and picked out several washers of different sizes. Using the biggest washer first, he attached one end of the wire to the washer by winding the wire tight around the rim of the washer. Then he cut off a length of wire about six feet and inserted that end through the washer and pulled it through until he had a loop on the washer end. That was just what he needed, but he decided to use the smallest washer.

The spike horn was always at the same place in the field every evening about half way on the left side. There was a lot of clover there.

Parnell waited until suppertime and then he made a beeline through the woods to the field. He knew that if the deer was coming out at the same place each evening, then the deer would have a well-worn trail. He found the trail without much difficulty and hung the wire snare about two feet off the ground. And secured the loose end tightly to another tree.

Then he stepped back about seventy-five feet, close enough to hear the deer thrashing, and laid down in a hollow in the ground and covered himself with dead leaves, to eliminate his scent. Then he waited.

He had to stay awake. He wanted to nap to pass some time, but he was afraid he wouldn't hear the deer in the snare then. It was getting dusky. That would put the time about 8:30 p.m. It would be totally dark in forty-five minutes.

Then he heard it, like rattling small saplings together and beating the ground. He hurried over. The deer didn't see him coming. He grabbed the deer around the neck and tried to wrestle it to the ground. He succeeded but not before the deer kicked him in the ribs, and once when the spike horn threw his head trying to free himself of Parnell's grip, the deer hit Parnell with one of his spikes below his eye.

Parnell finally had the deer under control and slit its throat with his knife. He lost precious time wrestling the deer. He had to hurry now. He cut the four legs off being careful not to paunch the deer. He took the saddles too. He put everything in his pack basket. But he wasn't finished yet. He broke off a crotched stick about thirty-inches long and picked the deer up, cape, head and all and walked out into the field and propped the deer's head up with the crotch stick and then brought the cape around front to make it look like a real deer. He made sure the eyes were still open and the head was pointing in the right direction.

He started for home. Trying to hurry without stumbling.

He was half way home when he heard the shot. He couldn't help but laugh. "What I wouldn't give to see their faces right now. I bet they are surely cussing at someone." He was still laughing when he unlocked the door of his root cellar. He put the pack basket on ice and left, locking the door. He left his boots in the shed portion of the cabin. He cleaned up and got out of his clothes without turning on a lantern. He fell asleep still chuckling.

* * * *

Just as everyone in the village would be eating supper Ian Randall was sitting in behind some small fir trees along the edge of the field not far from the village end of the field. He didn't expect anything to happen until later, once the lights had gone out for the night.

Nothing had come out to feed yet, the mosquitoes were biting, anxiety was increasing and he had to pee. He had no more than finished when he saw two shadowy figures walk by the field. They seemed to be more interested with something in the village.

They were; Hoggan and Lawrence wanted to make sure lights were out in the village. "Is your rifle loaded?" Hoggan asked.

"Yeah."

"Okay, we'll work our way along the field edge. Only as far as would be a comfortable shot. I'll shine the light and you take a quick bead and shoot." Hoggan said.

They worked their way along the edge and stopped not far from where Ian was concealed. "Okay, we'll wait to make sure all is quiet," Hoggan whispered. After a few minutes Hoggan said, "Get ready."

Hoggan snapped the four cell light on, "There, see the eyes." Bang! Ian saw the eyes also and he was already inching his way closer. He knew their full attention would be focused on the eyes and nothing else. They all saw the deer fall.

As soon as Lawrence had fired Ian stepped right behind them and said, "Hi, boys. My, that was a good shot." At the same time he reached out and grabbed Lawrence's rifle. That was now secured. "Boys, you are under arrest for night hunting."

Hoggan and Lawrence both were so surprised neither one could utter a word. "Jimmy, I'd better take that flashlight, just so you don't get any crazy ideas." There was no argument.

"Nice night isn't it? Air is clear and cool. Damn those mosquitoes, though. I bet they were bad walking up from Cut Pond." Still, silence.

"Well boys, let's go see what you shot." They walked over and Ian couldn't believe what he was seeing. "What in the hell is going on?"

Hoggan broke the silence; "Some cheap bastard set us up, Steve."

"Hey, don't look at me, Jimmy; this is as much a surprise to me as it is to you."

"Well, Mr. Warden," Steve was saying, "I guess you can't arrest us for shooting something that is already dead."

"But you didn't know it was dead, did you, Steve, any more than I did. Come on boys we have a long walk out of here tonight. You give me any problems and I'll drop you right here. Your choice."

They knew better than to give Ian any trouble. When they got to the iron gate Ian handcuffed them both to the gate. "I'll be back shortly boys. Sit down and relax."

Ian disappeared in the darkness. "Who do you suppose did this?" Hoggan asked.

"I don't know. But I'm not giving Ian any trouble, either. We're in the middle of the woods at night and he thinks nothing of it. He's more animal than man," Lawrence was scared.

Hoggan shook his head.

Ian went right to John Corriveau's cabin. This is something that he would be very capable of doing. He went out back; their bedroom window was always open. He waited. John was snoring peacefully.

Next he went to Parnell's cabin. The lights were out, no smoke, he knocked and then opened the door, "Hey Parnell, you home?"

Parnell rolled over and got out of bed. He didn't bother to pull his pants on, he walked out to the main part of the camp. "What's the problem, Ian? What you doing hollering at me at this time of night?"

Ian shinned his light at Parnell and saw his bruised eye. "What happened to you? Get into a fight?"

"No, a piece of wood fell off the top of the wood pile and hit me in the face. What's this all about, Ian?"

"Hold your hands out so I can see them," Parnell did and Ian shinned his light on them. Clean.

"Did you hear any shooting tonight?"

"I haven't heard anything. I've been asleep. That is until you woke me."

Ian just grunted and left the cabin without explaining any further. He knew Parnell was involved somehow. He just knew. But how had he done it. The field was empty when Ian arrived. There had only been the one shot. He had to have set it up after darkness and then traveled through the woods back to his cabin, he thought. "I could never prove it. I'll get you some day, Mr. Purchase."

Ian unlocked the handcuffs. "Come on, boys, we have a long walk."

"Where are we going?" Hoggan asked.

"My car is at Levesque City."

"There isn't any road from here to Levesque City."

"No there isn't, we'll follow a trail from Smith Brook Deadwater through the woods."

* * * *

The next morning Parnell got up and had breakfast just like he would any other morning. He cleaned up and then walked down to visit the Corriveaus. The gravel road was finally dry. The mill crew had all of the machinery dismantled and ready to load onto the railcars. The building would come down once the machinery was gone.

John was sitting on the porch drinking coffee. "Good morning Parnell."

"John."

"Had some excitement last night."

"Oh yeah? What?"

"Hoggan and Lawrence were arrested last night for night hunting, in the field across the tracks. Heard the shot, figured it was you.

"You know—funny thing. I was up before breakfast this morning and I walked over to the field. Just to see. It was you wasn't it?"

Parnell couldn't hold it back any longer. "Yeah, it was me, but I didn't plan on Ian being here. He must have already been here when I killed that deer."

"How did you do it? Stormi and me, we only heard the one shot."

Parnell started laughing. He just couldn't help himself. To think he not only got the deer and Hoggan and Lawrence, but unbeknownst to him, he had also gotten one over on Ian Randall.

"Well damn it, you going to tell me, or just sit there laughing."

"I snared the deer." They both laughed. Parnell then told John the rest of the story. "I thought we should have some fresh meat."

"We laugh now, Parnell, but I wouldn't want to be in your shoes right now."

"What do you mean?"

"You embarrassed Ian. Whether or not it was intentional. In time he'll figure it all out. But you embarrassed him and he won't forget. He'll keep after you until he has you. You will always have to be watching your back trail."

* * * *

The only thing left at the mill now was a smoldering pile of ashes. When the remains of the building and trash were burned, the hotel was being emptied, getting ready to be taken down. The restaurant had already closed its doors and moved. McBride was having a sale in order to unload as much as he could.

"Mr. McBride, I would take all of your food goods, if you offer me a good enough price."

McBride thought a minute and said, "How's a hundred dollars even sound for all the food goods?"

"Good." Parnell also bought more clothes, boots, gloves, snowshoes, tools, ropes, and brandy. He bought out almost the entire store.

There were only a few families left in the village. Some had had relatives in Oakfield and Smyrna Mills. Others had gone to Masardis and Ashland and had found jobs at Levesque's mill or in one of his wood crews.

The awful day came when John asked Parnell for help. "Stormi and I are leaving tomorrow, Parnell. Would you help me carry things up to the platform?"

"Sure thing." They were both choked up with sadness and neither one spoke.

Tomorrow came and Parnell met Stormi and John at the stationhouse. The restaurant had closed so they couldn't even have a last cup of coffee while they waited. Stormi's eyes were red from crying, and John's too. This was a sad, awful day. Ansel blew the train whistle signaling the train was about to leave. Parnell hugged Stormi and kissed her on the cheek. "See you, John."

John nodded his head. He was crying. Parnell stood on the

platform and watched as the train disappeared down the tracks.

The only ones left in the village now were the stationmaster and Parnell. "I'll be leaving tomorrow, Parnell. Then the wrecking crews will come in and take her down." Meaning the stationhouse, hotel and restaurant, all one big building. Even the old forestry camp beside the schoolhouse was empty. Because of cutbacks the forestry department had to eliminate several watchtowers throughout the state; and Howe Brook Mountain was one of them. The commissioner had decided that the towers at Number 9 Mountain and Oakhill in T8R5 could oversee the St. Croix drainage.

The next day the train arrived with the wrecking crew and a special car with a crane. Ansel shut the engine down and walked up the knoll to have a cup of coffee with Parnell. "Hi, Parnell, I brought you today's newspaper. Any coffee?"

"Sure, sit down. Coffee'll be ready shortly. Thanks for the paper. I guess I'm mayor of Howe Brook Village now, no one else wanted the job." They both laughed.

"You want some lunch while you wait?"

"Sure sounds good."

"How about some fried potato, dandelion greens, and fresh deer steak?"

"I think I heard about that deer. The story is all up and down the tracks. Except no one is saying who cut the legs off and propped the deer up. I guess the warden had been after those two for a long time. Although Ian isn't very happy about who did the dastardly deed while he was right there in the field."

"You know, I honestly had no idea he was anywhere around."

"This steak is delicious," Ansel said.

"It's fried in bear fat."

After lunch Parnell made another pot of coffee and they reminisced about the goings-on in the area. "The new bridge across the St. Croix River is finished and the crews are now cutting the right of way northeast to connect with the lower

Deadwater Road. It may be completed before winter. Levesque has two of those new skidders working on the right of way. They can sure haul a lot more wood than a team of horses or a crawler, for that matter."

The building was taken down in sections and loaded onto the railcars. Three days later the only thing left was again a pile of smoldering ashes. The train pulled out with all the workers. Ansel blew the whistle many times as he headed north. A final salute to Howe Brook Village and to the people who had called Howe Brook their home.

Tears welled up in Parnell's eyes. There wasn't a sound anywhere. He was alone. But now at least he had a clear view of the lake.

Chapter 4

It was 4:00 a m before Ian had delivered his two night hunters at the county jail in Houlton. "You boys are in luck; we have a brand new judge in Houlton now, Julian Werner. He takes a special interest in fish and game cases."

By the time Ian had filled out the booking sheet and written a synopsis of the case it was 6:00 a.m. Time for breakfast and he was hungry. After breakfast was over he decided he might as well stick around for the arrangement. Hoggan and Lawrence were not able to make bail.

The courtroom was full. The judge's room door opened and the bailiff announced. "All rise. The Honorable Julian Werner presiding."

Werner called for the warden cases first. He took a hard look at Hoggan and Lawrence before he read their charge. They were still dirty from the night before and the long walk out.

"You both have been charged with the offense of night hunting. How do you plead?"

Hoggan spoke up. "Your honor, we were out there to shoot a deer, but the deer was already dead and taken."

Werner looked at Ian, "I assume you brought these two in?"

"Yes, Your Honor."

"What are the circumstances?"

Ian told the court the whole story, except how he had come to be there and whom he figured had actually killed the deer and who had absconded with the meat.

"Mr. Hoggan, did your buddy fire a shot at what you thought was a deer?"

"Yes, Your Honor."

"When did you first learn that the deer you shot at was already dead?"

"When the warden had us walk with him up to inspect the deer."

"Mr. Randall, did they hit the deer with the bullet?"

"Yes, Your Honor, in the throat."

"Was there another bullet hole in the body of the deer?"

"No, Your Honor."

"So the deer was already dead when these two put their light on it and shot and you could only find one bullet hole in a deer that was already dead and the legs had been removed?"

"Maybe I'd better explain, Your Honor."

"Please do, because right now it looks as if these two missed."

"Your Honor, someone else that same evening had killed the deer with a wire snare, and then played a practical joke and propped the deer up in the field."

"But you two thought you were shooting at a live deer?"

"Yes, Your Honor," Hoggan replied.

"Guilty. Two hundred and fifty dollars each. Next time I'll put you in jail too. Now get out of here and go pay the clerk."

Werner looked at Ian and asked, "Do you know who hung the snare and took the legs?"

"I believe so, sir, but I'll never be able to prove it."

* * * *

Ian hadn't slept in three days now, and he was exhausted. When he drove in his driveway at Knowles Corner, his wife had her car out of the garage and all the doors were open. He walked by and looked in. From the boxes and suitcases it looked like she and the kids were going somewhere.

She met him in the kitchen. He knew a fight was brewing. "Ian, I'm taking the kids and we're leaving you. I have already filed for a divorce. You'll be getting served with the papers tomorrow. I've had it, Ian. I'm not even married to a memory of you, because we don't do anything together to remember. The kids and I go on vacation or go see my folks. It's always just me who goes to their school programs. And I don't have any friends because you have pinched every woman's husband around here! I won't live like that anymore.

"You can live fine as long as you are in the woods doing the only thing you know how to you, but out here in the civilized world you are a bore. The kids know their Uncle Jack better than they know their own father."

Ian just stood there flabbergasted. She was right of course. There was little sense in arguing. He couldn't even remember which grades his son and daughter were in. "Where are you going?"

"For now, my mother's. But when the divorce is final I'm going to have a beautician business of my own."

* * * *

The next day Deputy Crandall served Ian with divorce papers. He couldn't just stay home and dwell on it. She was right. His whole life was in the woods chasing poachers. The grandest game ever played.

He got in his car and drove to Houlton to see his supervisor, Virgil Brown. Virgil was sympathetic but he knew it was coming long before now. "Good game wardens don't make good husbands, Ian, plain and simple. I've tried in the past to get you to take some time off but you always had something in the woods that needed your attention.

"I tell you what, take a couple of days off. I'm working on something that just may interest you."

"What are you talking about, Virgil?"

"Can't say just yet. I haven't worked out all the details. Come back in two days. We'll talk."

* * * *

On his way home Ian stopped at the seniors' living center to say hello to John and Stormi. He found their unit and knocked on the door. Stormi answered, "Why hello, Ian. I haven't been fishing." They both laughed.

"Hello, Stormi. I just stopped to see how you and John were getting along out here in civilization."

"Oh, we're okay, John's in the living room. Go right in."

"Hello, John." John looked up from his book.

"Well, I'll be darned if it ain't the game warden. I'm afraid you're out of luck here. Stormi won't let me out of her sight these days."

Stormi brought a cup of coffee for Ian and a cup of decaf for John. They sipped coffee while reminiscing about the good old days in Howe Brook. Now that John was no longer a participant in the game, Ian quite enjoyed the ole reprobate's company and his stories.

It was getting time to leave. "One thing before I leave, John. I don't suppose you'd tell me who snared that spikehorn and absconded with the legs and saddle?"

"It wasn't me. No, I don't think I had better. That is unless you'd want to tell me how was it that you just happened to be there the night those two decided to shoot that spikehorn. Or how was it that you just happened to be in the area on so many other occasions?"

"I can't do that either, John. Let's just say that sometimes word just came out of the village."

"McBride! I knowd it all along—he was no good. That squealer. It was him, wasn't it?"

"See ya, John. Thank you for the coffee, Stormi."

"Come back and see us again, Ian."

Ian went home and that evening he went for a walk in the field across the road to watch the sunset. It was a glorious sunset. But Ian remained in the field long after dark. He couldn't just sit home any longer. He needed to go back to work, to get in the game again.

The next day Ian returned to his supervisor, Virgil Brown's home. "Well, I have some good news for you, Ian. You're aware, I believe that the Howe Brook forestry fire tower is no longer manned?"

"Yes."

"I have been talking with the district supervisor and he has agreed to let us have the use of the forestry camp at Howe Brook Village. It's all furnished; all we need to do is fly in food stores."

"That will be good. But there is only one person left in the village now, Parnell Purchase, and I have a score to settle with him. I'm sure that as soon as that part of the woods is opened to vehicle traffic more people will be using the area for recreation, and it'll be nice to have a camp there. When can the pilot fly me in with stores?"

"Today. He'll be landing soon at Drew's Lake and you should meet him there and then come back here and we'll put together a few things."

* * * *

Pilot Jack Dumont circled St. Croix Lake looking for hidden obstacles just under the water surface, before landing. Ian made sure they flew directly over Parnell's cabin, and then Jack put down softly on the lake and taxied up to the wharf at the forestry camp.

Parnell was inside reading when the plane flew overhead. Just above the treetops. He went outside to see. It had already disappeared, but he heard the prop as the plane taxied to the forestry camp. Being mayor of the village he went to investigate and was uncomfortably surprised when he recognized Ian carrying boxes of food into the camp.

Jokingly Parnell said, "What did, your wife kick you out?"

"She and the kids moved out," Ian replied without further explanation. "Warden service has the unconditional use of this camp now. Don't look so glum, Parnell. We'll be neighbors."

Now it was Parnell's turn to be quiet. The news hit him just as solidly as if Ian had hit him in the stomach. Would this be his revenge? Everything was unloaded from the plane and put away in the camp.

"Can't stay tonight, neighbor. We have to be going. But I'll be in one of these days. We'll have to be neighborly," Ian said as he grinned.

Parnell walked back up to his cabin. "Of all the rotten luck." In the evenings Parnell would sit out on his porch watching the warden's camp. Looking for signs of life. Ian had done this on purpose. To worry him, and settle the score, Parnell thought.

The days went by and still no sign of Ian Randall. Fall was almost in and Parnell decided to take a trip out to visit John and Stormi before the fall trapping season began. He put some food and water in a small pack, he picked up his rifle and locked the door and made sure the door was also locked to the root cellar. It was an eighteen-mile walk to town following the tracks.

The closer he got to town the air started to turn foggy with a slight mist. At Dudley Siding he stopped to rest and have lunch. He found dry shelter under a huge spruce tree on top of the bank along the right of way. He leaned his rifle against the tree and sat down, leaning his back against the tree.

After finishing his lunch he retied his boots and as he was standing up, he saw a small deer standing between the rails directly in front of him. He froze, so his movement wouldn't alarm the deer. This was a gift sent from heaven. He brought his rifle to his shoulder, slowly. And took a fine bead on the deer's head, just behind the ear. He squeezed the trigger and the blast echoed up and down the valley.

He dragged the deer off the tracks, into the bushes. He cut off the four legs and the saddles and put those in his pack. Now he wished he had taken his larger pack basket. But he would make do.

He left the scene of his crime as soon as he had everything secured. He knew he was only about three miles out of town, he found a place to wait for darkness at White Lake Crossing.

As darkness came, the air cooled and now it had a frosty bite. Parnell worked his way along the tracks until he came to the Great Northern Paper Company's road. This gravel road would take him very near to the Senior Citizen Complex. There wasn't much traffic on the main road tonight. He found the entrance to the complex—now to figure out which one. Fortunately each apartment had the occupant's name on the outside. The lights were already off. He knocked on the door. No answer. He knocked again, louder this time. Still no answer. He knocked louder. This time the lights came on and Stormi came to the door. "Who is it? And what do you want?"

"Stormi, it's me, Parnell. Open the door."

She opened the door and couldn't believe her eyes. "My gracious, it is you! What are you doing out here, Parnell? Come in, come in." She hollered for John. "Hey, John! Get up! You'll never guess who came to visit."

John came stumbling out of the bedroom, still wearing his pajamas and rubbing his eyes. "Well I'll be damned, if it ain't Parnell. What are you doing out here?"

"I came to visit, you ole reprobate."

"Couldn't you have come at a more decent hour?" John asked jokingly.

"Nope, I thought you might like a taste of fresh venison, so I shot a small deer and had to wait for darkness before I dared travel any further."

"We'd better take care of that meat before it spoils. We don't have a root cellar here, but our electric refrigerator has a freezer. We can slice the steaks and freeze 'em. Ain't that something? And out here we don't have to cut ice in the winter."

The three of them were two hours taking care of the deer meat. There were no scraps. Parnell told them the whole story of his hike down the tracks and Heaven giving him that deer, so he could give some fresh meat to his friends.

"Oh, I almost forgot! Ian Randall has taken over the old forestry camp in the village. He flew in some food stores yesterday."

111

John began laughing. Good naturedly, he said, "Well, Parnell, he'll be good company." All three laughed. Stormi went back to bed and left John and Parnell in the kitchen telling each other stories.

Parnell slept on the couch and had bad dreams all night about being chased by Ian Randall.

The next morning at breakfast—of deer steak and eggs— "I'll have to leave at noon today. Trapping season begins in two days and I have a lot of work to do."

Parnell said farewell and was on his way home. As he was crossing Route 2 in Smyrna Mills, Ian drove by and he stopped. Maybe he stopped because he saw the rifle. He got out and walked back to Parnell. "I didn't recognize you at first."

"I was visiting the Corriveaus."

"You had to bring your rifle with you to do that?" Ian asked good naturedly, but skeptical.

"Well, you never know what you'll see in the woods. Actually I wanted to get John and Stormi some fresh moose meat. But all I saw was deer. And tiny ones at that."

"I wished you had, cause you'd still have blood on your clothes. You heading back to Howe Brook?"

"Yeah."

"Want a ride to Levesque City? That'll save you about twelve miles."

"Well, I guess it won't hurt my reputation none to be seen with a warden."

By the time Ian stopped his car at Levesque's, there was still three hours left of daylight. If he'd walked up the tracks he'd have two or three hours of walking in the dark. "Thank you, Ian. I much appreciate the ride and the conversation."

* * * *

Parnell boiled his traps and scraped last years rust off. This year he had John's traps also. He would run a trap line around the lake for otter, mink, and muskrats. He also ran the same line as the previous year and made more sets for otter and mink. He didn't cross the new road at St. Croix Siding. He didn't want workers there to know he was trapping nearby. It might be too much of a temptation for someone to check his sets ahead of him some morning.

The new Levesque Road that came in from Route 11 was still too soft for the many log trucks that would be required to ship all the wood, so the wood was being piled down at St. Croix Siding, scaled and then loaded onto railcars. Parnell walked out to the clearing at the siding just to settle his curiosity.

He was watching the crane operator and hadn't noticed that the scaler had seen him and was now walking toward him. "Hello there." Startled, Parnell turned to see who was talking. Parnell waved.

The scaler kept coming. He was a big sort of fellow. He towered above Parnell and probably weighed close to three hundred. The scaler noticed Parnell's pack basket and traps and smelled the lure. "You trapping?" More statement than question.

What was Parnell to do? He couldn't very well lie when this guy obviously knew, "Yeah, just got started today."

"You alone?"

"Yeah. You drive in here every day?"

"Nah, I stay in here—that camp behind that pile of wood—during the week to get away from the ole lady and kids."

"How big is your crew?"

"Just me and the crane operator, Fred. He drives out each night. He has a new Ford pickup. My name is Max, what's yours?"

"Parnell."

They each went back to work.

He made his first tend two days later, after setting traps around the lake. He picked up two fox, a raccoon and one more mink; but at his last set, which was close to the log pile at St. Croix Siding, something looked out of place. The trap was still set but the ground looked like it had been disturbed and then smoothed out to look natural. He re-baited and thought about it all the way home. The next day instead of tending first around the lake, he went back to the trap by the siding. Again today the ground was a little more disturbed. Someone had taken the time to smooth the ground and reset the trap. Someone was stealing his fur.

He tended his line back to Howe Brook. Near the falls, he had a fox. An idea came to him. He put his gloves on and released the fox from the trap, but he held onto it. At first the fox struggled and was biting at his hands. After several minutes the fox relaxed in Parnell's hands.

He walked back to the fur stealing set and put the fox in the trap. By now the fox was quiet and not struggling. He lay on the ground. Parnell hated doing this to the fox.

Then he finished tending and put his catch in the root cellar. He ate an early supper and grabbed a warm blanket and hiked back to the trap near the log pile. The fox was still there and calm. He found a place to hide on a knoll where he had a clear view. He sat down to wait.

The sun was setting and he could see someone walking up the tracks. He waited with increasing anxiety. The same feelings he had found while on night maneuvers in Korea. His first instinct was to jump out and confront him. But it was Max, the giant scaler. He waited and he was surprised when Max placed his big foot on the fox's ribcage and put his weight on that foot. He stopped the fox's heart, killing it. He picked the fox up and put it inside his jacket. He reset the trap and smoothed out the ground. Parnell was seething with anger. But he waited until the thief was out of sight before he moved. He left the trap set but urinated on the set and bait. "There, there won't be any more animals dying in this trap."

He walked back to Howe Brook, wondering how to handle this. He skun the hides and put them on stretchers to dry, then he had a hearty supper and stepped out on the porch for a breath of fresh air. There were lights on in Ian's camp. "He sure isn't concealing his movements." He went back inside and went to bed.

He lay on his back thinking about what to do. Then the whole cunning scheme came to mind. If it worked, it would take care of ole Max for good. He'd teach him a sultry lesson. He went down to John's cabin. In the woodshed he had seen a coil of small wire cable. He would have to take it back to his woodshed and cut it. He cut off about twelve feet and made a snare with it, like he had done before.

He took his axe and a warm blanket. As he walked off his knoll towards the tracks he noticed smoke in the moonlight rising above Ian's camp. "He must be in." There was a well-used moose trail through the spruce and fir trees just before Beaver Brook. He looked at the tracks in the mud. There were several different sizes. He hoped the first moose to come along the trail wasn't a huge bull. In fact he didn't want a bull with antlers. A small cow or yearling would be fine. He followed the trail to the right side of the tracks about one hundred fifty feet back into a thicket of smaller trees. He made his snare loop and hung it about three feet above the ground and secured the other end to a large fir tree.

He walked back to the tracks and found a perch on a bank on the other side. He made sure he was out of sight and he lay down to sleep. This might be a long wait. He put his flashlight next to the axe so he wouldn't forget it.

* * * *

Ian left his car at Levesque City and walked to his new camp on St. Croix Lake. He was determined to catch Parnell. It was already dark when he arrived and he looked up towards Parnell's cabin. Lights were on.

Before lighting a lantern, Ian covered the windows with towels and jackets. He didn't want to alert Parnell of his presence, not just yet. He kindled a fire to warm the camp up and cook his supper. Every once and a while he would go outside to see if

Parnell's lights were still on.

After he finished eating and cleaning up, Ian turned the lantern out and removed his shades on the windows. He sat outside with a pair of binoculars, watching Parnell's front door. At 9:00 pm his lights went out. Ian watched for another half hour to see if Parnell would slip out in the cover of darkness.

There was no movement so Ian went inside and went to bed. Ian was up well before daylight. He went back outside with binoculars and when daylight started to break over the treetops, he went back inside and watched through the window. He didn't put wood in the stove or light a lantern. Hell, he didn't even eat. He was obsessed with catching Parnell.

By noon there still had been no movement on the knoll and no smoke rising from the chimney. It was trapping season so that meant he would be tending traps today. But there had been no activity. There was no possible way that he could have missed him.

Finally his curiosity was getting the best of him and he had to find out what was going on, on the knoll. He walked right up the middle of the road, as if he didn't care if Parnell knew he was coming. He walked right up to the porch and knocked on his door. No answer. It wasn't locked so he opened it and hollered, "Hey, Parnell, you home?" No answer. Ian looked in. He didn't see anything out of the ordinary. He went out back to the woodshed and tool shed. Parnell was not there. This perked Ian's curiosity even more. He went back and looked through the front door again. Parnell's rifle was in the rack.

Ian stood on Parnell's porch looking towards the lake, scratching his head. "What are you up to? You should be trapping. Your rifle is here so you aren't hunting."

He went back to his camp and ate a can of cold beans. He watched Parnell's cabin all day through the window of his camp. There was nothing. No lights after dark and no smoke in the chimney. Ian didn't go to bed that night. He moved the chopping block over next to his camp wall so he could sit on it and lean

116

back against his camp. He waited and watched all night, until daylight the next day.

Parnell slept fine that night. But nothing had crossed the tracks or come near the snare. He waited patiently all day without moving or making a sound. The only time he did move was to stand up and relieve himself.

That evening just before dusk two moose came up from the river and stood on the tracks for a few minutes, and then they sauntered off up the trail. The yearling cow was in the lead, a large bull following. Parnell waited patiently for the sound of thrashing branches. It came. Still he waited, hoping the bull would leave the cow. And he did. He crossed the tracks again and went back for the river. Parnell could hear him splashing in the water as he crossed to the other side.

Parnell grabbed his axe and flashlight; walking beside the muddy moose trail, so he wouldn't leave any tracks. The cow was tangled in several of the trees and down on her knees. Parnell inched his way around in front of her, trying not to spook her. He swung the axe and hit the moose between the eyes. He was becoming very proficient at quartering deer and moose in the dark, holding his flashlight in his teeth. He was careful not to paunch it or get blood on himself.

When he had finished he cleaned his knife off and put it back in its sheath. He laid his axe just behind the tree line. He shouldered one hindquarter and started walking towards St. Croix Siding. He detoured around the log pile through the woods until he had found Max's cabin and pickup. No wonder Max didn't drive back and forth everyday. It looked like a suicide vehicle. He laid the hindquarter down and covered it with branches. Lights were out inside and not much smoke. He went back for both shoulders. If everything went according to plan, he'd have the last hindquarter for himself.

He laid the forward shoulders with the hind leg and covered everything with branches. Then he crept over to look at the pickup. There was a lot of dunnage in back. There was even a piece of old canvas. "This'll do just fine." He went back to his cache to wait.

The temperature was dropping and he had left his blanket back at Beaver Brook. He had spent many cold nights like this on the front line in Korea. About 3:00 a.m. Parnell had to move to get his blood circulating again. Very carefully he slid the moose legs under the canvas and wiped all the blood off the tailgate and bumper and he made sure there were a few hairs on the floor of the body, just enough to attract Ian's attention.

When he was satisfied everything looked natural, he left and started for home. He picked up his blanket and axe. He was tired and it was a slow walk home.

It was just getting daylight when he crossed Howe Brook Bridge. He was between the rails and not paying too much attention to anything.

Ian was standing off to one side of the track waiting for Parnell to come near. He could see that Parnell was carrying something. But in that obscure sunlight he didn't know what it was. He stepped onto the tracks to greet Parnell. "Morning. You out for an early stroll." Now he could see that Parnell was carrying only an axe and a blanket.

"Actually I was coming to see you."

"How did you know I was here? You certainly haven't been."

"I left two nights ago after dark, and I saw smoke coming out of your chimney."

"What or where did you go that time of night?"

"That's what I came to tell you."

"I hope you're going to confess."

Parnell just looked at him and continued. "Someone has been stealing fur from one of my traps. I saw that big scaler, Max walking away once, but he didn't see me. So I went back to sit on my trap to see if he'd come back again. I waited two nights and a day and he didn't come back."

"What did you lose for fur?"

"As near as I could tell three pieces. Two fox and a fisher."

"Well, I'll go have a talk with Mr. Hartley. Max Hartley. He's in trouble everywhere he goes. A big bear of a man."

"That's him. But I ain't told you everything yet. Two nights ago when I went back to sit on my trap, two moose, a bull and a cow came out of the river and crossed the tracks toward the siding where the log pile is. This morning just before daylight I heard two rifle shots. They sounded real close, in the direction behind the log pile. I didn't see anything. I only heard the two shots. If you want, as soon as I have had some coffee and something to eat I'll go with you up the tracks."

Parnell invited Ian up for coffee and breakfast. "While I fix the coffee, why don't you go down to the root cellar and get a can of ham." Parnell gave Ian a magnetic key for the lock. "Just put this magnet on the bottom, you'll see how it goes, and the lock will open."

"I didn't know there was a root cellar."

"Go behind the outhouse over the bank."

Ian went around the outhouse and down over the bank. Sure enough there was a hidden door. He put the square magnet on the bottom of the lock. There was only one way it would fit. The lock opened. "This'll be interesting." It was dark inside, but his eyes soon adjusted. The walls were lined with canned goods, but there wasn't an ounce of meat anywhere. "Maybe he isn't the poacher that I've credited him with being."

They had a quick breakfast. Parnell changed his shirt and jacket and grabbed his pack basket and axe. Neither one spoke a word until Ian saw the moose trail near Beaver Brook. "Is this where you saw the moose cross?"

"Yeah. The trap that Max was stealing fur out of is up ahead here." He didn't want Ian dwelling on the moose trail and later coming back to look at it.

"My trap is right there at the tree line. See that dirt that has been disturbed?"

"Where were you?"

"Behind you. On top of the bank." Parnell jumped the ditch and pointed to a padded spot on the ground.

"You spent two nights and a day right here?'

"Never left."

They walked back to the rails. "I guess I can handle it from here, Parnell."

"Do you want me to go with you—just in case?"

"I'll be alright. Thanks."

Parnell watched as Ian disappeared up the tracks into some bushes. He was thinking that Ian had to be awfully gutsy to take on a brute like that alone. Then he got to thinking more, "He wouldn't be here if it were not for me." Parnell started to follow Ian, staying just out of sight.

There wasn't anyone in the log yard, which was strange. Parnell watched as Ian worked his way around to Max's camp, through the bushes. Max was loading his gear into the back of the pickup. Ian waited until Max came outside again with his arms loaded before he approached him. "Good morning, Max." Ian caught him by surprise and Max hollered and dropped the box.

"Holy Jesus! You scared me," Max exclaimed.

"You leaving early, Max?"

"Ah . . . I . . . I was just getting ready," Ian observed how nervous he was. This was all part of the great game.

"Had any spare time to trap, Max?"

"No, I generally work right up to dark."

"Do you see many people in here, now that there's a nice road from Route 11?"

"Not many at all. Maybe on the weekends, once Levesque gets the Black Water Road built from Masardis, there'll be people crawling all through here."

"Who's the crane operator?"

"You ought to know him. You arrested him twice—Fred."

"Old Fred! Is he trapping?"

"No, like I said we work 'til dark."

"You wouldn't have any water would you? I'm thirsty."

"I got water inside. I'll get you a jug."

Max was still nervous. He came back out carrying a jug of water and passed it to Ian. Ian took a long drink and set the jug on the porch.

"Mind if I look your pickup over?"

"Yeah, I mind. You got a warrant?"

"No. Actually out here I don't need one. If'n I was to leave and go to Houlton after one—well, by the time I got back here you probably wouldn't wait. So these are exigent circumstances, and I don't need one and I don't need your permission."

Ian could tell by Max's reaction that the word *exigent* had him confused.

Ian checked the front of the pickup first, looking for firearms or hidden fur pelts. There was a shotgun behind the seat. It was empty and under the seat he found Parnell's stolen fur. Two fox hides and one large fisher. "I thought you said you weren't trapping." No answer. He put the hides on the roof of the pickup.

Ian took his time; everything was in his favor right now. The game was getting exciting. He started to drop the tailgate and noticed a spot of blood on the bumper. He ran his finger through it. It hadn't congealed yet. He opened the tailgate and found a few moose hairs Parnell had left for him to find. He folded the canvas back and exposed three moose legs.

Ian stopped and just looked at Max. Max couldn't say a word. "Where's the rest of it"

"I didn't shoot it."

"I didn't say you did. But it is hidden in your pickup."

"That ain't mine! I didn't shoot it! You're just trying to frame me."

"Max, we have a real problem here? First you're in possession of illegal fur pelts. Either you're trapping without a license or you lifted them from someone else's trap. Second, you are in possession of three moose legs. It doesn't matter none if you shot the moose or not. What does matter is that I found them hidden under your canvas in your truck. You're under arrest, Max, for illegal possession of moose and possession of illegal furs."

Parnell was watching all this and could barely contain himself.

"What you going to do with me, Ian?"

"Well, I just placed you under arrest and now I'll have to take you to jail in Houlton."

"I ain't going to no jail!" Max started for the driver's door and Ian cut him off and slammed the door shut. When he did that Max pushed Ian over backwards and was coming at him like a huge grizzly bear. One step at a time, head down and his arms stretched out. Ian saw the predicament he was in and jumped to his feet and hit Max in the solar plexus as hard as he could.

All this seemed to occur at once. When Ian went down Parnell couldn't see him any more. But he could see Max going after him. Parnell took his pack and jacket off, left his axe and ran to assist Ian.

Max had recovered from the blow to his mid-section and had Ian around the neck. He hit Ian in the face once and started to hit him again. Parnell was running now. Max hadn't seen him. Parnell sprang through the air at Max with his legs coiled and just before he contacted Max's head, he kicked out with both feet. Max let go of Ian and fell to the ground. Parnell was on the ground too. They recovered about the same time, and Max hit Parnell in the face with a huge fist and Parnell went down again.

Ian had regained his feet by now and was welding a broken axe handle at the back of Max's head. He went down and stayed there this time. Ian got out his handcuffs and cuffed Max's hands behind his back.

Ian looked at Parnell, "You okay?"

Parnell was rubbing his face, "I will be in a couple of weeks. How about you?"

"A couple of weeks ought to do it." They both laughed. "There wasn't any need of you interfering, I was getting the best of him."

Parnell laughed again, "Yeah, I noticed. While you were lying sprawled out on the ground."

"Your fur is on the roof. You might as well take it. I won't charge him for stealing fur. He has more serious charges to face now. The judge would just throw this one out."

Max was coming to. "Are you going to walk him out of here, like you did me?'

Ian laughed, "No, I'll have to take these three legs too. I'll commandeer his truck."

"What will happen to the moose legs, from here?"

"Do you want one?"

"Thanks, but that's not why I was asking. I know some people who would really enjoy it, the people living in the complex where John and Stormi are living. I am sure John could take care of it and see that everyone had some."

"He probably could skin and slice it with his eyes closed. I'll do that. I'll keep a couple of pounds for myself too."

"I'm sure they would all appreciate the meat."

Max was groaning. "Who hit me?"

"I did and I'll hit you again if you don't behave. Now I'm charging you with assault on top of the moose. Parnell, help me stand him up."

Ian rolled Max on his back and he took one arm and Parnell grabbed the other. They got him to his feet with difficulty.

"Do you want me to ride out with you?" Parnell asked.

"I don't think that'll be necessary, will it, Max?

"Max, you get in the passenger side. You stay handcuffed. Parnell, don't forget your fur. Thanks for your help." Ian got in and shut the door and drove off.

Parnell was satisfied, except he had not anticipated the fight with Max. He pulled his trap where Max had been stealing the fur, and at Beaver Brook, he gathered his snare and made sure he had left no evidence or tracks, and then he shouldered the fourth moose leg and headed for home. He still would have to make another trip to tend his traps, but now he had to put the moose leg on ice.

He shoveled the sawdust aside in his root cellar and put the leg on ice with the last of his deer meat. Then he covered the meat with plastic and recovered his cache with sawdust.

Before making the last trip up the tracks he made lunch and some coffee. He really needed to lie down and rest, but he had to tend traps, and tomorrow he would have to tend around the lake.

It was a long tiring walk back up the tracks. But at least on this trip he didn't have to go as far. He wondered how Ian could stay out here for days with little food and rest. Something about that man bothered him.

By the completion of his tend, Parnell had one more fox, one fisher, an otter and two mink. He was pleased, but before retiring that night he had to skin them and put the hides on stretchers. It was ten o' clock when he had finished and turned out the lantern and he fell asleep almost as soon as he lay on his bed.

* * * *

Parnell slept late the next morning and then he was in his canoe checking traps around the lake. He had a muskrat in each of his rat sets and he picked up another otter at the mouth of Howe Brook and on the opposite shore he had another fisher and two mink.

He watched a huge buck on shore between Tracy Brook and Emerson ridge. He had a nice rack but Parnell was too far away to count the points. He would watch for him in another month.

He paddled up Smith Brook and some animal had wreaked havoc with all his land sets. The traps were all dug out and the bait taken. There weren't any visible tracks in the disturbed ground, but Parnell knew it had to be an animal.

For the rest of that fall every time Parnell tended his trap line up along Smith Brook, all his land sets had been disturbed. He did rather well with otter, mink, and muskrat traps though.

When the trapping season came to a close he had more than quadrupled his previous year. With more otter and mink than other furs. He had one problem, though. How was he going to get his fur to a buyer?

B&A still operated a passenger service. But the train no longer stopped at Howe Brook. "I suppose I could back pack my furs out to Masardis and take the train to Ashland or Presque Isle." But he didn't know if there was a buyer in Ashland. He would have to wait for Ian to return. He should know where the closest buyer would be.

He had taken all the hides off the stretchers and hung them up in the root cellar. Then he grabbed an arm full of firewood from the shed. He was almost out of wood. "Damn! I've forgotten all about getting more wood. John had so much wood worked up that I never even gave it a thought."

He took the armload inside and then went down to John's camp. He still had some wood left, probably enough to last Parnell a month. He still would have to work up some. He got John's sled out of the shed and piled on some firewood and hauled it back to his cabin. Then he put his axe and bucksaw on the sled and headed out the back road to cut some wood.

He cut mainly dead trees that were mostly dry. On occasion he'd take a green one. His sled would only handle a few four or five foot lengths of wood. He had to make several trips back to the woodshed to have enough even for a week's supply. And then he would have to chunk it to fit the stoves. This was going to be a lot of work.

It was deer season and there was snow on the ground, but Parnell worked every day getting firewood. After a week of working up firewood he figured he had about two cords. All the wood would have to be chunked up into twelve-inch pieces, in order for it to fit in the stoves easily. By the time he had finished the two cords he had a large pile of sawdust.

November, deer season was coming to a close and he needed to shoot a deer. The lake was frozen, but not safe enough to walk on. He went down to the field where Ian had arrested Hoggan and Lawrence for night hunting. There were a lot of tracks, but mostly does and lambs. He decided to try the deeryard at Beaver Brook, where he and Ansel had shot bucks the previous year.

Parnell noticed this year the deer trail was in the same place, as the deer wound their way up along the side of the brook. He had to go a bit further than last year before he started jumping deer. He waited, instead of hurrying on. He didn't want to alarm the deer. He picked a large wide track and started following it. He hadn't gone very far at all when he spotted a flickering tail. All he could see was the hind end and he didn't want to waste any meat.

The deer was intent on something in front of it. The deer stomped its front foot and then blew. Parnell was caught by surprise and he jumped. The deer blew again and suddenly wheeled and took a jump towards Parnell. He didn't have time to bring his rifle to his shoulder or aim. He brought it up to his hip, pointed and fired at the approaching deer. In that instant Parnell saw that it was a huge buck and he was about to be run over, but the bullet hit the deer in the chest and it dropped at Parnell's feet. It wasn't dead yet. It was kicking wildly trying to get up and spraying foamy blood on Parnell. His first thought was to cut its throat with his knife, but he decided against that when the deer kicked him. He shot it again in the base of the skull and then it lay still. He counted the points, fifteen.

He dressed it and started dragging it towards the track. He could hear the train coming by the time he got the deer to the cleared right-of-way. He stood by the deer, exhausted, and waited for the train to pass. Ansel Snow leaned out of the engine cab window and saw Parnell with his deer. He blew the train whistle several times acknowledging Parnell and his deer.

The deer was too heavy to drag back to his cabin by himself. He would have to get the sled and come back. Just as he stepped between the tracks he heard something coming through the bushes. He had already unloaded his rifle, so it was of no use to him now. All he could do was wait. He could just make out movement, but wasn't sure what it was. Then it emerged through the bushes. "Hello, Ian. I wasn't sure what was coming through."

"I was out in front of you when you fired. My heart skipped a few beats. I see your face healed okay."

"How's your face?" They both laughed. "That's a nice buck. Need any help dragging that back to camp?"

"Sure, if you're going my direction. You looking for anything special in there?"

"There's a new scaler at the siding now. A nice fella from Squapan, Rusty Jalbert. He said there's been an awful flock of raven's circling over the tracks between the siding and Beaver Brook. I was on my way to camp anyhow, so I thought I'd hike in this way and see what those ravens were circling over. Of course that was five weeks ago. Ravens are gone now. I found where a moose died though. I kicked through the snow and I couldn't find any legs. Bears had chewed the head and neck up pretty much. The ravens probably cleaned up the slimy innards. Maybe the bears dragged the legs off and ate 'em. A lot of deer tracks. We'd better start dragging or it'll be dark soon."

Now Parnell was worried. He knew that Ian now knew about that moose lying dead on the other side of the brook, with no legs. He began to worry.

Even with help dragging, they had to stop often to catch their breath.

It was dark before they had the deer at Parnell's woodshed. "Let's leave it right here and go inside and I'll throw some wood in the stove and get a lantern, so we can see to hang it up. I'd like to put it in the root cellar, so it won't freeze."

Parnell unlocked the root cellar door and hung the lantern on a peg so they could see. "These are nice pelts. You'll get top dollar for these. I like the way you take care of your fur."

"John showed me how."

All while they were hanging the deer and looking at the fur pelts, Ian was taking a mental inventory of the contents, still nothing but food stores and the deer. But then Parnell wouldn't let him in the root cellar if there had been anything illegal.

Parnell reached up into the chest cavity of the buck and ripped out the heart. "You might as well stay for supper. We have fresh deer heart, potatoes and canned carrots."

While Parnell was cooking supper, Ian went down to his own camp and started a fire in the wood stove. Then he came back. He was hungry.

"What did Max get for a sentence?"

"For assaulting me, the judge gave him thirty days. For the moose the judge fined him five hundred dollars. He kept telling the judge he didn't kill no moose and he didn't know the legs happened to be in back of his truck. He was more angry about that than the jail time. I wonder why." Parnell thought he saw Ian smile just briefly.

"How can I tag this deer, Ian?"

"I know you have it and that it was taken legal. I'll fill out the tag for you. What about your fur?"

"Is there a buyer in Ashland?"

"The only buyer around is in Presque Isle. But he comes to Ashland, at the fish and game headquarters, every Thursday. You could get a ride out with Rusty. He traps too. Probably you could ride with him.

"It won't be long now and I'll be able to drive in here from Route 11. Levesque's road crew only has the bridge to build across Howe Brook on the Horseback Road. They are about a month ahead of schedule."

Ian thanked Parnell for supper. "Thanks for your help, Ian." He left and never said why he had come in. Unless it was only to make Parnell uneasy about the moose that died at Beaver Brook.

The next morning there was no smoke from Ian's camp. He had left during the night. He left as mysteriously as he had arrived.

* * * *

Parnell made arrangements to go to Ashland with Rusty. "Be here at 3:00 p.m., if you're going."

He carefully folded and rolled his pelts and packed them in his pack basket. He had six fox, four fisher, two raccoons, three pine martin, five otter, seven mink, one deer hide, and twenty muskrats.

It was an interesting ride for Parnell out the new Levesque Road, or Levesque Street, as it was being called. He was hoping to see one of the talked about skidders, working. "They have all moved in across the river now. They were being used to clear the right of way for the Horseback Road, but I think they are now on this end of the new Blackwater Road," Rusty said.

They didn't stop at Rusty's house in Squapan. They drove on to Ashland so they wouldn't be late. There were several trappers at the headquarters building, and Rusty and Parnell would have to wait their turn.

It was finally Parnell's turn. The buyer never said a word as he examined each pelt thoroughly. He ran his fingers through the hair and inside the hide. "You have a nice catch here, Mr. Purchase. You do an excellent job stretching and preening." He picked up a pencil and paper and began figuring.

"For the lot I'll give you twelve hundred and ninety dollars." He paid Parnell in cash. Rusty was next. He only had a few fox and three otter.

"Before we leave town, Rusty, I'd like to stop at a food store if you don't mind."

"Not at all."

Parnell bought twenty-five pounds of potatoes, a gallon jug of brandy, books and magazines. "You have quite a load there Parnell—I tell you what. We'll stop at the house and I'll give the Mrs. this trapping money, and I'll take you back to your cabin and I'll spend the night in the scaler's camp at St. Croix Siding."

"That's awful considerate of you, Rusty, I hate the idea of imposing on you, but this is a heavy load to carry all the way back. Only wish you would let me give you twenty dollars for your trouble."

"Done." That was two days wages.

At 11:00 p.m. Rusty stopped in Parnell's camp yard. Parnell gave him the twenty dollars. "Thank you, Rusty. I suppose where the train no longer stops here, I should get me a pickup truck. Thanks again, Rusty."

Rusty waved goodbye and left. The wood stoves were out and the cabin was cold. After kindling fires in each stove, he poured himself a glass of brandy and sat down in his one relaxing chair.

* * * *

The ice was still too thin to be safe. So he put beaver trapping aside until colder weather and worked on his firewood. The trail he had been using was frozen now and that made it easier to pull the sled loaded with wood. He worked steady for four days and had a cord and a half, almost enough now.

On the fifth day, or that night before, the temperature dropped below zero. He set up Tracy Brook first, and the small streams that feed into it. The next day he set traps along Smith Brook and this time he explored Smith Brook Deadwater. He found two more colonies and set those. Instead of tending the traps he had set yesterday along Tracy, he decided to set up the Lower Deadwater and Boom Branch.

Every morning since the village was no more, Ansel Snow on his morning southbound run to Oakfield, he had thrown a daily newspaper for Parnell. Two days after all his beaver traps were set, Parnell walked down to the tracks to look for the paper. Ansel had always put the newspaper in a bread bag to protect it from the weather. This morning Ansel had put a note in along with the paper.

Parnell sat down at his kitchen table and removed the newspaper from the bread bag. He found the note and read it.

> *Parnell. John Henri had a severe heart attack*
> *and was taken to the Houlton Hospital.*
> *He is asking for you.*
> *Stormi*

There was no hesitation. Parnell put some clothes in his pack basket, money in his pocket, a warm hat, jacket and blanket. He was out the door and started walking towards Smyrna Mills.

He was just six hours walking eighteen miles. He knocked on Stormi's door at 3:00 p.m.

She answered the door. She was crying. "Oh Parnell—" she sobbed some more, "—I'm so glad you're here. Come in. John Henri died just before noon, Parnell. Sit down, Parnell. Would you like some coffee?"

"Yes, please."

"John Henri knew he was dying. He had known it for several months. He really wanted to see you again before. . . before." She started crying again. Parnell went over to her and hugged her. In between tears, she said, "You were like a brother to him, Parnell."

Parnell sipped his coffee and he and Stormi talked until supper and once the dishes and kitchen were cleaned they talked way into the night. "When is the funeral, Stormi?"

"Day after tomorrow at the Methodist Church in Smyrna Mills. He is being cremated tomorrow. He wants you, Parnell, to take his ashes back to Howe Brook with you and in the spring put them in the water at the mouth of Tracy Brook."

"I would be honored to fulfill his wish, Stormi."

It was late and Stormi didn't feel like she could talk any more. "I'm going to bed now, Parnell. I need some quiet time alone to talk with John Henri."

He didn't say it, but he understood.

* * * *

Parnell didn't sleep at all that night. How he wished he had been able to say goodbye to the best friend he had ever had. The next morning Stormi was up early and she fixed a nice breakfast for the two of them.

"I have decided to sell the camp next to the lake, Parnell. I know I'll never go back now. Not sure I would want to, without John Henri. If there is anything you want inside the camp, Parnell, it's yours. And everything in the sheds, and the canoe. It's all yours."

"Thank you, Stormi. You and John have been the best friends I ever had."

For the rest of that day friends of the Corriveaus would stop by to offer Stormi their condolences. A few would even share a few stories. Parnell found it intriguing how two people who probably never traveled more than a few miles from Howe Brook had affected so many lives.

The next day Stormi awoke very unsettled and nervous about the funeral. She would have to face so many people today. Her sister from Oakfield drove Stormi and Parnell to the church. "Stay with me through this will you, Parnell? Please." She was in tears.

Parnell hugged her and said, "I'll be by your side all day, Stormi." As they walked into the church, Parnell had his arm wrapped around her. They were seated in front.

On their way to the front row, Parnell saw Ian Randall sitting by himself, all dressed up in a nice suit. He looked genuinely sad. If he didn't know better, he'd say there were even tears in his eyes. What a truly strange enigma. Parnell couldn't understand it. To listen to either one, John Corriveau or Ian Randall, talk about the other, you would have thought the other person was the lowest heap of crap on the earth. But here was Ian at his supposedly archenemy's funeral. What does he think? That this is just a game to him?

Parnell turned to look at Ian. It was easy to see that Ian was genuinely sad. Like he, too, had lost his best friend. Parnell turned to look at Ian again. That was it! That was the bond between these two. The Outlaw and the Law. Ian had lost his playmate, and this duty of his to find poachers and John's so-called right of duty to poach now and again, was in fact only a game between the two. The Great Game.

Parnell smiled then and his eyes filled with tears, with this sudden recognition of the real truth.

Ian was one of the last to go through the line offering condolences. He hugged Stormi and said, "I'll miss the ole reprobate, Stormi. There has always been a special place in my heart for you and John."

"I know'd all along you and John were more friends than either one of you would let on," He hugged her again.

"Hello Parnell."

"Ian."

* * * *

Parnell stayed with Stormi for another day. "But, Stormi, I need to get back. The inside of the cabin will be as cold as the outside."

He left that morning. The cold wind blowing from the north almost took his breath away. He met the southbound and stepped off the tracks and waved to Ansel Snow. He returned the greeting with a blast from the whistle.

The walk out had taken six hours and the return was going on to nine. It was dark and the earlier gray clouds were threatening snow. He wished he had his flashlight. He recognized the Corriveau camp when he walked by. He'd be home soon.

But the inside of his cabin was indeed as cold as the outside. He had not emptied any water containers and those were all frozen solid. He was also cold. These last few days had been stressful. A stress from sorrow and loss that can be as devastating as—well, that was the worst.

He unpacked his pack basket and lovingly removed the blue and gold covered urn that held John's ashes. He put the urn on the top shelf of the bookcase.

It was comforting to sit back in the lantern light of your own home listening to the fire crackle in the wood stoves. He could have very easily gone to sleep, but he was hungry and the cabin was still cold. He put more wood in the stoves and went out to the root cellar to get some food.

It was beginning. A nor'easter. "This is going to be a bad one." He boiled a potato and cabbage and fried some deer steak. With his belly full and the cabin finally warm, Parnell picked out one of the new books he had purchased a couple of weeks ago. It didn't matter which book. He'd read them all before winter was over.

As he read he listened to the wind howl outside. He was thankful now he had left Smyrna Mills when he did. He would hate to have been caught still walking the tracks in this storm. He poured himself a brandy and lit a cigar. He had never been a smoker, but he liked the aroma of a good cigar and between brandy and cigar, he was feeling relaxed.

* * * *

The storm lasted for two days and then the wind blew for a third. When it was all over, Parnell had to shovel snow away from his windows and off the roof. It was difficult to say just how much snow fell. The wind blew it around so much. When he shoveled the path to the root cellar, the new snow was up to his waist.

Before tending any of his beaver traps he had to wait and let the snow settle and compact or he'd never be able to snowshoe through it. The weather started changing. Each day the thermometer read a little warmer, and it stayed in the high twenties for a week. Then one night the cold returned, below zero.

This was okay with Parnell; the snow would be compacted now. The next morning he donned his snowshoes and headed for Tracy Brook, a shovel in one hand and an ice chisel in the other. His axe was in his pack. He had decided that whether or not he had beaver, he'd pull all his traps and those he couldn't bring back, because of a full pack of pelts, he would hang in a tree. Then if the cold weather broke, he would reset. Trapping bobcat for now was out.

* * * *

There wasn't much ice, but there was an average of about twelve inches at each one of his traps. That first day he only tended six traps and he had six beaver. That night he did flesh the hides before he rolled the hides up and put them in his woodshed to freeze. He'd put them on drying boards later.

The going was easier the next day. He had a frozen trail until he got to the last set tended yesterday. He only had four traps left on the Tracy Brook drainage. He had a beaver in each of those traps also.

He was home earlier than yesterday so after fleshing, he put those four on drying boards. They were all big beaver and the hair was shiny.

He next tackled his traps along Smith Brook Deadwater. He had a greater distance to travel and he was three days before he had tended and pulled all his traps. The traps he had on the deadwater, he brought back as far as where Little Smith Brook joins Smith Brook.

This time he had two otter. That he thought was strange, considering the traps were baited with wood and otter ate meat. They must have been curious.

His last ordeal was up Howe Brook to Boom Branch Deadwater. He only had four traps here, but he had a devil of a time breaking out a snowshoe trail from the lower deadwater to Boom Branch. He had four beaver, but they were only blanket size. There were only two traps on the lower deadwater and he was glad of that.

By the time Parnell found his last two sets on the lower deadwater, he was exhausted from the ordeal of breaking trail through the deep powdery snow to Boom Branch. The four beaver he had rolled up in his pack basket were beginning to weigh him down. The load wasn't that heavy, but he was tired and four blankets carried like they were a dozen. He stumbled often and had to pick himself out of the deep snow. He was beginning to wish he had waited until the snow had settled more before snowshoeing to Boom Branch.

The two sets on the lower deadwater were empty. And he was just as glad for that. He put the two traps in his pack basket and shouldered it and started following his trail down to the lower end of the deadwater. He noticed that water had seeped into his snowshoe trail, beyond where his traps had been and now the trail was full of slush. He had to break out a new trail in order to stay out of the slush.

Parnell wanted to drop his pack basket and leave it. "I could come back tomorrow after it." He was that tired and not thinking altogether correctly. He didn't drop it. He couldn't imagine having to do this again.

He could see the end of the ordeal, as he approached the lower end of the deadwater. He was watching the tree line and where his snowshoe trail left the ice through the trees, and not paying too much attention to the ice directly in front of him. He stepped through a soft layer of snow into a spring hole. There was no ice under the snow. He went through, snowshoes, pack basket and all. His alertness returned immediately, but it was too late. He was already up to his neck in ice-cold water, realizing he was in a terrible fix.

But he didn't panic. He was standing on the bottom. The bottom wasn't that solid, not sand or gravel, probably black muck. His snowshoes helped to distribute his weight just enough so he didn't sink in that ooze. His pack basket had to come off though before he could get himself out. Fearing there was more open water under the snow ahead of him, he decided to turn around, if he could, and work his way back to solid ice.

Turning around in that black muck with snowshoes on was difficult at best. Once he had turned completely around—which took an eternity—he could see solid ice only three feet away. He had to hurry because he was getting cold as all get-out, hypothermic. In order to remove his pack basket he had to submerge his head below the water line. The buoyancy of his pack basket and fur helped him to slip out of the shoulder harness. With all the strength he could muster, he threw the pack over his head, onto the ice.

There was no way he could remove his snowshoes unless

he submerged again to cut himself out of the harness. He was afraid that if he did, he wouldn't come back up. No, he would have to try to crawl out with his snowshoes still on. He put both of his arms on the ice and pulled himself over and then took a deep breath, before trying to pull himself out, and then he rolled onto the ice.

If he had not succeeded in that first attempt, Parnell doubted if he would have had enough strength to try it again. He was exhausted and cold. He forced himself to roll in the snow so the snow would soak up as much water as it could from his clothing. He was still in a fix. His matches were now as soaking wet as he was and there would be no way of starting a fire. His only alternative now was to get to his cabin as fast as he could. He shouldered his pack basket; it was heavier than ever now. Now that his attention was back on the deadwater and not the tree line, he could see where the snow had sunk, because the ice had melted, making a huge dish shape. He started out, detouring away from the ice, inland and down the shore to his trail through the trees.

By the time he was through the trees and back on the road to his cabin, the sun had set and the wind was beginning to blow. He was still cold, but now he could feel his blood circulating through his muscles. Once back in his snowshoe trail in the road, he picked up his pace. He didn't know what was keeping him going. If he were to fall, he knew he would never get up again. If he stopped to rest, he knew he would never get started again. As cold and as exhausted as he was, he kept forcing himself to pick up the pace. Placing one snowshoe in front of the other. Faster, and faster.

He turned off the main road, onto the one that would take him to his cabin. He could see the end now. He could just make out the shadowy outline of his cabin. He pushed the back door open and with his snowshoes still strapped on, he went through the shed to his main camp and collapsed onto the floor in front of the wood heater. There was still a fire in the stove. He could feel the heat on his face, as he lay there, trying to regain enough strength to get up off the floor.

He started laughing. That was a good sign. He suddenly remembered what John had said about the ice on the lower deadwater. He laughed again and then pulled himself up into a chair and he unstrapped his snowshoes.

* * * *

Now that all his traps had been tended and pulled, he spent the next several days fleshing and putting hides on drying boards. For all his efforts he had twenty beaver. Eight were super blankets and the rest only blankets and two otter.

The snow started to come down again. At first it just floated down to the ground and Parnell doubted if it would amount to much. Then overnight it changed to another nor'easter. Then the wind started to blow and the temperature fell too, one morning it was –35 degrees Fahrenheit. Parnell was glad he didn't have to go out.

There was nothing to do but sit and read. His brandy was almost gone. Then he wondered if John might have a bottle hidden somewhere that Stormi had never found. But he soon discovered he was on a fool's errand and he returned to the warmth of his woodstove.

The train didn't run during the blizzard and Parnell was lost without the newspaper. That was his only link to the outside world.

* * * *

The weather cleared, Parnell made a snowshoe trail down to the tracks. He went back and forth, back and forth packing the snow firmly. When he was done his path looked like a trench. The train was running again. And this meant he could walk down to Corriveau's camp and make another snowshoe trail, but when he got to the camp the roof had so much snow on it, he was afraid of it collapsing. He kindled a fire in the kitchen stove. Then he found a ladder hanging on pegs inside the woodshed and it just reached the roof of the camp. It only took Parnell a couple of hours to clear the snow.

When he had finished he started looking for a bottle John may have hidden away. There was nothing in the shed or woodshed. He went inside to get warm. Stormi had said he could have anything. He needed new blankets and sheets if there were any. He checked dresser drawers, closets, under the bed and finally found bedding in a window bench seat. There was storage room inside. There were three blankets and a clean set of sheets and much to his surprise a new bottle of French wine. "This must have been Stormi's. If only I could tell John," he laughed.

* * * *

Winter was coming to an end and before the wood crews quit for spring break-up, Parnell walked up the tracks to see Rusty at St. Croix Siding. "Rusty, do you know when the fur buyer is going to be in Ashland?"

"Yeah, it was in the local paper. But not the Bangor Daily. Every Friday afternoon from 2:00 p.m. until 8:00 p.m. until April fifteenth. Do you have some beaver hides to go out?"

"Yes."

"I could take them out for you tomorrow; it would save you a trip."

"Thanks, but I need to pick up some supplies too. What time are you leaving tomorrow?"

"3:00 p.m. sharp."

"I'll be here. If not, leave without me."

* * * *

Rusty and Parnell arrived at the headquarters storage building at 4:00 p.m. Again there was a line, but shorter this year. It had been a hard winter for trapping, because of the snow depth. Only the die-hards ventured out very far.

The price on both beaver and otter was better this year. Mostly because of the shortage of hides. Parnell was paid sixteen hundred dollars this year. He couldn't believe it. Between his winter and fall trapping he was making as much money as he would have if'n he'd stayed fishing.

Rusty stopped at the food store and waited outside while Parnell shopped. He bought two jugs of brandy this time, some more magazines, and soap and blades for his razor. "I'll take you to the station in Masardis. You have missed the southbound. I told the Mrs. I would be home for supper."

"Thanks, Rusty. I can walk home from here. It might take me all night, but that won't be a problem. Thanks, Rusty." Parnell got out and put his pack basket on.

"Come spring I'll have to buy me a pickup truck." He left Masardis and started for home.

After two hours he stopped and sat on the snow bank and rested. The stars were bright and a quarter moon was beginning to appear. He wanted to have a drink of brandy. But he knew if he started here he'd never make it safely back to his cabin. So he moved on in the star-studded night.

It was only a mile or two more from Masardis than from Smyrna Mills, but it seemed twice the distance by the time Parnell got home. He kindled a fire and fixed a sandwich before having a drink.

There were only a few hours before daylight so Parnell spent the rest of the night in his chair.

* * * *

There wasn't much to do until spring came and the snow melted. There was more firewood than he had thought and he would have enough to last him now until fall. There was no one to visit. No one visited him. No one to talk with. There wasn't much of anything to do, so he drank.

The two jugs he had purchased lasted almost three weeks. Rusty was gone now until summer. So once each month he would walk to Masardis, and if he timed it just right he could catch the northbound to Ashland. But then he would have to hitch a ride back to Masardis and then walk back to Howe Brook.

The snow was finally gone but there was still ice on the lake. The roads were dry so he spent a lot of time walking. He walked across the Horseback Road to where it intersected with the Blackwater Road.

One morning in late April, as Parnell stood looking out his front window, he suddenly realized the lake was free of ice. He pulled his canoe out of the shed and got his fishing gear and John's ashes.

He paddled straight for Tracy Brook, threw out the anchor and picked up the urn. "John—" he paused and cleared his throat. "John this was your last wish." He took the top off the urn and poured the ashes into the water and sat there watching them scatter over the surface of the lake. "Goodbye, John."

* * * *

The roads were dry and crews were beginning to go back to work. Levesque had more roads to build and crews began cutting the right of way.

Parnell caught a ride to Masardis with one of Levesque's foresters. There in Masardis he caught the afternoon train from Presque Isle to Ashland. There was one used car dealer in Ashland, Lilly's Autos.

He bought a 1955 Studebaker-Packard pickup truck. It was like new, only ten thousand miles. The salesman was surprised when Parnell gave him five hundred dollars in cash. "I assume you'll fill the gas tank."

"Yes, Mr. Purchase, of course."

Before leaving Ashland, he bought four, five-gallon gas cans and filled them with gas. He bought two jugs of brandy and some food stores.

When he got back to his cabin Parnell parked his pickup in the tool shed and shut the doors.

Chapter 5

Several years had come and gone since John Corriveau's death. Gray was now streaking through Ian's hair, and his hairline had receded some. He walked with a limp now, and he used his car more to get around now than walking, and he didn't stay in the woods weeks at a time. But neither was he willing to give up the Great Game. Not just yet.

Two winters ago, he had had an accident that had nearly cost him his life. And the odd thing about the accident, he was not that far from his home.

The Township of Merrill had been closed to beaver trapping for two years and one day in January, he had received information that there was some illegal trapping taking place on Hastings Brook near Sholler Mountain. There was no convenient place to leave his car along Route 212, so he left from his home on snowshoes to investigate. There was four inches of powdery snow on top of a well-packed base. Excellent conditions for snowshoeing. Since he would be in his own back yard, so to speak, he didn't take any food.

It was all down hill from his house, and he was making good time. He came to an active flowage a quarter of a mile from the main brook. The beaver had backed the water up, covering about two acres. And in front of the beaver house, next to the feed bed, were two trap stakes sticking above the ice. Ian paced off the distance and they were twenty-one feet from the house. That was legal. The stakes had been scarfed with an axe and the names of the trappers were written on the wood. *Tom and Vern Trout, Smyrna Mills.*

Why would anyone set traps in a closed town and write their name on the stake? Something wasn't right. Ian knew the Trouts, and although they might poach occasionally, they were not this stupid to leave their name. Could the informant have set the Trouts up to take a charge for illegal trapping?

Ian chopped the two traps out and had one small beaver. He put the traps and the beaver in his pack basket and continued on his way to Hastings Brook. He hit the brook downstream of the small feeder brook that comes off Sholler Mountain. He followed Hastings until the brook ran through a gorge on either side. He had walked the brook before during the open water fishing season and he wasn't aware of any flowage below there. He turned to make a swing back to the feeder stream.

The landscape was rugged. The snow gave way under him and he fell into a deep crevasse. He hit his head on the ledge wall of the crevasse and was now unconscious. When he awoke his head hurt where he had hit the ledge wall and his right leg was broken below the knee. Both snowshoes were still on his feet and the pack basket probably had prevented him from breaking his back. He was wedged in and he started to drift in and out of consciousness. He tried to focus his mind on something, anything to stay awake, but he kept drifting.

It was a good thing he had dressed warmly because darkness was setting in and the weather had turned foul and beginning to snow.

Just before daybreak, Ian regained consciousness. His head and right leg were still hurting, but at least he was fully aware of his present circumstances. He needed help soon or he would die. He looked at his watch—6:05 a.m.

No one knew where he was and last night's snowstorm would have covered all of his snowshoe tracks. He had no way of signaling. There wasn't much snow on him from the storm. Then he remembered that he was amongst some tall spruce trees when the crevasse opened up. Probably the wind had drifted snow over the opening of the crevasse, making it appear like solid footing.

His immediate concern was to get himself out of the crevasse and put a splint on his leg. He remembered trying to get the pack basket off yesterday, without any success. He had to keep trying or surrender. Then he chuckled to himself, "Ah, the Great Game ain't over yet."

The first time he tried to slip his left arm free of the basket, it had come free without any problem. Now he wondered what the matter had been yesterday, or had he tried his left arm at all. With his left arm now free it was easy to free himself from the pack basket. He could now stand in the crevasse by putting all of his weight on his left leg. Before he could do anything about crawling out of the crevasse, he had to first remove his snowshoes. That presented a problem in itself, but he eventually had them both off.

Standing on his good leg, he beat the snow down using a snowshoe and packing it as much as he could before crawling forward. He was an hour going four feet. But he kept doing it, four feet at a time until he found a small spruce tree growing at the edge of the crevasse that he used to pull himself out. He first threw his pack and snowshoes up, and then pulled and dragged himself out.

He rested before trying to splint his leg. After he had recovered, he removed his T-shirt and ripped it into cravats to tie off the splint. He cut two small fir trees and cut them to length. He placed one on each side of his leg, and tied a cravat on either side of the break, and then another below and above, and another by his ankle.

He was exhausted and he knew he should not attempt to start backtracking. He found he could move around better with his leg in a splint, but he knew enough to be careful. He hollowed out a spot close to the ground and kindled a fire. There was plenty of dry wood within reach of his little hollowed out hole. He soon had a warming blaze going. He leaned back against a spruce tree and rested in the comfort of his fire. The worst of his ordeal was over, but he wasn't out of danger yet.

He was hungry and he soon had the beaver skun and was roasting a hind leg over the fire. He could survive as long as he had food. With the hot meat in his stomach and a little snow for water, Ian felt surprisingly fine. But he wouldn't attempt to move again until the morrow.

During the night, about every hour-and-a-half or so, he would have to get more wood for the fire. At daylight, he roasted a forward leg of the beaver and ate that with more snow. He put the fire out and decided that it was time to travel.

His trail had frozen, but not enough to support his weight without snowshoes. He put his snowshoes on and started backtracking. He hadn't gone far when hc soon realized that he needed something to use as a crutch. He pulled his axe out of the pack basket and cut down a maple sapling. He cut two poles to use like ski poles and help to support his weight. The going was easier now, but still difficult at best.

By the end of that day, he had only traveled as far as the intersection of the stream coming off Sholler Mountain. He made camp there where the two brooks came together, making sure he chose a sight with plenty of dry wood.

He roasted more beaver meat and rested quite well that night.

* * * *

The morning after the snowstorm, Ian's supervisor, Virgil Brown, stopped at Ian's house. Ian was supposed to go with his supervisor to a meeting in Ashland. Ian's driveway and yard were still plugged with snow. There was snow still covering his car. There was no smoke in the chimney and Ian wasn't home. Virgil opened the door and hollered, "Ian! You home?" No answer. Virgil checked the counter top and the table for a note. There was nothing. This wasn't like Ian. *Maybe he had an emergency somewhere? But why is his car still here?*

He called Ashland from Ian's phone and canceled the meeting. No one there knew anything about Ian's whereabouts either. When Ian hadn't shown up by night, Virgil called the plane base in Eagle Lake and had the plane on stand-by for daylight the next morning. Virgil remained at Ian's house all that night. He knew Ian had stayed out before, but not under these circumstances. Something was wrong and Virgil was worried.

* * * *

By daybreak, Ian had his fire replenished with wood and was roasting more of the beaver meat. He was hungry. He roasted the last leg and ate it. Then, he sliced strips off of the back, and roasted that and ate until he was full. He washed it down with a handful of snow. He left the remainder of the carcass. It would be that much less weight on his back.

His leg was stiff and sore this morning, so he hobbled slowly and stopped often. He had just gotten to where the land started to incline towards his home. The rest of the way would be uphill. And then he heard the drone of an airplane. It was low and was looking for him. He hurt too much to rush downhill, to the clearing in the heath. There was no going back. Maybe, if he plugged along uphill, he'd come to an opening large enough to build a smoke signal and wait.

The pilot, Jack Dumont, saw Ian's fire and circled back to follow his trail.

"Pilot to Virgil—come in."

"Virgil to Pilot. Go ahead. What have you found?"

"I found his fire and he is now heading for his house. A compass reading of north, 360°, will put him in his backyard."

"Okay. Jack, I'll go out to meet him. Thanks."

"Do you want me to hang around?"

"Negative. Go home."

Virgil put his snowshoes on and started out through the woods. He cut Ian's trail. It was obvious, once he was in the woods, where the wind hadn't drifted snow in it.

When Virgil found Ian, he was still looking for that clearing. "Well. What happened, Ian?"

"I fell into a crevasse and broke my leg and knocked myself out."

"Is that all?" Virgil questioned with humor in the tone of this voice. "I thought maybe something serious had happened to you."

They waited there for more help. Virgil had his radio and called back to the other wardens, waiting at Ian's house, to come in with a Ski-Doo. ". . . and be quick about it. Follow the snowshoe trail."

Ian was embarrassed, but he was glad for the help.

* * * *

At the doctor's office, Dr. Stevens said, "You did a fine job setting your leg, Ian, but it isn't exactly where it should be."

"Well, move it."

"The break has already started to mend, and I will have to re-break it."

"Go for it."

"I'll give you something that'll knock you out for about an hour."

"No, just break it and be done with it."

After Doctor Stevens had reset the leg, he examined Ian's head. "That's a nasty bruise."

"Don't tell me you have to re-break my skull, too?"

"No, the swelling should be gone in a couple of days. You were lucky. Most people wouldn't have been able to get themselves out of the crevasse, let alone apply a splint and then snowshoe."

Ian stayed at home, recuperating, for the rest of the winter. When Doctor Stevens removed his cast in April, he said, "You will probably walk with a limp for the rest of your life. Your leg will get stronger once you start using it, and that limp will fade with time. But it'll always be there."

Ian missed the smelting season and the good early spring fishing. So, with nothing else to do, he decided to drive to Howe

Brook and stay at the warden's camp for a few days and do some early fishing.

* * * *

Through the years, Parnell had seen a lot of changes around Howe Brook. The Kennedy Tote Road that came in from Smyrna Center now went all the way to Levesque City. The road had been extended beyond the old (removed) roll dam on Smith Brook Deadwater, and joined the Kennedy Tote Road that went to Cut Pond. The Blackwater Road, which came out of Masardis, now connected with The Horseback Road. There was a new road that went into the Beaver Brook country which by-passed the Blackwater Road. Levesque had moved his city to T9-R3, just across the town line. Levesque had abandoned his first road in from Route 11. It went through low, wet ground, and twisted too much for all of the trucks that were now hauling wood. The new Levesque Road came over the top of McNally Ridge, from Route 11, just north of the upper McManus farm. And there were dozens of spur roads off each of the main gravel roads.

The new roads and extra harvesting that was going on all around didn't bother Parnell as much as the thought of all the people—people he didn't know—now in his hunting and trapping territory, his domain. He was a bit jealous.

Parnell hiked out one day, on one of the new roads, to see one of those skidders and watch it work. At first, while sitting parked in a yard, the thing just looked like a big, over-proportioned farm tractor. But when he watched it work, he couldn't believe it. The thing didn't need a road. It made its own through the woods, as it went. And the loads it could haul out were unbelievable.

He returned to his cabin, sick to his stomach, for he could see the future of his beautiful and tranquil world. "I now know how Crazy Horse felt, when he tried to stop the westward expansion of the white settlers."

Because the roads were plowed so close to the lake during

the winter, there were even people ice fishing on the lake, almost every weekend. He was glad John and Stormi didn't live to see the goings-on now. Stormi died two years after John. And because more people were around now, Ian Randall was around more and Parnell found it very difficult to get a piece of fresh meat.

Parnell had changed also. He had stopped shaving, he was now sporting a full beard, well trimmed, and his hair was longer, almost reaching his shirt collar. He drank brandy when he had it, and water when he didn't. His savings had grown from his trapping, but he had yet to file an income tax form.

The B&A train still went through Howe Brook, but there was no longer a passenger service north of Oakfield. This was only a minor inconvenience now, since Parnell had bought a pick-up some years back. He never licensed it. He only used it in the woods, or went only as far as the old train station in Masardis. And he never used it to joyride around on the wood roads.

Parnell read in the newspaper one day about Ian's ordeal with his broken leg, and the months at home to recuperate. He could have taken advantage of Ian's absence and gone out and gotten himself a nice young moose. But he didn't. It wouldn't be fair, or right to take advantage of his situation. It wouldn't be a fair play in the game, so out of a deep respect for Ian Randall, Parnell would not poach during his recuperation.

But there were others who were not as respectful. Lately, while sitting on his porch in the evenings, there had been several times when he had heard rifle shots in the distance. Sometimes one shot, and sometimes several. And with each shot Parnell heard, he'd clench his teeth together so tight his jaw would hurt.

There was no longer a bounty on bear and bobcat and the price for good beaver had increased to seventy dollars a hide, for a super blanket. Fox, otter, mink and fisher were worth more and pine martin were being caught everywhere in large numbers.

Moose were on the increase and the deer herd had remained

stable, but for the last few years, there was a new predator called the coyote, or coydog, in the southern part of the state. Parnell had yet to trap one while a few other trappers had.

Some were saying that they had come here from Canada, while others said that biologists for the fish and game commission had introduced the coyotes.

One thing that had not changed was the swarms of black flies and mosquitoes that reined the air in spring and early summer. In the evenings in warm weather, Parnell enjoyed sitting on his porch, watching the sunset and listening to the many loons on the lake. Sometimes, the hoard of black flies and mosquitoes would drive him back inside. He started smoking cigars more often during these evenings in order to ward off the pesky wing marauders.

Parnell sat watching the fiery sunset, but more spectacular was its reflection on the lake surface. He poured himself a brandy and lit a cigar. A loon cried across the lake, then the loon screamed its warning, and scolding tone. Parnell knew that something had disturbed the nesting loon around the point from Tracy Brook. He didn't believe it would be an otter or a mink. Then the silence was broken by a sound he had never heard, only read about in books. He listened again. There it was, the unmistakable sound of a howling wolf. "But wolf, or coyote, that everyone is talking about?"

Then the howling changed. Now it sounded like two or more animals were squabbling or fighting. Then all was quiet. Even the loons stopped their calling. Parnell listened and then remembered years ago, how his traps along Smith Brook had all been dug out and the bait stolen. "I wonder if that had been coyotes."

Although Parnell had chosen long ago to withdraw from society and the crazy political arena, he still stayed current about what was happening around the world. His only source of information was the Bangor Daily News, delivered almost every day, by Ansel Snow.

What he found most profoundly interesting was the United States involvement in Vietnam. At first he thought it just another small country's struggle for independence, but the U.S. was losing the war in the news media, the home front and the battle lines. It didn't seem to Parnell that the congressional officials should have as much authority how the battles were fought on the front lines, as they seemed to empower. The fighting should be left to the military.

Parnell noticed another alarming trend. He read the paper in its entirety every day. He followed the New York Stock Exchange, what was printed in the newspaper. He was particularly interested in the corporations that were in the business of making war materials. Then he began to wonder how many politicians had investments in those same corporations.

When one is locked away from general society, as Parnell had isolated himself, the mind can often see things more clearly or at least the mind can think that way. In Parnell's case, he needed something to occupy some time, each day. And one way was solving all of the world's problems himself. He needed to keep his mind busy.

Another evening, while Parnell was watching the sunset, he heard coyotes howling down the tracks beyond Corriveau's camp. The next morning, after breakfast, since the Saturday newspaper wouldn't be delivered until Monday, he grabbed his rifle and followed the road as far as Corriveau's. Then he started walking the tracks. Before crossing the Smith Brook Bridge at Weeksboro, he found the remains of a moose. Upon closer inspection, he decided that the train had probably struck the moose and the smell had attracted the coyotes. Something had been feeding from it and there were dog-like droppings everywhere.

He started to swing back through the woods to hit the Smith Brook Road. Just as he stepped into the woods he heard a rifle shot. He waited. There was only one shot from a small caliber rifle. He wasn't sure in what direction. He came out to the road between Quigley Brook and Long Brook. As he walked by a branch road next to Quigley Brook, he saw something odd lying next to the bushes. He walked up the road. There was a little yearling doe deer, dead. Blood dripped from a small hole in the rib cage. *This must have been what the shot was about,* he thought. Back on the gravel road he began looking at the tracks in the soft gravel. "They never even stopped. They shot that doe and drove on." He was disgusted at the idea of shooting something simply for the fun of it.

He went back to his cabin and put his rifle up in the rack. He thought about going back to take the quarters and saddles, but he didn't want a confrontation if those responsible were to come back for it. And he certainly didn't want Ian to catch him cutting the legs off.

The next afternoon, Parnell went for a walk up to the old fire tower on Howe Brook Mountain. Forestry had removed the tower but the view was still pretty good. Parnell stood at the concrete base, where the tower had been anchored, and looked out across St. Croix Lake. All he could see was an endless ocean of trees. Simply beautiful. Lonely and tranquil at the same time.

He left the mountain and crossed Howe Brook and walked up to the top of the Horseback and stood and looked out across the lower deadwater. Here too, everything seemed so peaceful. He followed the road out to the intersection with the Blackwater Road. He knew that he wasn't far from Levesque City, but he turned around and headed for home.

He hadn't gone very far when he came to a winter road on the right. The banks alongside this road were covered with blueberry bushes. He went to see if there would be enough berries to come back in a couple of months to pick. Out of sight of the Horseback Road, lying in the middle of the road was a dead cow moose. Her sides were bloated and aromatic gases were escaping. Parnell saw a small caliber bullet hole in the rib cage. Probably the same person. Nothing had been taken. Disgusted, he returned home. He longed for the days of the quiet habitat of the village.

The next morning he could hear equipment running behind his cabin. After breakfast, and a quick scan of Saturday's paper, he went for a walk to investigate. He took a compass reading and headed up through the woods.

The more he walked, the louder the noise. He could hear the chainsaws running, skidders running and a huge bulldozer making a new road. He found a forester running ribbon lines to the west, off the new road. Parnell walked over to query this young fellow.

"Good morning. What's going on here?" Parnell asked, hoping he wasn't too abrasive.

"We're putting in a new road from the Blackwater Road to the Howe Brook Road. It'll be a crosscut across Diamond's land. As soon as we can connect with the Harvey Siding Road, we'll start harvesting these strips that I'm laying out."

"Where is this Harvey Road?"

"It's coming in from Route 1. East of here. That crew has about another two miles to build. Then there'll be a woods road connecting Route 1 in Monticello with Route 11 in T8-R5."

"What is this strip cutting? I have never heard of that term," Parnell inquired.

"We clear cut everything in strips ninety feet wide, then leave a sixty foot strip uncut then clear cut another strip and so on."

"Why?"

"Well, we do less damage to the trees left standing this way and the uncut strips will act as wind buffers for the new growth. Also, there is a spruce bud-worm epidemic that is killing most of the fir trees. By clear cutting this way, Diamond is looking to slow down the epidemic."

"How wide spread is the spruce bud-worm epidemic?"

"All over northern and western Maine. The large landowners are losing millions of cord of lumber each year to the bud-worm. Some companies are spraying insecticides. They work good, but you can't always spray the trouble spots, because of the wetlands. And, it isn't good for the environment. Plus, it is expensive to hire DC-3s. If we can control the spread of the epidemic by strip cutting, it'll be more cost effective and better for the environment."

"I miss the days when the mill was up and working at Howe Brook, when people and families lived in here."

"I understand what you're saying, but unfortunately, cost and profit make the decisions today."

"Perhaps," Parnell offered to shake hands, "I'm Parnell Purchase."

"I have heard of you. I'm Rick Clark, from Merrill. The warden, Ian Randall, has told me some interesting stories about you. He should watch some of these guys on the job. They need watching." That was all Clark would say about that.

Parnell left Clark to his work and he wandered out to see this new road under construction. He still couldn't believe what a skidder could do. He watched in fascination. The huge bulldozer ripped through the ground like it was snow. Nothing could stop that monster.

Sadly, Parnell walked home. Wishing the happy days of village life would return.

* * * *

That evening, after the air had cooled, Parnell went for a walk down to the field where he had slept, his first night here, so many years ago. He walked around the edge of the field. One could hardly recognize it as a field today. Alder bushes had taken over and there was no green grass or clover. Deer no longer came here to feed.

He left the field and started for home. He no sooner got out onto the road than a pick-up with two younger men in it stopped. "Do you want a ride?" the passenger asked.

Parnell was feeling down in the dumps and lonely, so he accepted. "Where are you going? Hi, I'm Steve Michaels and this guy here is Buster, Buster Morgan."

"I'm Parnell."

"Where are you going, Parnell?"

"My cabin, follow this road and hang a left."

"Want a cold beer, Parnell?" Steve asked.

"That would go good, thanks."

"You boys are welcome to come in. I haven't had any company for a while."

Buster turned the truck off and grabbed the last three bottles of beer. "You live here all year?" Buster asked.

"Yeah."

"What are you hiding from?"

Already, Parnell took a disliking to this fat, uncultured idiot. Parnell noticed the .22 mag. rifle resting on the seat next to him. It was an automatic and the clip was inserted. That meant it was loaded. Probably these two are responsible for the dead animals left to rot along the roadsides.

"I'm not hiding. I simply enjoy living here."

"To each his own," Buster commented.

They all went inside and sat at the table. Buster had finished his beer and was opening another. "You ready for another, Parnell? How about you Steve?"

Steve gulped the last of his beer and then said, "Sure."

"What brings you two way in here at night?"

"We're cutting the right of way for the new cross-cut road. I run the skidder," Buster puffed up, "and Steve here cuts for me."

"Do you drive back and forth?"

"Nah, we're staying in a trailer camp parked next to Beaver Brook on the Blackwater Road."

"We come in Sunday evenings and go out Friday afternoon," Steve added.

Buster had already guzzled his beer down and was looking for more. "There ain't no more beer, Buster. You've drank it all," Steve said.

"You got anything to drink, Parnell?"

"I don't have any beer, but I do have some brandy."

"That'll do just fine."

Parnell poured him a tall glass full and sat back at the table.

"What about your families? You living in here all week must be difficult, especially for your wife."

"Steve here got a divorce last month. He can't afford to live out to town. I have five kids that scream and nag all day and a bitch for a wife. Besides, if I'm caught at home, the old lady's food stamps and welfare will be taken away."

Steve was yawning. Apparently, he did more work than Buster.

"What do you do for excitement in here?"

"Well, that depends. There are no movie theaters, bars or restaurants. I find surviving is excitement enough."

"You must shoot all of the moose and deer that you want, you living in here, just you."

"Nah, now that's illegal. I shoot a deer each season, and I'll shoot a bear when I need some bear fat for cooking."

"Me…I like to hunt. I was brought up on moose and deer meat and all the potatoes we could steal."

Steve got up, "I've got to go outside and relieve some water."

"What rifle do you hunt with, Parnell?"

"A .35 Marlin."

"I use a .22 mag. I hit 'em in the lungs or liver and they wander off the road before they drop. Out of sight. Then I come back later and take what I want of the meat. Ole Ian, he ain't caught me yet," he bragged.

Parnell was already scheming a plan to take care of this blowhard.

"I got a nice bull last week, but some lousy skunk stole my antlers."

"What happened?" Parnell asked.

"Me and Steve, we were coming in Sunday evening and just as we turned onto the road from Route 11, this huge bull stepped into the road and stood there, I shot him low in the brisket so he'd run off the road. He ran all right. Hundred yards, down through the woods. I got out and grabbed my axe and Steve, here, took my truck and drove up the road and waited. I whacked those antlers off with my axe and drug 'em back to Levesque's Road. They were huge. Steve and me loaded them into the pickup and we drove down to the sand shed on Route 11 and hid the antlers out back where nobody would find them. But some lousy skunk did! And if I ever find out who, I'll break both his arms.

"I really enjoy the woods and hunting."

"Yeah, that's indelibly so," Parnell noticed. A strange expression suddenly appeared on Buster's face. He had never heard the word *indelible* before, let alone understanding its meaning. But Parnell wasn't so sure that he enjoyed hunting or just the thought of killing something and getting away with it. He was a killer, a bully.

Steve was almost asleep. "Hey Steve," Buster shook his arm. "It's time to go. We'd better get some sleep before morning."

They both got up to leave and Buster stopped and said, "I'll come in some evening and you and me, we'll go shoot us some game."

Parnell didn't answer and the two left. He didn't know if Buster and Steve knew Ian had a camp in here or not. Although, he hadn't used it in several months.

A few days later, Parnell was awakened by what sounded like a pack of coyotes fighting. It seemed to be coming from up the tracks beyond the Howe Brook Bridge. He dressed, trying to make as little noise as possible, without lighting a lantern. He took his rifle out of the rack and closed the door quietly. He didn't need to load his rifle. It was always loaded, just in case.

He didn't have to go far at all before he realized what the coyotes had found and were fighting over. Who was going to feed first? About two hundred yards beyond the bridge, he saw three dog-like creatures scatter as he approached. One ran across the tracks towards the lake. Another ran into the woods away from the lake, while the third ran up the tracks a ways, then stopped and sat between the rails, watching Parnell.

The smell of a rotting carcass was getting stronger the closer Parnell came to the putrefying mess. A large cow moose was lying between the woods and the tracks. At first, he thought that a train had probably hit the moose. That is until he saw a small caliber bullet hole behind the chest. This was looking like Buster's work. Just then, there was a rifle shot to the north. It was just getting light.

The report didn't sound like a large caliber rifle. Then he thought again of Buster and Steve and wondered what they had shot now to run off and die.

He decided to go see. "The boys will be working by the time I get there." When he came to Beaver Brook, he crossed to the other side and started following the brook upstream. The two were supposed to be camped where the brook crosses the Blackwater Road. The temperature was already rising. It was going to be a hot day. He wiped the sweat from his face.

He moved through the woods as quiet as a deer, making hardly any noise. But as he was getting closer to the road, he stopped to listen. He moved forward even slower and quieter. There was a path coming from their trailer camper. Out of curiosity, Parnell followed the path to the brook. There, in a spring pool, Buster and Steve had made a watertight box and anchored it to the brook bottom. A cool storage box. He opened the lid. There were two fresh deer hindquarters. *This was probably shot last night.* He closed the lid and followed the path back to the camper. He hadn't heard any voices or commotion from the boys yet. But—he stopped in his tracks. Buster's pickup was parked in the shade under a tall spruce tree. Not wanting to be discovered, he crouched down behind some cedar trees.

There was no noise coming from inside the camper and no movement. After a several minutes, he felt safe enough to come out from behind the cedar trees to have a closer look. The .22 mag. rifle was still in Buster's pickup. Now Parnell could see that a second vehicle had been parked there and fresh tire tracks, where it had been backed out onto the gravel road and driven towards the new crosscut road.

He felt safe enough now, so he walked around the camper. The boys had thrown garbage everywhere. There was a fifty-gallon barrel filled with trash, and on the ground around it. These two were nothing short of pigs. There was a dirt spur road across the Blackwater Road that appeared to still be following Beaver Brook.

Again, curiosity prevailed and Parnell decided to see where it went. There were fresh man tracks in the dirt, one larger than the other. Buster and Steve. He walked along the edge, being careful not to leave any tracks. There were deer tracks going both ways in the road. Up ahead, in a tall, dead pine stub, there was an eagle's nest.

Only a few large spruce trees had been cut. Probably, these were used to build the bridge over Beaver Brook. Around the next corner, Parnell found a small dead deer lying just off the road. The hind legs had been cut off. And there was an eagle, lying dead beside the deer. This really angered Parnell. Now he was going to make these two killers pay. He had seen enough for one day.

He sat down in the shade to think on it. How to scheme a plan so Ian would arrest the two of them without having to bring him here. He lit a cigar, so the smoke would keep the flies away. He went back to look at the deer again. It had been shot behind the head with a small caliber. Parnell turned the head over, looking for an exit wound. There wasn't one. That meant the .22 mag. bullet would still be inside the deer's head, and ballistics could match the spent bullet with the rifle in Buster's pickup. He looked the eagle over. There was fresh blood on the breast and no exit wound.

He had his plan. He cut the deer's head off. Just the head. Then he dragged the deer out of sight, through an alder wet hole. He was sure that Buster and Steve wouldn't find it in there. Parnell hoped that they would think that a bear had dragged it off. He picked the head up, along with the eagle, and went through the woods to the gravel road. He waited to make sure all was quiet.

All was clear. He followed their path down to the brook, and then found what he wanted, a little downstream from the box cooler; cool moss was growing next to the water. Very carefully, he pulled a small section of the moss loose. There were small rocks underneath, as he had expected. He dug out several and put them in the stream. That way, nothing would look out of place. He put the deer head and eagle in the hole he made and then he laid the moss back on top, covering the cache. They wouldn't spoil in the cool ground until he could complete his plan.

* * * *

Parnell left and walked back to the tracks and then back to his cabin. It was past noon, and he hadn't eaten breakfast yet. He fried up some ham and eggs. He thought of the two hindquarters in the box cooler and wished he had some fresh venison. When he had finished eating, he went out and sat on the porch, thinking. Thinking about how to complete his plan. He needed Ian here.

Little by little, Parnell drifted off to a peaceful sleep. His belly was full of food and he had been up and walking since before daylight. The afternoon sun was shining directly on him and he finally awoke, covered with perspiration.

The northbound train was coming. It was still a long ways off, coming up the grade from Dudley Siding. The engines were working hard, making a lot of noise. Parnell sat on the porch, waiting for the train to go through and thinking about life in the village, when there was a real village, with happy families and celebrations. "Those were good years. Too bad that era had to come to an end."

The train was just coming into view and it was picking up speed. The engineer blew the whistle and waved, but it wasn't Ansel. No matter.

Parnell stood up to go inside and he looked down towards the tracks. Ian was just driving across the crossing, towards his camp. He had his plan now. First though, he would have to keep him in his camp tonight.

Ian was unloading his gear from the car. It looked as if he might stay a few days with all of those food stores. Parnell was glad for that. "Hello there," Parnell called. "You haven't been around for a long time." Parnell noticed the limp.

"Had a little accident this winter. I'm just getting back to work now."

"I read about you falling into that crevasse. That was damn careless of you, with as much as you're in the woods. Did someone push you? Or are you just naturally clumsy?" Parnell said jokingly.

"That's what I thought, too. Anything new around here?"

"Just all the new roads that are being built. Pretty soon, this'll be like New Jersey. All roads and no game. Hey, how about you and me doing some fishing? The water is just right for some big brookies off Blackpoint."

"I'd like a fat trout for supper…we might as well take my canoe. I have to get it out of camp anyhow." Ian wondered why Parnell was suddenly being so friendly. Perhaps he had just developed an overly suspicious mind over the years.

The canoe was loaded and both men had fly rods. Parnell borrowed one of Ian's. "I'll paddle you around so you can troll until we get to Blackpoint," Parnell offered.

"No objections here." Parnell paddled out and guided the canoe effortlessly. He paddled on the right, without ever taking the paddle out of the water, while Ian trolled on the left. So far, everything was working fine for Parnell's plan, but it would prove to be a long night for him, with no sleep.

About twenty yards directly out from Blackpoint, Ian hooked a big one. It was a fight. Three times it jumped out of the water, trying to shake loose of the hook. "We didn't bring a net, did we?" Ian asked.

162

"Guess not. Bring him alongside and I'll grab him by the gills." Parnell brought him in and released the streamer. "Hmm, a warden's worry. I'll have to try that sometime."

Ian measured his trout. "Seventeen inches, and look how orange the belly is. I can almost smell him in the fry pan now."

Parnell geared up, using a royal coachman fly. There was a slight breeze, which was moving the canoe. Trout were jumping all around them. After many casts, Parnell paddled back to where Ian had caught his. "Try it again, Ian. I'll keep the canoe moving a little." He no sooner had said this than Ian hooked into another fish, the same size as the first.

"There, that's supper. We can go eat now," Ian said.

As they paddled back to camp, Parnell was hoping they wouldn't hear any rifle shots. If they did, he was sure Ian would go and investigate, and that would spoil his plans. Instead, "Hear that? Crews are working tonight."

"Where are they?" Ian asked.

"They are making a new cross-cut road through Diamond's land from the Blackwater Road to Harvey Siding, eventually." Parnell hoped that would be Buster and Steve's skidder making that noise.

Parnell cleaned the fish, and Ian peeled the potatoes and put them on to boil.

The trout were fried with salt pork and that too was eaten when there was no more pink trout left. "That was delicious," Ian said as he cleaned up. "Game of cribbage?"

"Sure thing. It's been a few years. The last game I played was with John." Ian was playing right into his hand.

As they played cribbage, pegging hole for hole, "You know, as much poaching that went on here before the mill and station house were dismantled and the families left, I'd still rather have those days back again. In spite of all the walking I had to do. Now, I can practically drive wherever I want to check something."

"I was thinking the same thing recently," Parnell said.

As far as the game of cribbage, these two were pretty evenly

163

matched. The score was two up. "One more, Ian, to break the tie, then I've got to get some sleep." He hoped his yawn was convincing. He stretched and yawned again. He was making himself sleepy.

They went right to the last six holes, hole for hole. Parnell pegged two holes with a pair of eights and Ian pegged six with the third eight. Ian played his last card and pegged the finish hole for last card. "That was a good game, Parnell; we'll have to do it again."

"Any time you're in, Ian. Now I've got to get some sleep. Maybe I'll see you tomorrow if you're not too busy. Goodnight."

Parnell actually walked as if he was exhausted. If he wasn't, he should have been. He was playing the game well. He walked slowly back to his own cabin. He opened his door and closed it so Ian could hear the slam, if he was listening, and he probably was. There were two kerosene lanterns, one full of kerosene, the other only had little more than fumes. He lit the later, knowing it would soon burn out. He changed his clothes, put his axe in his basket and set the lantern on the stand next to the bed. He shouldered his pack basket and put a flashlight in his jacket pocket. He walked outside through the woodshed door in the back.

He waited momentarily, listening. All was quiet. He walked out the back trail, and then circling north, crossing Howe Brook and back to the tracks. There was supposed to be a full moon tonight, but it still hadn't risen above the horizon. Total darkness made it terribly difficult. Once he found his trail that crossed the brook, and circled down to the tracks, he didn't have as much trouble. Once on the tracks, he couldn't see the ties and he kept tripping. He had all night, so he took his time until the moon was up. Then he walked like he had a single purpose in his mind.

Rather than sneaking through the woods, trying to follow Beaver Brook in the dark without a flashlight, Parnell walked to St. Croix Siding, and then down the Backwater Road to their camp. The trailer camper was just a shadowy silhouette.

He walked right up to the camper, stopped and listened. The only sounds were those of the two men snoring. He tested the passenger door on Buster's pick-up. It was unlocked. "Good."

Even with the full moon out, Parnell still had a difficult time to navigate the path down to the brook where he had earlier buried the deer's head and the eagle. He didn't use his flashlight, fearing they might awaken and see his light.

On his hands and knees, he searched for the mossy spot. He was beginning to damn himself for being too cautious. He finally found the spot, after ripping his pants and scraping his knee. He removed the eagle and head and laid the moss back and smoothed it out. His heart was racing and each beat sounded like drums in his ears.

He wound his way back along the path and made sure the two were still snoring before he very gently opened the passenger door. The door hinge squeaked. Parnell stopped and listened. This time, he lifted the door as he opened it. No problem. He brushed the dirt and moss off the deer head and slid that under the seat. Then, he brushed the eagle off and put that behind the seat and pulled some old rags over it, to conceal it. Then he had an idea. He pulled several of the tail feathers out and a few of the pinfeathers. Those he left on the front seat. The tail feathers he put in the glove box. Then, to make sure that Ian would look in the glove box, Parnell took his knife and stuck his finger. It drew a drop of blood. He lightly smeared the blood on the glove box latch and on the corner of the lid next to the passenger door.

He closed the door, trying to latch it without having to slam it. Next, he went back down the path to the box cooler and took the two deer legs out and put them in his pack basket. The stage was set and now it was time to clear the scene. He was afraid that if he walked the road back to St. Croix Siding, someone might come along and see him. He couldn't take that chance, so he followed the brook through the woods to the tracks. When he thought he was a safe distance from the camper, he turned his flashlight on. But, once he was on the tracks, he didn't need the flashlight and he put it back in his pocket.

It was just breaking daylight when Parnell got back to his cabin. The two hindquarters went in his root cellar under the sawdust and on top of the ice. "There. They'll keep now. I'll have fresh deer steak for supper. Now to go see Ian." To make his story convincing, he took his rifle with him and unloaded it. The game had to be played just right.

There were no lights on at Ian's camp, but there was smoke coming from the chimney. As Parnell walked around the front corner of the camp, Ian was just coming out of the outhouse. "What brings you here so early, Parnell? Come on in. I'll turn a lantern on. I already have coffee boiling."

After the light was on, Ian saw Parnell's rifle, the condition of his clothes, and the blood on his hand. "I hope that's deer blood on your hand."

"Not this time, Ian. I fell down and stuck a thorn in my finger. Tore my pants and skinned my knee."

"What have you been doing out so early?" Ian looked at Parnell rather sternly.

"I woke up about 3:30 a.m. I had to pee. Coyotes were making an awful racket, up the tracks, across the bridge. There's a dead moose lying beside the tracks." He saw the look on Ian's face. "No, I didn't shoot it. Someone did though, last week, with a small caliber rifle. Hit it behind the chest. I figure the moose wandered down to the tracks and died. It was probably trying to get to the lake. Anyway, when I heard those coyotes yapping, I took my rifle and went up to see if I could get one."

"Did you?" Ian was hoping. Shooting, even coyotes at night, would be a charge of night hunting.

"They heard me on the tracks and left."

"Is your rifle loaded?"

Parnell opened the lever action so Ian could see for himself. "I wished you had. 'Cause, then I'd have you for night hunting. Even if it was nothing but a mangy coyote." Ian said this in goodwill.

"But I did hear some shooting up towards Beaver Brook, where the road crosses the brook. There is a trailer camper parked there. Two real dirt bags. They gave me a ride back to my cabin last week. The loud mouth one had a .22 mag. rifle with him. He made the comment that you *weren't smart enough to catch him.*"

"Oh? How many shots this morning?"

"Just one."

"Have you been hearing a lot of shooting?"

"Not a lot. But when I hear a shot, I usually take notice."

"Okay, I'll take a ride over and see what's going on."

* * * *

Parnell was glad that was over. For a minute, he didn't know but what Ian was going to arrest him for night hunting. As he was leaving, he noticed that Ian was buckling a gun belt. This was the first time that he had ever seen Ian carry a revolver.

"What is, the game getting so rough you have to carry a gun now?"

"New regulations from Augusta. We have rules to follow, too."

He went back to his own cabin, cleaned up and lay down. He was exhausted and relieved.

The bridge on the crosscut road over Howe Brook was completed and the new road connected with the Horseback Road, but Ian didn't want to let the crews know that he was in, not just yet. So, he drove around and came in from the Blackwater Road.

Buster's old, brown Chevy pick-up was still parked in the same spot. Ian knocked on the camp door. No answer. He walked around the camper and found the path to the box cooler. He lifted the lid. It was empty, except for a few hairs. He picked a couple up and looked at them. "Deer alright. But where's the meat?"

He followed the path back to the camper. He wasn't sure, but it looked as if he might be too late. "Maybe the meat is gone already." He walked over to the driver's door of the brown Chevy and looked through the window. He could see a small caliber rifle, but from that angle, he couldn't tell if it was loaded. It was a typical culls' work truck—greasy towels, rags, old gloves, *and, and feathers on the passenger seat.* From the passenger side, Ian could clearly see a clip inserted into the rifle. That was enough probable cause to check it, but he waited. There were some papers on the dash. Old scale slips and on one was the name, Buster Morgan. He knew Buster, and he knew that he was capable of anything illegal if he felt safe, particularly in the woods.

Then he noticed a speck, just a speck of blood on the glove box latch button. "That's good." But still, he didn't open and search the interior. Instead, he looked through the dunnage on back. There was deer hair on the body and moose hair on the inside of the plywood box, Buster had on back in which he carried gas, oil, tools, rags and such.

Today was Friday, and probably he and his helper would leave the woods early. Rather than searching the inside now and checking the rifle, he'd wait and watch and see what Buster would do. Ian would not approach the pickup until Buster was in and attempting to leave. There'd be a stronger case for safety than for finding the rifle loaded now with no one around.

He parked his car in the road where Parnell had found the dead deer and eagle. As he was walking back to the gravel road, he smelled the air. There was a strong, pungent odor of rotting meat. He followed the scent, where it had lain and noticed a lot of dry blood on the ground. He continued following the rotting scent into the alder growth and found a small rotting deer carcass. The head was gone, and both hindquarters. "But this can't be the shot Parnell heard earlier this morning. It's too old."

He went back to the edge of the gravel road to wait for Buster. He just happened to pick the same spot Parnell had, behind the cedar trees. As he waited, he tried to think of a way to connect Buster with the dead deer. Probably, the deer had been shot in the head and he had cut that off and thrown it. "But where is the meat now? I suppose they could have eaten it all. It was only a small deer."

The mosquitoes and black flies were terrible. Ian prayed that Buster would show up soon. He could hear a loaded truck coming. The driver must be new because he was having some trouble shifting, grinding the gears. He went by Ian in a cloud of dust. When the dust settled, and the air was clear again, Ian had a layer of dirt covering him.

Another truck loaded with spruce drove by, and behind that, in a cloud of dust, were two pickups. They went by, following the big truck. When the dust had settled again, Ian could hear another pickup coming and it turned and stopped at the trailer camper. Two men got out. Buster was the passenger. He grabbed his chainsaw out of the back and walked over close to his truck and then tossed his saw into the back of his truck. Then both men went inside. Ian was getting excited. The Great Game was building in climax. Soon, he'd make his play. Not yet. The adrenaline was flowing, and he had to pee, but he'd have to wait.

The other fellow came out of the trailer carrying a box of dirty clothes and put the box inside of the pickup. He went back in and came out with his bedding and put that inside too. "We sure had a good week. I need the money. I'll see you at the pay office, Buster."

"Okay, you have everything?"

"I think so. Don't forget the scale slips on the table." Steve got into his pickup and drove off.

Buster was coming out, carrying his dirty laundry and bedding. He closed the trailer door and locked it. He put his clothes inside of the pickup, got in and started it. Ian had stepped out from behind the cedars and was walking towards Buster's pickup, keeping the back corner post of the cab between him and Buster.

Buster had his pickup in gear now and was backing up. He never saw Ian coming. When the warden tapped on the window, he surprised Buster. "Hey! Damn, you scared the hell out of me, Warden!"

"You all done for the day already?" Ian asked, trying to get Buster off the defensive.

"Ya, me and Steve. We quit early on Fridays so we can pick up our pay checks at the office before they close."

"A nice load of spruce went out."

"Ya, it's real cream stuff."

"Who are you working for?"

"Right now, the Diamond Corporation. We're cutting the right of way for the new roads."

"That's a nice looking rifle there. What make is it?"

"It's a Remington," Buster replied. Now he was showing signs of nervousness. "It's a .22 mag."

"Nice looking rifle. I'd like a good look at it, if you'd pass it out to me."

Buster hesitated at first, and then he thought about popping the clip out, but Ian had already seen enough. "I suppose you know it's loaded."

"I can see the clip. Why don't you shut your engine off? No sense in wasting the gas."

Buster turned the truck off and handed Ian his rifle. Ian popped the clip out and it had live rounds inserted. He put the clip in his pocket and pulled the action back. A live round was ejected. He picked that up from the ground and put that in his pocket. "Do you have any other firearms or handguns?"

"No, that's it. Steve and me, we go out target shooting after work sometimes. Not much to do in here."

Ian laid the rifle on the hood of his pickup. He knew that there was nothing on the seat under the clothing, so he didn't have to look. But, he did bend down to look under the seat. "What ta-hell?" He pulled the deer head out by the ear and held it up. The expression on Buster's face was priceless.

He also said, "What ta-hell? I didn't cut no head off! Steve must have put that under the seat. That's why he left so fast!" He was getting angry.

Ian looked the head over and saw a small caliber entrance wound. Now he understood. These two were poaching in Parnell's backyard and he didn't like it. And the game plays on.

"Where would Steve get a deer head to put under your seat?"

Buster clammed up and wouldn't answer.

"Looks to me, this deer was shot right behind the head." Ian turned the head around so Buster could see the small entrance hole.

"Do you want to tell me where this head came from?"

"Not likely. Don't you have to advise me of my rights or something?"

"That's right. It's called your Miranda Rights. Do you need me to explain them to you?"

"Why don't you enlighten me?"

"Well, basically, it's telling you: *You have the right to shut up and if you give up that right, anything you say, can, and will, be used against you. If you want to speak to an attorney before you answer any of my questions, you can. If you can't afford an attorney, one will be provided.* Now, are you going to answer my questions?"

"No."

"Okay. Then I'll tell you where I found the rest of this deer." Ian noticed that Buster was really nervous now, and fidgety. Buster gave Ian the impression that there was more to this. Ian nodded with his head, indicating the road across the way. "There's a small deer, just lying in those alders, with no head or hind legs. Then I've got to ask myself, 'cause I can't ask you, remember? Why did someone cut this deer's head off? Then, low and behold, I find a head under your seat that's been shot right behind the head. And you know, this is still fairly fresh, compared to the rest of that deer. But I bet I'll be able to remove a rifle slug from this head." He held the head up to emphasize his point. "And I bet that ballistics will match it to your .22 mag. rifle. What do you say? Don't answer. Just think on it."

"You can't pin that on me! I didn't put that head under my own pickup seat. Why would I?"

"You tell me, but remember, I can't ask you."

Ian could see that Buster's anger was growing and growing. "Could be you were only going to take this home to your dog."

"Can I leave? I need to pick up my check before the office closes."

"No, you can't. You are under arrest for possession of deer parts in closed season and for having a loaded rifle in your motor vehicle. And I ain't done looking yet." Ian put the deer head on the hood with the rifle. Then he opened the glove box. "Well, well. Will you looky here?" Buster stepped over to the driver's door so he could see.

"Damn him! I told him to get rid of those eagle feathers! I'll fix him!"

"Who are you talking about?"

"Steve, that's who."

"Did Steve shoot an eagle?"

"No, we found one and he wanted some feathers."

"Can you take me back to where the eagle is?"

"It wasn't anywhere around here."

Ian put the feathers on the hood with the rest of the items. "You know, just possessing eagle feathers is a crime." No comment.

Ian walked over to the driver's door and looked under the seat. There were several empty .22 mag. shells. He picked up three and put them in his pocket.

"Why did you take those?"

"Because, soon I'll find out where the eagle was shot and there's bound to be empty shells lying around somewhere."

"That won't mean that I shot it."

"No, not that alone. But it will prove that you were there."

Ian looked behind the seat on the driver's side. Nothing of interest. Then, he walked back over to the passenger side and looked behind the seat. Nothing but a large pile of rags.

Something just didn't look right and Ian felt at the pile of rags. He pulled the rags back. "Well, what do you say about this? That wasn't a question, you understand."

"Damn him all to hell! I told him to leave that damned bird alone!"

Ian was handling the bird, looking it over, "Will you look at this?"

"What now, Mr. Warden?"

"A bullet hole, and an awful small caliber too. I wonder if this could have been shot with a .22 mag. Now, I'm just wondering, mind you, that wasn't a question. You know, Buster, there doesn't appear to be an exit wound here either. Guess I'll have to do an autopsy.

"Just so you understand, Buster, you're also under arrest for possession of parts of a bald eagle.

"You know, maybe I should have a look in the back of your pickup also." Ian looked in the wooden box, under all of the dunnage in the body. He shook gas and oil cans and even opened the toolbox. Nothing.

"Well, I guess I have everything. Now, I'm going to leave everything right here on your hood. You and me are going to walk across that road and go in that one." He pointed. "My car is in there only a step. Now you have a choice. I can either handcuff you right now, or you can behave yourself. Which is it?"

"I'll behave."

"Walk with me." When they were almost at the spot where the deer had been when Parnell had found it, Ian said, "Eagles go for the eyes first when they find a dead carcass. They pluck 'em out and toss them up, like we do popcorn, and catch 'em and swallow them whole. They probably slide down real easy. I noticed that both eyeballs on that deer's head were gone. With a little work, I bet I'll be able to come up with some eagle feathers somewhere around here. I found where you dragged the carcass into those alders."

"I didn't drag no deer nowhere. Can't you see I'm being framed?"

"Well, if someone did—and I doubt that, but if someone did frame you—then he did an awful good job of it." Then to himself, "Yes, Parnell, you did a good job."

* * * *

Buster's bail was set at five thousand dollars cash. He remained in jail.

Ian went home and before fixing himself something to eat, he dissected the deer's head and the bald eagle. He was very careful, taking photographs as he proceeded. When he was finished, he wrapped each separately in plastic and put them in his freezer. The spent bullets looked alike to him. After eating, he wrote up his report and then sat on his porch until long after dark, sipping a brandy, inwardly laughing.

Parnell went to bed early that night, after eating fresh deer steak and potatoes.

* * * *

The next day, Saturday, Parnell decided that he had better can the rest of the deer meat before Ian paid him an official visit. Ian would have been able to figure out where the meat had gone when he checked the box cooler. He didn't want to be caught with fresh meat. So all that day, as warm as it was, Parnell kept the wood cook stove going, boiling water to cook and seal the canning jars. He kept enough steak for one more meal.

That night, as he sat on his porch watching the sunset, sipping a brandy and smoking a cigar to ward off bugs, he couldn't help but feel the satisfaction with the help that Ian had given him. Buster was nothing more than a killer. He killed for the simple pleasure of pulling the trigger and watching his prey die, or wander off to suffer. He didn't kill to eat, to feed his family. Parnell wasn't feeling smug about what he had done, but someone like that should not be allowed in the woods.

The next day, Parnell had a lot of nervous energy and needed something to do. He backed his pickup out of the shed and put his chainsaw, gas and oil in the back. He drove out the back trail to work on some firewood. It was warm, but for some strange reason, he had to keep busy.

He didn't wake up the next morning until the southbound train went through and Ansel blew the whistle, signaling the morning newspaper and Saturday's paper had arrived. Parnell kindled a fire and made a pot of coffee and set it on the stove to boil while he walked down to the tracks after the newspapers.

On the front page of this morning's newspaper, in bold headlines: POACHER NABBED FOR SHOOTING BALD EAGLE.

The only satisfaction Parnell had from reading the article was knowing that, for now at least, no more birds or animals would be shot simply for the thrill of it.

The next few days turned off very warm. Parnell had intended to work on his firewood, so he wouldn't have to do it during trapping season. Instead, he put his canoe in the water and canoed around the lake, just looking and exploring. He floated down the outlet, as far as he could go, and found many new beaver houses. He would remember those for this winter.

He pulled his canoe onshore at Blackpoint and explored the point. He found an old fireplace. Someone had been there before him. This took some of the interest away from Blackpoint. He sat down on top of a knoll, not looking at anything in particular, but seeing in his mind, life in the village when the mill was in full operation and all of the cabins were full of families. No one griped about not having enough money or new clothes or anything about the outside world. People had been content with their lives and willing to help those who were not so fortunate. That's exactly how John and Stormi had lived. By the living standards of those outside, the Corriveaus would have been deemed penniless and poor folk. But in here, they were as rich as they came. They gave away more than they kept.

How Parnell wished he could turn the time back again to

175

those rich and wonderful days. Tears began to cloud his vision. He stood up and walked back to his canoe and continued with his journey around the lake.

As he paddled up to the railroad trestle, across Smith Brook, he looked up at the tracks. There was a reddish brown coyote standing between the rails, watching Parnell. Parnell sat still in his canoe and the coyote stood still. It had stopped panting. Parnell knew that the coyote would not attack, but he couldn't understand what this standoff was about.

A mosquito lit, and bit Parnell on his cheek. He slapped the bug. The coyote ran off, tired of the game. Parnell canoed back to the lake and then home.

Later that night he was sitting on his porch thinking. There was something wrong, but he couldn't identify it. There had been restlessness inside of him since the night when he had been at Buster and Steve's trailer camp. He was full of nervous energy, but he couldn't stop his mind from wandering. There was nowhere where he could go to escape this feeling. It was almost like there was something, some entity that possessed his mind and body. Had he been too long in the woods, alone?

He poured himself a brandy and started to light a cigar, but decided not to. "Bugs ain't bad tonight." The sunset looked threatening. Gray clouds lit up with golden rays, making them look like solid, rugged mountains. Heat lightening flashed, but no thunder. The waning moon reflected off the lake surface, making it appear as gray slate. There wasn't a breeze. All was still. Even the loons were quiet tonight.

The southbound train could be heard in the distance, coming down the grade from Pride Siding. It was late tonight. The whistle blew at the St. Croix crossing. The engines were making more noise now, as the engineer opened the throttle, anticipating the incline into Weeksboro. From there, he would have to slow the train's momentum on the downgrade, through Shorey and Dudley Sidings, into Smyrna Mills.

There were five engines tonight, hauling a long train of

cars. Parnell started counting. The train kept increasing its speed and the cars were going by faster. Many of the cars were loaded with sawed lumber, some with wood chips for the paper mills. No passenger cars. No wonder they needed five engines. He counted over a hundred cars.

When the train was no more, the eerie silence returned. The only lonely creature out tonight, besides Parnell, was a bat, swooping down to catch some flies.

A slight breeze from the north started to blow. The breeze brought cooler, dryer air. It was a welcoming relief. There were streaks of lightening in the north also, accompanied with a dull, thundering roll. This echoed through the valley.

The slight breeze changed into a steady wind. Not strong yet, but no troughs. Lightning flashes were coming faster and the thunder was louder. No longer was it just rolling through the valley. Sharp cracks, followed by more zigzag lightening flashes, followed by louder thunder. The wind was stronger now. But no rain yet. Parnell sat still on the porch, amazed at the storm. The wind was really blowing now, like a winter blizzard. Then hail started, driven by the wind, hitting the ground so hard, it was bouncing up six inches. In five minutes the ground was all white. Then it stopped hailing as soon as it had started. Now the rain poured forth, driven by the wind. Parnell had to retire inside, or he'd get drenched.

The rain slamming against his cabin was deafening, almost so that he couldn't distinguish the thunder from the noise the rain was making. The storm was so close that thunder immediately followed lightening flashes. The wind was driving the rain through the cracks around the windows on the north and west sides of the cabin. There was really nothing he could do about the storm or the water leaking through the cracks. He turned his lantern out and went to bed.

By morning of the next day, the storm had passed and the sun was out, already evaporating moisture back into the atmosphere. Parnell looked at the windows that had been leaking and decided that there was nothing he could do about it. So, he decided to take a walk out along the back trail and swing over and look at the new bridge on the crosscut road.

Caught in pools upstream from the bridge were several peeled poplar sticks that had floated downstream last night in the heavy rain from a beaver flowage upstream. He would remember this for this winters beaver trapping. A blue pickup stopped as Parnell was standing on the bridge, thinking about beaver.

"Any fish in this brook?"

"Not here, up at the next bridge. Who are you? I haven't seen you here before."

"Merle Yates. I'm the contractor for the landowner. Right now, we're just putting in roads. This fall I'll have ten crews in here working. The company forester wants a hundred cords a week trucked out of here. You must be Parnell Purchase. You're the hermit who lives at Howe Brook. I've heard a lot about you."

"Oh, how's that?"

"Stories are, you're not a man to cross. And that you're buddies with the game warden."

"Well Merle, I don't know what you've heard. The warden and I are friends and he put me in jail once for fifteen days."

"Fifteen days! What did you do?"

"I had a summer deer in my canoe."

"And you got fifteen days for that? I guess you're not buddies. I lost a good man last week cause of the warden. Nabbed him with an eagle in his pickup. That was a stupid thing to do. I don't know why he just didn't throw the damned thing in the bushes after he shot it. You know, I can't cut trees within a quarter of a mile of an eagle's nest! That makes it hard on the crews and we lose a lot of good trees."

"I met Buster once. He didn't impress me much. A loud-mouthed blowhard."

"Maybe so, but he could sure cut wood. I don't know when he'll be back. The bail is set so high he can't come up with the money, so he sits in jail, waiting for his trial. I've heard he has quite a surprise coming up for the warden."

"How's that?" Parnell asked.

"Not sure. It was something to do with the trial." Then in the same breath, "You looking for a job?"

"No, I get by just fine."

"What do you do?"

"I trap."

"Well, I do have a job for you. Trapping nuisance beaver. Every time they plug one of my culverts, it costs me thousands of dollars."

"Sure, I'll do that, as long as you clear it with the game warden first."

"I'll give you twenty dollars for each nuisance beaver you catch. I'll get a permit from the game warden first though. My crews are waiting for me. I'll be in touch as soon as I get the permit."

The job offer sounded good to Parnell. Trapping nuisance beaver would give him something to do. The strange feelings he had experienced yesterday were gone now.

So Buster is still in jail. Good.

Chapter 6

When the turnkey at the county jail closed and locked the cell door, Buster sat on the narrow bed and cried. He had never been in jail before and he was scared. There was no way he or his family would be able to come up with the bail, not that much. That meant he would have to sit in his cell until he could be arraigned Monday morning.

No one came to visit. Not even his wife. He didn't know any attorneys. Even if he did, he couldn't afford one. He began to realize he was in a bad kind of fix. He wasn't allowed to mingle with the other detainees. He was allowed out of his cell only once, to shower.

* * * *

Monday morning finally arrived and Buster was handcuffed and escorted across the street to the court building. Ian was standing in the hall when Buster entered the building. He wanted to sneer at him, but decided against it. He had developed a new sense of respect for Ian Randall. He was ushered into the courtroom and told to sit in the second row from the front on the right side. The courtroom was starting to fill with accused violators.

Ian came in and sat across the aisle from him. There were other officers present, but Ian was the only game warden.

The court bailiff called the room to order. "All rise for the Honorable Julian Werner." They were then seated.

"Is there anyone here today that doesn't understand why you are here?" No one responded. "Good."

The first few cases were speeding violations. Then an assault case, an arson case and then the judge picked up the complaint on Buster.

"Buster Morgan." Buster stood up. "Mr. Morgan, you have three charges against you. One: having a loaded firearm in a motor vehicle. Two: illegal possession of deer parts, to wit, head only." The judge hooked his glasses on the end of his nose and looked over the top of them, down at Buster. "Only the head? And three, the most serious: you did have in your possession one bald eagle. Do you understand these charges, Mr. Morgan?"

"I was framed! He put those in my truck!"

The judge hit his gavel several times. "Order! There will be no more outbursts like that, Mr. Morgan. Do you understand?"

"Yes."

"We are not going to try the cases today. Do you understand the charges against you?"

"Yes."

"You do not have to plead guilty. You are entitled to a trial. And because of the seriousness of two of these charges, I would recommend that you do ask for a trial. Have you had a chance to talk with a lawyer yet?"

"No, and I can't afford one."

"If you are indigent, the court will provide one for you.

"Mr. Barnes, how is your agenda?"

"I can make room."

"Okay, Mr. Morgan. Ralph Barnes is now your lawyer. Mr. Barnes, you may want to consult with your client before we go any farther with this matter."

"Thank you, Your Honor." Attorney Barnes escorted Buster to a small anteroom where they could discuss the case.

A few minutes later, Buster and his lawyer returned to the courtroom. "Now, Mr. Morgan, do you better understand what your choices are?"

"Yes. Not guilty."

"Do you wish a trial by jury or in district court?"

"District court."

Judge Julian Werner looked through his docket schedule and then said, "Will two months be sufficient?"

"Yes, Your Honor," Barnes replied. "There's a matter of bail. My client feels it is too high. He can't come up with the necessary funds."

"Are you working Mr. Morgan?"

"Yes, for Merle Yates, in the woods. At least, I was when I was arrested."

"Does your wife work?"

"No, she collects welfare."

"Then I presume that you have children."

"Yes, five."

The judge thought about it for a minute, and then said, "I am going to let the bail amount stand. And furthermore, I don't want your wife using any of the welfare money she receives to bail you out. Is that clear?"

"Yes," Attorney Barnes replied.

Once outside of the courtroom, Buster asked, "So what does that mean?"

"You remain in jail until your trial the first of September, unless you can come up with the money for the bail."

Ian walked out of the courtroom just then. "All this because of you, Warden!" Buster said rather loudly.

"Let me handle this, Buster. Not another word."

"I can't believe you would stoop so low as to do something like this," Barnes said to Ian.

"What are you talking about?"

"My client claims you framed him."

"Let him moan and cry all he wants." Ian walked off.

* * * *

Ian had the day off, so he returned home to work on home projects.

Buster Morgan went back to jail, and he was allowed to join

the other inmates in the fenced in compound outside. Now he had an audience.

Attorney Ralph Barnes didn't waste any time. He wrote up a complaint against Warden Ian Randall for harassment, false arrest and planting illegal contraband in his client's pickup. After he had posted the complaint, he telephoned the Attorney General's office.

* * * *

Two days later Ian was finishing his breakfast when his supervisor, Charles Vernon, knocked on the kitchen door. Virgil Brown had retired and Augusta had combined the two northern divisions. Charles Vernon was now Ian's supervisor.

Ian waved for Charles to come in. "Good morning, Charles. What brings you out so early?"

"Do you have any coffee?"

"Sure. All made."

"Maybe we should sit down and have a cup and talk."

"This sounds serious, Charles."

"It is, Ian. I received a phone call last night, from the Chief Warden. He has placed you on administrative leave, pending an investigation. This is coming down from the AG's office in Augusta."

"What's going on, Charles?"

"I can tell you only a little. I've been told to stay out of it and let the AG's office investigate the matter. Apparently, Buster Morgan filed a complaint against you through his attorney, ah…a Ralph Barnes, stating that you framed his client."

"Well, I didn't. What happens now?"

"You'll be interviewed by an internal affairs investigator. Then he'll discuss his findings with the Chief Warden and myself.

"Has the ballistic report come back from the lab yet?" Ian's supervisor asked.

"I should have it by tomorrow, or the next day. I'm not

worried, Charles. I did everything correct."

"I believe you, Ian, but the District Attorney has called my office too, wanting to know whether to proceed or dismiss the charges."

"You can tell the DA for me, Charles, that if he dismisses any of those charges he'll have to answer to me," Ian said, not blinking.

"Do you know how the head and the eagle were put in his truck or why? I'm not supposed to ask that, so just say yes or no."

"I suspect how they happened to be there. But I don't have anything I can give internal affairs."

"You tell me that you didn't set Buster up, and I believe you and I'll support you."

"I had nothing to do with it, sir. But…I do find it rather comical." Charles made a sour looking face. "Perhaps, down the road, I can tell you more."

"Okay, but no games, Ian."

"No games."

* * * *

The next day, Ian received the results of the ballistics tests from the lab. He sat down at his desk and opened the envelope. The two spent bullets had been fired from the same rifle, a .22 Remington magnum. These same bullets came from the .22 Remington magnum rifle submitted by Game Warden Ian Randall for ballistic comparison.

Ian filed the report with his report on Buster Morgan. Ian didn't have any doubt that Buster had killed the deer and the bald eagle, but he didn't have to prove he killed them; only that he was in possession.

The next day, while Ian was mowing his lawn, a black sedan with government plates drove into his yard. He turned the mower off and figured this had to be internal affairs.

"Ian Randall?"

"Yes."

"Good morning. I'm Jeffrey David, State Trooper assigned to Internal Affairs in the AG's office. Can we talk?"

"Sure. Come in and have a cup of coffee." While Jeffrey David organized his papers on the table, Ian made two cups of instant coffee.

As Mr. David sat at the table, removing some papers from his briefcase, Ian stepped into his office and then came back and placed a tape recorder on the table and turned it on. Jeffery David looked questioningly at Ian before speaking. "I'll want a copy of that recording also."

"Not a problem," Ian commented, and then he got the two cups of coffee.

"Do you understand why I am here to talk to you today, Mr. Randall?"

"It has been explained."

"Then before we continue, I must advise you of your Miranda Rights."

"Is that necessary? I'm well versed in Miranda."

"It's only a formality." Trooper David read Ian his rights from a plastic card. Ian never carried a cheat card. He knew Miranda by heart.

"Can you describe for me the circumstances that led up to searching Mr. Morgan's vehicle?"

"I was sitting at the warden's camp at St. Croix Lake in T8-R4. This would have been June 27th and 28th. On the morning of the 28th, I had a conversation with Parnell Purchase, the only year-round resident now of Howe Brook. He had advised me that morning that he had heard a small caliber rifle shot off in the distance, towards Beaver Brook, also in T8-R4. There was a trailer camper parked near the brook, just off the gravel road. I left my car in another road across the way. While walking back to the camp, I could smell rotting meat. I followed the scent to a small deer carcass that had been dragged into some alders. The hind legs had been removed, and the head. I knocked on the camper door to see if anyone was there. There was no answer. I walked around the camper and I saw a path leading towards the brook. I followed it and found a homemade wooden box cooler sitting in the brook. I opened the lid. It was empty except for several deer hairs. I checked the pickup. Then, looking in the passenger window, I could see a clip inserted into a .22 mag. rifle."

"Did you open the door at this time to check the rifle?" David asked.

"No. Not until later."

"Okay, continue."

"I also saw some small feathers on the passenger seat. And there was a small speck of blood on the glove box latch button. In the body of the pickup, I found deer hair and inside the plywood box, I found a moose hair. I observed scale slips on the dash and I could read the name on one of them. Buster Morgan.

"I decided to wait until Buster returned before I searched his vehicle and I wanted to see what would be brought out from inside the camper."

"At this point, did you know anything about a bald eagle?"

"No, not at all."

"When Buster and Steve returned, they went into the camper. I waited to see what they would bring out. Just dirty clothes. Steve left in his truck and as Buster was getting ready to leave, I stepped out and approached him. When I searched his truck, he was there and he saw when I discovered the deer head and bald eagle. At this time, he kept saying he'd get even with Steve for putting those in his truck."

"Why do you think they were there?"

Ian thought long and hard before answering. "I don't know. The bald eagle I could understand, but it seems rather stupid to have just a deer's head in your truck. Unless, perhaps he was using that to bait the eagle or some other animal."

"When you first noticed that the clip was in the rifle, you had enough probable cause to secure the rifle and check it. Why didn't you?"

"Because there wasn't anything unsafe about the situation at that point. When the situation became unsafe, when Buster started to drive off, I used that for my probable cause to conduct a more legal and thorough search."

"Did you ever find the hind legs of the deer?"

"No. It was, after all, a small deer. It wouldn't be unrealistic that two working men could have eaten most of it, or given it to some other workers."

"It seems extremely odd that anyone would stuff a deer's head under his seat. The bald eagle might be understandable though. There must have been a terrible smell."

"Actually, there was no smell at all."

"That too seems strange. Right now, I can't find that you went beyond any scope of search and seizure. You were, in fact, professional in the manner in which you performed your duty. What you say about finding the head and eagle, for now I'll have to take your word on it. But, I will have to interview Mr. Morgan to get his side of the story. He is still in jail, I understand."

"As far as I know," Ian said.

* * * *

Trooper Jeffrey David went to interview Buster Morgan after leaving Ian's house. Before he did this though, he needed another cup of coffee and something to eat. He stopped at the local café and ordered a coffee and danish. While he waited for his order, a group of four had seated themselves in the booth behind his. As he waited, he listened to their conversation. They were apparently talking about Buster Morgan.

One of the four said, "I don't feel sorry for that bum at all. He deserves to sit in jail."

Another added, "The wardens have been after him for a long time. It's about time he was caught for all the deer and moose he has killed."

"Ya, but why an eagle? They're such a pretty bird."

"You know Buster, he likes to kill."

"Maybe, but I don't think it was fair play for the warden to put that deer head and the bald eagle in his truck."

"Well, there ain't a doubt that he shot them, is there?"

Jeffrey laughed to himself, but he also wondered if Ian did plant the evidence in Buster's pickup.

Jeffrey couldn't interview Buster without his attorney present, so he stopped first at Ralph Barnes' office. He knew where to find it. He had had to investigate many complaints filed by Ralph Barnes.

When Jeffrey and Ralph Barnes arrived at the county jail, Buster was still in his cell. "Do you have a conference room we could use, Deputy?" Jeffrey asked.

"At the end of this hall. Go right down, I'll get the prisoner."

Seated at the conference table, Mr. Barnes introduced Jeffrey. "Buster, this is Trooper Jeffrey David from Internal Affairs in the AG's office. Mr. David, this is Buster, my client."

"I have already interviewed Ian Randall and I have his observations as well as what he did and why. I'm not here to discuss with you what Ian said. I want to hear why you think he is framing you.

"First, though, I must advise you of your Miranda rights." Again, Trooper David read Buster his rights from a plastic cheat card.

"Before he starts, I want to just make one statement," Mr. Barnes said. "I will not allow my client to admit to killing either the deer or the eagle."

"That isn't why I'm here."

"Isn't it obvious to anyone that I am being framed? Why in hell would I, would anyone, have just a small deer head under the seat and no meat? And the head just happens to have a bullet in it? My pickup was not locked. There is nothing to say that the warden didn't shoot my shell from my rifle into that deer head that he found somewhere."

"What about the bald eagle?"

"Same thing. Why would I have it in my truck? He could have picked that up anywhere and blamed me for it. It's obvious, at least to me, that he has had it in for me. My rifle was loaded. My mistake. Steve and me went target shooting the night before, and I just forgot to unload it before putting it in my truck. But I didn't put no eagle or deer head in my truck!"

"Well, that's all I need. As I said, it's not up to me to determine if the warden framed you or not. I gather the information and someone else will have the final decision."

* * * *

The next day, there was a meeting of the minds in Augusta, at the Chief Warden's office. Trooper David, the Attorney General, in person, and Supervisor Charles Vernon were there.

AG Smith said, "I have another meeting, so I'll have to hurry through this. There isn't enough information to believe that Warden Ian Randall did or did not plant evidence inside of Mr. Morgan's vehicle. As much as I would like to take the warden's side, there is the fact that no deer meat was found in the truck, or anywhere except for the rotting carcass. And, there is no logical reason why the deer head was there, except for a ballistic test to prove that Morgan had indeed killed both the deer and the eagle. Warden Randall is going to have to have more evidence to support his story or I'll have no choice but to recommend to the District Attorney to dismiss all charges against Morgan. And, until Warden Randall can provide this needed information, I recommend that he remains on administrative leave."

Attorney General Smith and Trooper David left the meeting. "What do you think, Charles? You know Ian better than anyone," The Chief Warden asked.

"I believe Ian. That man wouldn't do anything to disgrace himself or the warden service."

"I'm inclined to believe him also. But damn it, to any reasonable person, it looks like the deer head and eagle were put inside his pickup, pointing a finger at Morgan. And any court will think the same and I don't want this case to be tried and kicked out."

"All we can do is talk with Ian again. We may have to dismiss the charges." Chief Warden John Smallwood said. "You have four days to come up with the information or the cases are dropped."

"Okay, I'll talk with him."

* * * *

On his way home from Augusta that day, Charles Vernon stopped to see Ian. "The AG needs more information, Ian, why you didn't find any deer meat and only the head. And why the head was in that pickup. The eagle, one can understand. He may have intended to cut the beak and claws off and remove the cape. Maybe with the intention of selling the parts. But no one can understand why anyone would have a deer's head hidden under the seat. He said that, unless you can give him some information, he would have the District Attorney dismiss the charges."

"Like hell he will! I'll charge him with dereliction."

"You can't do that, Ian. You can't charge the AG or the District Attorney."

"Who says? You watch me!"

"Think, Ian. There must be something that you missed. As they say, the hand was too pat."

"There is one possibility."

"What is it?"

"Parnell Purchase. He is the one who said he had heard the shot that morning, about daylight."

"How would he know anything, or how could he help your case?"

"This guy is…well he is different. I don't mean weird or anything. Talk to him, you'll see. He plays the game better than we do, Charles."

"How do I find him? Game?" Charles looked surprised at Ian.

"Howe Brook Village at St. Croix Lake. He has the cabin at the north end of the siding."

"You think he can help? Why?"

"Just a suspicion. That's all."

"I think I'll ask the DA to ride in also. Time is short. You need this information soon or the cases are out the window and you too, Ian, if Ralph Barnes convinces his client to sue you. Can I use your phone? I'll call the DA from here."

Vernon talked with the DA and convinced him to ride with him and talk to Mr. Purchase. "We'll leave your office at five o'clock."

* * * *

District Attorney Barney Small was not used to getting up before breakfast, let alone before the sun was up. Charles Vernon was at the DA's office ten minutes early and had to wait fifteen minutes before Small arrived.

Charles decided to drive in from Harvey Siding. The only traffic he encountered were log trucks hauling their second load of the day.

"What time do these people go to work?" Small asked.

"Well, the wood cutters usually are on the sight an hour before daylight and the truckers are on the road, usually by 2:00 a.m."

"I never realized the hours the woodcutters and truckers worked, or how early they go to work."

"Sometimes you just have to get out in the real world, Barney."

"What's this guy Purchase like?"

"I have never met him. Ian just said unusual."

At 6:15 a.m., Charles and Barney drove up the knoll to Parnell's cabin. "He lives here all by himself, all year?"

Parnell was already up. For an unknown reason, he had spent a restless night and at 4:00 a.m., he had decided to get out of bed and go for a canoe trip around the lake. He was just walking up from the shore when he saw a car drive up to his cabin. When Charles and Barney stepped out of the car, Parnell was behind them.

"Good morning." Barney practically jumped out of his three-piece suit.

Charles turned around and said, "Good morning."

"What brings you gentlemen out here so early this fine morning?"

"Parnell Purchase? I'm Charles Vernon, Ian Randall's supervisor, and this is District Attorney Barney Small." They all shook hands.

"Well?"

"We'd like to talk about Ian."

"He didn't get himself hurt again, did he?"

"No, nothing like that. Could we go in where we can sit down?"

"Sure, where's my manners?" Parnell pulled the table out from the wall. "Sit down," he offered. "I'll make some coffee." Water was already boiling in the kettle and it didn't take Parnell long before he had three hot cups set on the table.

"Now, what's this about Ian?"

"You are acquainted with Buster Morgan?"

"Yes, unfortunately."

"He and his attorney, Ralph Barnes, have filed a complaint against Ian for false arrest and claiming that Ian framed Buster by putting the deer's head and eagle in Buster's pickup. Ian said you might be able to help us."

"Why isn't he here?" Parnell asked as he sipped his coffee, looking over his cup at the two.

"He has been placed on administrative leave until this matter is concluded."

"Are you going to shit-can him?"

"If Morgan wins his claim that Ian framed him and arrested him from the information he gathered, then termination is a strong possibility for Ian."

"Ian is a damn good game warden. He arrested me once." Barney's eyes lit up. "I've never held a grudge."

"That's why we're here, Mr. Purchase."

"What do you want from me?"

"The Attorney General said he needs more information that will support Ian's claim that he didn't put the head and eagle in Morgan's pickup. Ian told me I should talk with you. That's all."

"Well, that's easy. I put 'em in that louse's pickup."

Barney choked on his coffee and spit it all over the table. "Why?"

"Because that blowhard needed to be caught."

"You decided that on your own?" Barney asked.

"Yeah, that's right. Morgan doesn't poach to feed himself or his family. He poaches to kill. He gets a thrill out of killing. When I found that deer and eagle he had killed, I knew what I had to do."

"Instead of putting the evidence in Morgan's pickup, why didn't you just tell Ian what you found?"

"Because, there was no way he could have legally connected Morgan to the dead deer I found, and the eagle. I left enough clues for Ian to discover the evidence on his own and not taint the discovery."

"Where did you find the eagle?"

"Right beside the deer, across the road from Morgan's trailer camper."

"And you were sure he had shot them both?"

"Absolutely."

"Will you testify to this in court?" Barney asked.

"If it'll help Ian and help put Morgan in jail, yes, most certainly."

Barney was trying to keep notes and keep up with the discussion.

"Now you gentlemen look hungry. It won't take but a few minutes to fix breakfast. I'll have to go down to my root cellar for the fixings. I'll be right back."

Parnell brought back eggs and the last of the deer steak he had on ice.

"How do you like your eggs?"

"Over easy."

"Same here."

"This is delicious steak. What is it?" Barney asked.

"Deer."

Barney almost spit it up. While he was trying to clear his throat, Parnell saw the questioning look on Charles face. "I get a big deer each fall and I keep it on ice in my root cellar. This is the last of it. That is unless I poach one. Nah, that would be illegal."

Just then, the southbound train went through and Ansel blew the whistle. "What was that?" Barney asked.

"The engineer, Ansel Snow, telling me today's newspaper has been delivered."

"You mean you have the paper delivered to you in here?"

"Ansel does it because he's a friend. Every day almost, since the station house was taken down."

Charles had really enjoyed his time with Parnell. He was indeed an unusual person. He laughed to himself, and thought, "You, indeed, play the game well."

Barney Small had to get back to his office, so they said goodbye. "Ian will let you know when the trial will be. Tentatively around the first of September."

"Does that mean Ian goes back to work?" Parnell inquired.

"Yes, today."

"I guess there won't be more deer steak until the season opens. Have a nice ride out, gentlemen."

* * * *

Ian went back to work and Merle Yates had his nuisance beaver removal permit. "There are two problem areas, Parnell, on the new Levesque road. One on Harper Brook in T8-R4 and the other a mile and a half beyond Harper, Mack Brook in T8-R5. Take all the beaver in each colony and I'll give you twenty dollars apiece. You do have traps?"

"I have Blake and Lamb leg holds, number three and four."

"Do you have any conibear?"

"I have never heard of them."

"They are killer type traps. You can get some at the hardware store in Ashland." Merle explained to Parnell how the conibear trap worked. Parnell thought he understood, but he was still doubtful until he could see one set and actually catch a beaver.

In the meantime, he set the two brooks using his number four Blake and Lamb leg hold traps. The surest way to catch summer beaver was to set a trap in a trough on the dam. With the permit, this was now legal.

Parnell felt confident with his traps, but he wanted to see these conibear traps. So he drove his pickup out to the Masardis Siding and hitched a ride to Ashland. The storeowner showed Parnell the traps. "But the man you want to be talking to is two aisles over. Game Warden Dan Glidden, he's also a decent trapper."

Dan explained, "What you want for beaver is the 330 conibear." He explained how to fence off a beaver run and where and how to set the trap. "While handling the trap, you will want to make sure the safety catches are hooked across the springs. If the springs snap on your fingers, hand or wrist, it'll hurt. If you set the trap right, it'll take the beaver right behind the head."

"Thanks, Dan."

"Good luck."

* * * *

The next time that Parnell checked his traps, he had only one beaver at each trouble spot. He staked off two new runs in Mack Brook and set two of the conibear traps.

The next day he had three beaver at Mack Brook; one in each of the conibear traps and one in the trap set on the dam. It didn't take a genius to see that the conibear could certainly be useful.

He removed the beaver out of those two flowages and cleaned the culverts. He had nine beaver at twenty dollars apiece. Merle paid him for those and told him of another nuisance colony on the Blackwater Road between the new crosscut road and the turn off for Levesque City. "You can't miss it. The water is over the road."

"Okay, I'll get up there this evening." The dam near the road was four feet high and there was a meadow behind the dam. He had to break the dam out and drain the water so he could find the runs. With the water gone it was easy to see which runs the beaver were using. He set all six of his conibear traps and at the last one, he went to move a branch away from the trigger wire. He slipped and accidentally hit the trigger and the trap snapped shut on his right hand. "Ouch! Damn!" His hand was stuck between the jaws. He couldn't just pull his hand out, it hurt too much. "It must be broken. Now what do I do?" He pulled the trap stakes out of the mud and stood on the bottom jaw and pulled, bending the other jaw. He slid his hand out. It was broken all right, and swelling.

He couldn't reset the trap with a broken hand. So, he picked the trap up and walked back to his pickup. It was no easy ordeal, trying to drive and shift with his left hand. Once he had the transmission in second gear, he left it there and drove home.

He chipped some ice from his root cellar and wrapped it in a cloth and tied it to the back of his hand. The swelling was reducing. He'd have to go to Ashland in the morning and see a doctor and have it set.

It was still dark when Parnell left for Ashland in the morning. His pickup wasn't licensed and he wanted to get most of the driving done before too many people were out. He drove in second gear all the way to the paved road in Masardis. There was a stop sign at the junction to Route 11. He kept the transmission in second and when he reached Route 11 there was no traffic, so he didn't have to stop. Once he was at the top of the hill, heading for Ashland, he managed to steady the steering wheel with his knee and slide his left hand through the steering wheel and move the lever into high gear.

At the medical center, he simply coasted to a stop and shut the engine off.

"Well, what did you do to your hand, Mr. Purchase?"

"I got caught in a beaver trap. In one of those new conibear type traps."

Doctor Hatford set his hand and put a short forearm cast on. "In two weeks you can take this off yourself. But be careful of your hand for another two weeks. There were two bones in the back of your hand that you fractured. They were clean breaks. You were lucky."

"Thanks, Doctor Hatford."

On his way back to Masardis, a county deputy sheriff stopped Parnell. He explained why the pickup was not licensed and about the emergency. The young deputy gave him only a warning this time.

At least he could use his right hand to shift now. "Damn those conibears."

* * * *

Ian was waiting for Parnell in his cabin. "I was going to ask if you were out trapping nuisance beaver, until I saw your hand. What happened?"

"I got caught in a 330 conibear yesterday. Those damn things should be against the law."

"Morgan's trial begins tomorrow. I'll stay in tonight and we'll drive out early tomorrow and have breakfast in town before court."

"I don't have any fancy clothes."

"You won't need any. Just be clean and well groomed and have clean clothes on."

"Is this going to be a jury trial?"

"No, his attorney thought Morgan would stand a better chance appearing in front of just the judge, instead of twelve people who might be offended by someone shooting a bald eagle. You better plan to stay over at least one night. I don't believe they'll get through it in one day. The county will pay for your lodging and meals."

197

"Does it bother you when you're on the witness stand? Do you get nervous?" Parnell asked.

"Actually, I enjoy it. That's when I finally have my say. I look at it like it's sort of the icing on the cake. You'll do just fine from what I've seen of you through the years."

"What time does the trial begin?"

"10:00 a.m. We should be there at 9:30 a.m., so we can talk with the District Attorney. We should leave right at daylight."

That night, Parnell trimmed his hair and beard and washed in cold water. He laid out the best clothes he had. Blue jeans and a forest green shirt. He didn't have shoes, but he did have a brand new pair of Bass leather boots. He put extra clothes and toilet articles in his knapsack. He didn't have a suitcase.

* * * *

It had rained during the night. Now there was only a lingering mist. At least the road to Harvey Siding wasn't dusty. "I have never been out this way before. Never been north of Houlton, actually." After Harvey Siding, they drove by many large potato farms. Most of the fields were planted to potato, some had wheat or oats. Everything was a rich color green.

They stopped at the Elm Tree Diner in Houlton. Parnell ordered bacon, eggs, fried potato and homemade toast and coffee. When he saw how large the platter was he wasn't sure if he would be able to finish it. Ian had just bacon, eggs and coffee.

They had some time to spare, so they had a second cup of coffee. "When this is all over, Parnell, you and me, we need to sit down and really talk. But for now, we'd better go talk with the DA."

The courtroom was beginning to fill with spectators. Buster and his attorney hadn't come over from the jail yet. The district attorney came out of the clerk's office and motioned for Ian and Parnell to follow him to an anteroom.

"I know you never have any problems on the stand, Ian. How are you feeling, Parnell? Nervous?"

"Not really nervous. I have never testified on the witness stand before. I don't know what to expect."

"Just remember to speak clearly so the judge can understand you. Be precise, but don't elaborate unless you are asked. Don't offer information, particularly when the defense is asking you questions. And above all, be completely honest."

"I'll put you on first, Ian, but only briefly, then I'll put you on, Parnell, to describe what you did and why. Okay? Any questions?

"Wait in here until I come to get you. Neither Buster, nor his attorney, are aware that you are here today. I want to keep it a surprise as long as possible. I'll be back in a few minutes."

"This is going to prove to be most interesting, I think," Parnell said and smiled.

"You're enjoying this, aren't you?" Ian commented.

"Yeah."

"Me too." They both laughed.

The door opened and the DA motioned for them to follow. The courtroom was full. The DA went to a table up front on the left and motioned for Ian and Parnell to sit right behind him. The bailiff came out from the judge's chamber.

"All rise for the Honorable Julian Werner." The judge walked in and sat down behind the bench. Parnell recognized him as the young attorney he had spoken with when he had been arrested for the illegal deer. That seemed like another lifetime ago now.

Everybody was seated and the judge was arranging some papers. "Are we ready?" He looked first at the district attorney. "Yes, Your Honor." Then at the defense attorney. "Yes, Your Honor."

"Buster Morgan." His attorney motioned for him to stand. "You have been charged with, one: possession of a loaded firearm in a motor vehicle; two: illegal possession of deer parts in closed season; and, three: illegal possession of a bald eagle. Have you changed your plea?"

"No, sir."

The judge looked at the DA. "Are you ready for opening statement?"

"Yes."

"Your Honor, I'd like to stipulate…"

"I'll hear what you stipulate to later. Right now, I want to hear the prosecutor's opening statement."

"Your Honor, I have brought two new charges against Mr. Morgan. They should be with the papers in your folder. Your Honor, we will not only prove that Mr. Morgan did possess in his vehicle a loaded rifle, parts of a deer, to wit, deer's head, and a bald eagle, but we will also prove that Mr. Morgan did shoot and kill the deer and bald eagle. We will prove all these charges, Your Honor, beyond a reasonable doubt. Thank you."

"Okay, Mr. Barnes, your turn."

"I would like to forego an opening statement, Your Honor, and stipulate to the possession of the deer's head and bald eagle with testimony of probable cause which led the warden to search Buster Morgan's pickup truck."

Judge Werner looked at the District Attorney and said, "Any problems with that?"

"No, Your Honor."

"So stipulated. You may call your first witness." He was looking at the prosecutor.

"The state calls Game Warden Ian Randall."

He was sworn in and then he sat down. Parnell noticed how much at ease Ian appeared.

"State your name for the court, please."

"Game Warden Ian Randall."

"On the day in question what information led you to stop at the trailer camp, where Mr. Morgan's pickup was parked?"

"Earlier that same morning—it was about daylight—I had a conversation with Parnell Purchase."

"And what was the conversation about?"

"Mr. Purchase said he had heard coyotes fighting over a dead moose up the railroad tracks from his cabin. He said while he was standing near the moose he had heard a small caliber rifle shot in the direction of Beaver Brook, where it crosses the Blackwater Road."

"Then what did you do?"

"I had driven by this camper the day before and I recognized Mr. Morgan's pickup. I didn't want to drive by where he was working, so I took a detour around on another road. When I stopped at the trailer there didn't seem to be anyone around, so I knocked on the trailer door. No one answered. I then walked around the trailer and found a path that led to the brook. There I found a wooden box cooler in the water. I opened the lid and it was empty, except for some deer hair. I closed the lid and went to look at the pickup. From the driver's door, I could see a small caliber rifle. From the angle, I couldn't see if the clip was inserted or not. I walked around to the passenger side and now I could see a clip inserted into the rifle."

"What next?"

"At this time, I noticed a small speck of blood on the glove box and latch button. Then I gave the body a cursory check. I found deer hair in the body, and moose hair in the plywood box that was in the body."

"Did you find anything else?"

"Not at this time."

"What did you do then?"

"I wanted to get my car out of sight. There was a small road across the Blackwater Road, directly across from the trailer. As I was walking back towards the gravel road, I found a dead deer. The head was missing and the two hind legs were also gone."

"Did you look the carcass over for an entry wound?"

"I didn't see any bullet wound."

"What then?"

"I went back to watch the trailer and pickup and wait for Mr. Morgan to return."

"That's all for now, Your Honor. I will recall this witness again."

Defense Attorney Barnes stood and cocked his head, then asked, "Did Mr. Purchase have a rifle with him when you were conversing?"

"Yes, he did."

"Then one could assume Mr. Purchase had the rifle with him when he heard the shot, while standing over the moose?"

"I also assumed this."

"Why didn't you arrest him for night hunting?"

"His rifle wasn't loaded. I checked. And I had no corpse. I had seen nothing."

"When you said you saw a clip inserted into the rifle, did you check the rifle at this time to see if it was indeed loaded?"

"No."

"You didn't open the door and open the action of the rifle?"

"Your Honor, asked and answered," the prosecutor stated.

"Move on."

"Why didn't you open the door to check the rifle? Wasn't it a violation?"

"It was a violation if the rifle had been loaded, but then there was nothing unsafe about the circumstances at the time. I decided to wait to see what Mr. Morgan would do when he got into the pickup."

"You said you found hair in the box in the stream."

"Yes, deer hair."

"But there wasn't any meat?"

"No, there was nothing but the hair."

"What if I were to tell you that when Buster left that morning there were, indeed, two deer legs in the box."

"Perhaps. But not when I checked."

"Did you find anything elsewhere or near where you found the deer carcass?"

"No."

"Did you hear any shots that morning or the night before?"

"No, and the night before I was playing cribbage with Mr. Purchase."

"Did you take the two deer legs out of the wooden box?"

"There were no legs when I looked."

"No further questions."

"You're excused for now, Mr. Randall," the judge said.

Parnell observed how much interest Judge Werner was finding with the case.

"Call your next witness," Judge Werner directed to the prosecutor.

"The state calls Parnell Purchase."

The judge looked up, surprised. "One doesn't often forget a name as uncommon as yours, Mr. Purchase. We meet again."

"Yes, sir. I remember."

After Parnell was sworn in, the District Attorney said, "Sit down, Mr. Purchase. Relax. For the record, is your name Parnell Purchase?"

There was a long silence. No, his name was not Purchase. In those few seconds, so much was being flashed across his mind. He couldn't lie in court, but then the court would know that he had been lying all this time.

"No. I can't lie, Your Honor." He turned to look at Judge Julian Werner. Everybody in the courtroom was talking. Ian and the District Attorney looked shocked. "My name…my name is Parnell Peasley." Again, the courtroom became noisy and disrupted. Morgan was smiling.

District Attorney Barney Small was probably more surprised and shocked than anyone. "Your Honor, I ask the court for a few minutes to confer with the witness before we continue."

"I think that would be a splendid idea, Mr. Prosecutor. Ten minute recess."

Outside in the anteroom, "What in hell is going on, Parnell?"

"I couldn't lie in court. My name is actually Peasley."

"Boy, is Barnes going to have a field day with this. Are you wanted by the law or anybody?"

"No, of course not."

"Well, we can get through this. I'll put you back on the

stand and we, not the defense, will bring out who you are and so forth. We'll be the good guys, not him."

Parnell looked at Ian. He was almost laughing.

Back on the witness stand, "You have been sworn in, Mr. Peasley. State your name for the record."

"Parnell Peasley."

"You have hidden behind the identity of Mr. Purchase for almost thirty years. Would you explain to the court, why?"

"Actually, it all started by accident." Parnell was looking at Julian Werner. "Thirty years ago, I was Captain Parnell Peasley, United States Army, stationed in South Korea. I commanded an infantry squadron on the front lines. I lost many good, good men for no reason. I saw too much blood and guts on both sides. When it became time for me to cycle back to the states, I resigned my commission, vowing never again to fight in a politician's war.

"I returned to my home in Boothbay and I became a drunk, so much so that my mother told me to get out and never come back. When I bought my train ticket in Bangor to come north, the ticket agent asked me my name, I said, 'Parnell' then absently read the sign at the ticket window that said 'Purchase your tickets.' When I said 'Purchase' the agent thought that was my last name.

"I liked how it sounded and I kept it. I was that determined never to be called up to fight a politician's war."

"Did you receive any commendations while you were in Korea?"

"Yes."

"What are they?"

"A Silver Star, a Bronze Star and two Purple Hearts."

"Did you squirrel away at Howe Brook because you were wanted by the law? Or were you hiding from an unsavory reputation?"

"No sir. It was nothing like that. I liked the life I found at the village. The people there made me feel at home. I fit in well."

"Have you ever violated the fish and game laws of our

state?"

Before answering, he looked at Ian, who was trying not to smile. "Yes, I have." Now the judge was smiling.

"Were you ever caught and arrested?"

"Ian Randall arrested me once, years ago, for illegal possession of a deer." The courtroom broke into laughter.

Even the judge made the comment, "I remember that incident also, you wouldn't let me defend you. You said you were guilty. And if I remember correctly, you did fifteen days in jail."

"Your memory is correct, sir."

"As a captain in the U.S. Army, you must have had a formal education?"

"Yes sir. I worked my way through four years of college and got my master's degree in business administration. I also had two years of ROTC."

"Your Honor, I object to the prosecutor wasting the court's time. I'm sure everyone here has had a good laugh about Mr. Purchase now coming forward about his real name. Captain Peasley's decorations and his poaching reputation—"

"Your honor, I'm only trying to show the court the sincerity of Mr. Peasley's intentions when he did what he did, and his honesty."

"I agree. Objection is overruled. Continue."

"After you finished your time in jail, Mr. Peasley, did you harbor any ill feelings towards Ian Randall?"

"No sir. None at all."

"Did you shoot the deer, Mr. Peasley?"

"No, I didn't."

"Who did?"

Parnell turned to ask the judge. "Do I have to answer that, Your Honor? That was a long time ago."

"Is it relevant, Mr. Prosecutor?"

"I guess we can sidestep it."

"Now Mr. Purchase—excuse me, Mr. Peasley—getting to

the conversation you had with Warden Randall the morning of the incident; can you tell the court why and what transpired?"

"About a week or so before this, Mr. Morgan and this friend, Steve Michaels, gave me a ride back to my cabin. Mr. Morgan gave me a beer to drink and I invited them into my cabin. I don't get many opportunities these days for conversation. Most of Mr. Morgan's conversation was centered around killing animals."

"I object, Your Honor. Hearsay."

"The witness can testify to conversations he was a participant in. Overruled."

"What did the defendant have to say?"

"He said he used a .22 mag. rifle, small caliber rifle, and shot deer and moose just behind the chest. That way, the animal would still be able to stumble off the road before dying. Then it would be out of sight of anyone on the road."

"Were you a witness to any of these shootings?"

"Was I there at anytime when he shot? No. But, I did find a moose shot a short distance from my cabin that had been shot by a small caliber rifle behind the chest."

"I object to this, Your Honor. Testifying to finding a dead moose that my client is not even charged with shooting..."

"Your Honor, it goes to frame of mind. Why Mr. Peasley did what he did later."

"Overruled. Get to the point."

"What led you to discovering the dead moose?"

"Coyotes were howling and fighting. I went to see what the commotion was all about."

"What did you find?"

"The moose was about a five minute walk away, lying beside the tracks. There was a small bullet entry wound on the right side behind the chest."

"Would this have killed the moose immediately?"

"No, the bullet had probably entered the lungs or liver, the moose still being able to run off and die later."

"Could you tell from which direction the moose had come?"

"Yes. There were moose tracks in the mud and it had come from the direction of a woods operation on what is now the cross-cut road, just a short distance through the woods."

"Where was Mr. Morgan working?"

"He told me, he and Steve were cutting the right of way for this new road."

"Okay, then what did you do?"

"I have to back up some. I got ahead of myself. As I stood looking at the moose, it was just getting daylight. I heard a small caliber rifle shot to the north in the direction of Beaver Brook."

"Okay, what did you do when you left the moose?"

"I went to see what the shot was about."

"How did you get there?"

"I walked up the tracks until I came to Beaver Brook, then I followed the brook upstream where it crossed the Blackwater Road. Mr. Morgan had said earlier, that was where they had a trailer camper set up."

"Was anyone at the camper when you arrived?"

"No. But before going right to the camper, I found a narrow path leading from the camper to a pool in the brook. There was a wooden box anchored to the stream bottom."

"Did you look inside?"

"Yes, there were two fresh hind legs of a deer."

Everyone was now looking at the warden, assuming he had taken the two legs.

"Continue."

"When I looked in Morgan's pickup there was a .22 mag. rifle. Like the warden had said. There was a dirt road on the other side of the Blackwater Road and I walked out there."

"What did you find out there?"

"Next to the road, I found a freshly killed deer with the hind legs cut off and a dead bald eagle." Everyone in the courtroom gasped. Even the judge showed displeasure.

"Did you make any observations of the two?"

"Yes. I found a small caliber entrance wound just behind

the deer's head and the eagle also had a small entrance wound in its breast."

"Could you tell which one died first?"

"I object, Your Honor. The witness is not a forensic expert."

"Your Honor, taking into account Mr. Peasley's military background and his knowledge—oh, let's say of poaching—I think it will become clear to the court if I'm allowed to continue."

"Overruled for now. Make it happen quick, Mr. Prosecutor."

"Could you determine which of the two died first?"

"Yes, the deer died first. When an eagle finds a fresh kill, they will often eat the eyeballs first. The deer's eyeballs had been removed. When I picked the cagle up, I could still feel some body heat."

"What did you do then?"

"I carried the eagle and dragged the deer into an alder wet hole, out of sight of the road. I cut off the head of the deer." Everyone knew what happened next, even Buster, and he was glaring at Parnell. At that moment, he would have liked to kill him.

"What did you do with the eagle and the deer's head?"

"I crossed the Blackwater Road and went to the brook. A short distance downstream from the box, I found a cool, mossy area. I pulled some moss back, exposing small rocks. I dug out the rocks and put them in the brook, then I put the eagle and head in the hole I had dug and folded the moss back over to keep them dry and cool."

"That's a good place to leave Mr. Peasley's testimony for now. We'll break for lunch and continue at 1:00 p.m. Mr. Peasley and Warden Ian Randall, I must instruct you that during this lunch break, you are not to discuss the case, or your colorful testimony, Mr. Peasley, to anyone. And that includes the District Attorney."

Buster Morgan could be overheard talking to his attorney, "I can't believe he would frame me! Set me up like that!"

"Sshh, not here, Buster. This isn't the time. We'll have our chance later," his attorney assured him.

Inside the judge's chamber, Judge Julian Werner was laughing so loud, the clerk burst into his room to see what the matter was.

* * * *

Parnell and Ian walked passed Buster and his attorney in the hall as they were returning from lunch. Buster sneered at them both. His attorney, Ralph Barnes, wasn't feeling so sure about his client's case now.

Everyone was being ushered into the courtroom. There seemed to be more media people in the afternoon. Some of the folks who had been in the morning session had to leave, because now, there were not enough seats for all.

The bailiff called the courtroom to order and Judge Julian Werner seated himself behind the bench. "Are we ready to proceed, gentlemen?" Both attorneys nodded that they were.

District Attorney Small stood and addressed Parnell, "You may take the stand. Remember, you are still under oath."

"After you put the head and eagle under the moss, what did you do then?"

"I walked through the woods, back to the tracks, and went home. I met Ian; he had just arrived. We went fishing, had supper and played several hands of cribbage."

"During the time you were with Ian, did you, at any time, discuss with him what you had found, or what you were planning to do?"

"No. I was trying to keep him from going out, if my plan was going to work."

"So, as I understand it, you were not going to inform Warden Randall what you were doing, is that correct?"

"That's correct."

"Maybe you better continue, so we don't get confused. What happened after you finished playing cribbage?"

"I went back to my cabin and made it appear as if I was

going to bed. I had a lantern lit that would burn out in a few minutes. I put my axe in my pack basket and shouldered it and circled through the woods to the tracks."

"Why did you circle through the woods?"

"Well, sometimes Warden Randall watches me. This night, I didn't want him suspecting anything was up." More laughter.

"Continue."

"I walked the tracks up to St. Croix Siding and then I followed the Blackwater Road back to Beaver Brook where Morgan's trailer and pickup were parked. When I got to the trailer, I waited to make sure both Morgan and Michaels were inside. I could hear them both snoring. I retrieved the head and eagle and replaced the moss. I put the eagle behind the seat, under some old rags, out of view. I had pulled some tail feathers out and put those in the glove box and to make sure Warden Randall would look inside. I stuck my finger with my knife and smeared just a bit of blood on the glove box latch button. I slid the head under the seat and closed and latched the pickup door. Then I went down to the box cooler and put the two deer legs in my pack basket. I then went through the woods to the tracks and home."

"So you took the two deer legs. That clears a lot up. Where are the two legs now, Mr. Peasley?"

"They're gone. You ate the last steak, sir."

The entire courtroom burst into laughter, even Judge Julian Werner. DA Small's face was scarlet red.

Morgan would have killed Parnell, except he was in enough trouble already. He was seething with anger and contempt for Parnell.

"Continue, Mr. Peasley."

"I put the deer legs on ice in my root cellar." He looked at Ian. "Then I went to see Warden Randall. This is when I told him I had just heard one shot in the direction of Beaver Brook."

"So you set the stage, sort of, so Ian would follow up with his own inquisitive curiosity and discover the deer's head and the eagle on his own. Is that correct?"

"Yes, sir."

"At any time, did you inform Warden Randall what you were doing?"

"No, sir."

"I have to ask, why?"

"I didn't like Mr. Morgan's bragging about the brutal, senseless killing. There was no sense in what he was doing. I saw too much senseless killing in Korea. And when I found that bald eagle, I had to do something."

"Thank you, Mr. Peasley. That's all for this witness Your Honor."

It was the defense's turn to cross-examine Mr. Peasley. Mr. Barnes strutted back and forth in front of Parnell, thoughtfully rubbing his chin. "Mr. Peasley, you are an excellent entertainer. You have kept the entire courtroom entertained with your heroic poaching tales, done only to protect the little animals, but you yourself admit that you poach. Oh yeah, I forgot, you're a decorated war hero too—"

"Your Honor, I object. The defense is editorializing."

"Sustained. Get on with your questioning, Mr. Barnes."

"You said your own mother threw you out of her house because, I believe you said, you had become a drunk. Do you still drink today, Parnell?"

"I like a brandy in the evening and a cold beer goes down nice."

"The day that Buster and his friend, Steve, gave you a ride, you were drinking, correct?"

"Mr. Morgan gave me a cold beer. At my cabin, I also had some brandy and so did Mr. Morgan."

"Did you get drunk, Parnell?"

"No."

"How much does it take to get you drunk?"

"Objection."

"Sustained."

"When was the last time you were drunk?"

"It was many years ago, after a celebration dinner at the village. After dinner, a few of us got together and had a few drinks."

"Were you drinking while you played cribbage with the warden?"

"Yes. We were both drinking coffee." Ian was smiling. Julian suppressed a grin.

"Are you AWOL from the Army, Captain Peasley?"

"No. I resigned my commission."

"But you said you left your name changed to Purchase, one reason, because you didn't want to be called back to fight another political war."

"That's right. Commissioned officers can be recalled to active duty."

"Do you have any proof that these medals or commendations of yours exist?"

"Here? No. I suppose they are still in my mother's house."

"So, we only have your word for this. You want us to believe your story, even though you used to be a falling down drunk and, by your own words, you, too, are a poacher?"

Parnell sat there not knowing if he was supposed to answer or not.

"You said you didn't like the conversation you had with Mr. Morgan. Did he make you angry?"

"Yes."

"You were angry because he was telling stories about killing animals, and you didn't like this, did you, Mr. Peasley?"

"No, I didn't."

"So, you took it into your own hands to get even with him for telling stories, by framing him. Isn't that so, Mr. Peasley?"

"I was angry enough that I wanted to do something to stop him, but I didn't know what. At least not then."

"Did you even consider that everything he said about killing animals might be lies, only stories to show how much of a man he was?"

Parnell thought before answering. "At first I thought that Mr. Morgan was simply a blowhard. Making up stories to impress me." Morgan didn't like being called a blowhard.

"What happened to change your mind?"

"When I found that dead moose on the tracks, just above my cabin."

"But you didn't know for sure who shot that moose, did you, Mr. Peasley?"

"For sure, no, but—"

"Thank you.

"So when you found a moose that you didn't know who shot it, there and then you decided to frame Mr. Morgan, because you had been angered by his story telling. Is that it, Mr. Peasley?"

"No. I didn't know what I was going to do. I only knew I had to do something to stop him."

"So you took it upon yourself. You decided to take the law into your own hands and deal out your justice to my client. Why didn't you just tell the warden about Morgan's story telling and the dead moose and let an expert make the decision?"

"I hadn't seen or heard from Warden Randall since before his accident. I didn't know if he was still working, or back to work. Several months may go by before Warden Randall makes his presence known. I didn't know when he would be in next or how many more animals would die until then."

"So you decided to frame, Mr. Morgan?"

"I decided I had to do something."

"Why did you go to the box in the brook first?"

"Because I found the path between the brook and the trailer as I was following the brook upstream."

"In direct examination, you said you walked the tracks to St. Croix Siding, then down the road to the trailer."

"That was later, after it was dark."

"Seeing a box in the brook and a path going back to the trailer, didn't you think that this might be someone's personal property?"

"I didn't stop to think about it."

"But you opened the lid, regardless?"

"I opened the lid, yes."

"You said the deer's eyes had been removed. Did you examine the eagle to see if it had eaten the eyeballs?"

"No."

"Then anything could have eaten them. A raven, fisher, a blue jay, almost anything. Isn't that right, Mr. Peasley?"

"Perhaps. I don't know for certain if those you named eat eyeballs. I know from experience that bald eagles do."

"How far is it from your cabin to St. Croix Siding?"

"Almost four miles."

"So, you walked the round trip, what twice? How far is it from St. Croix Siding to Beaver Brook, along the road?"

"A little more than a mile."

"So in about twenty four hours, without sleep according to you, you made two round trips to Mr. Morgan's trailer, walking a distance of what maybe twenty miles? You went fishing and then you played cribbage with the warden. How old are you, Mr. Peasley?"

"I'm fifty-five."

"So, at fifty-five you'd have us believe you did all this in twenty-four hours without sleep?"

"I was tired. Yes."

"After you found the deer remains and the eagle, why didn't you make an effort to go see a game warden and tell him what you had found? Instead of framing my client."

"Well, I live where there are no telephones. I do have a Studebaker pickup. But it is not licensed and I use it only in the woods."

"That's fine, Parnell, but later you met with the warden. You fished and played cribbage! I would think that any reasonable man would have told the warden what you had seen instead of taking the law into your hands and framing Mr. Morgan. Why did you not inform Warden Randall?"

"I wasn't sure if he would have been able to make the connection legally between the dead deer and eagle, or if he would be able to prove it. If a bear or coyote had carried the head and eagle off, then there would have been nothing."

"But you put the head and the eagle under the cool moss. Why did you do that?"

"At this time I had decided to return that night, if Warden Randall was around, and put them in Morgan's pickup. I didn't want them to start rotting and Morgan smell them and get rid of them both. Then Warden Randall could find them."

"Okay, but later that same day, you admitted to talking and spending time with the warden. Why didn't you tell him then what you had found, Mr. Peasley? Why?"

"I wanted to make sure Morgan was caught. I knew, my way, he would."

"Is that the truth, Mr. Peasley? Or by doing it your way, you could carry off two deer legs? No more questions, Your Honor. I'm finished."

"Does the prosecution wish to redirect?"

"No, Your Honor. I think everything is clear to the court."

"Then we'll adjourn until 10:00 tomorrow morning."

Small asked Ian and Parnell to wait in the courtroom until everyone had left. "You did a fine job testifying, Parnell."

"I felt like I was on trial."

"In a way, you are. The defense was trying to convince the court that you framed Morgan, only because you didn't like him. I think you did a good enough job explaining, so that's why I didn't redirect. I don't want to confuse the court. I think we'll do all right tomorrow, too.

"Remember, you can't discuss the trial with anyone. Parnell, I hope in the future, you never get teed-off at me. See you tomorrow."

* * * *

A deputy escorted Buster back across the street to jail.

Ralph Barnes went back to his office. There was something about Parnell's testimony that sounded just a bit familiar. But he wasn't exactly sure. It had something to do with another case he had defended years ago. He pulled out his file cabinet and started looking.

Parnell wasn't ready to go back to his motel room just yet. He walked over to Market Square and located a men's clothing store. He bought a pair of casual pants, a long sleeve Arrow shirt, three chamois shirts, one green, one buckskin and one red. He bought socks and underwear too. It had been a long time since he had been in a men's store.

He took his packages back to his room and then he walked around for a while, to stretch his legs. He saw a movie at the cinema, a John Wayne western. Then he ate supper and went back to his motel room.

Parnell was feeling restless after eating so he went for another walk around. He had forgotten how a town looked at night, illuminated with electric lights. He was wondering why Ian didn't have supper with him, instead of rushing off.

Ian did meet Parnell the next morning for breakfast. "You know, when this trial is over, you and I are going to have to have a long talk."

At 10:00 o'clock everyone was in the courtroom. The media people were back. Some drew figures, while others took notes.

Judge Julian Werner sat and rearranged papers in the file folder, then said, "Are you both ready to start?"

Ralph Barnes spoke up, "Your Honor, may we approach the bench?"

"Come on up. What's the problem?"

"Your Honor, I'd like to recall Mr. Peasley."

"You said you were finished yesterday."

"I know, Your Honor, but there was something he said yesterday that I'd like to explore further. It goes to motive, why he did what he did."

"Any objections?" he directed the question to DA Small.

216

"As long as he doesn't go fishing. No."

"Okay, let's wrap this up, though, by noon. Mr. Peasley, would you take the stand again?"

Attorney Barnes appeared to be more confident this day, like he might know something that no one else did.

"Mr. Peasley, have you ever, in the past, done anything similar, to anyone else who might have crossed you?"

"Yes, there have been times."

"Would you enlighten the court, please?"

The prosecutor stood. "Your Honor, I object to this line of questioning. The defense is wasting the court's time."

"Your Honor, the prosecutor opened the door, trying to show the court Mr. Peasley's good intentions. I'll show that Mr. Peasley had an ulterior motive. One that suited himself."

"I'll let you continue, Mr. Barnes, but do not try my patience."

"Mr. Peasley, does the name Max Hartley ring a bell with you?"

"Yes, sir, he was a thief."

"He stole from you didn't he, Mr. Peasley? I believe it was animal hides."

"That's right."

"Explain to the court, if you would, how you chose to take care of this little problem."

Ian's face was dead serious. He had suspected all along, but there was no evidence to warrant his suspicions.

"Max Hartley was scaling wood at St. Croix Siding. I had traps set along the railroad tracks near the siding and I observed Mr. Hartley one night, stealing a fox from my trap. But this wasn't the first time, either. I had already lost two animals from that same set.

"I told Warden Randall that I had heard a shot in the direction of St. Croix Siding."

"Knowing fair well that the warden would investigate."

"Yes, he's good like that."

"You watched while the warden was talking with Max Hartley, didn't you?"

"Yes."

"And a few minutes later, you kicked his face in, isn't that so, Mr. Peasley?"

"He had assaulted Ian, and I helped Ian to subdue Hartley."

"Okay, you helped the warden from being beaten. What did Warden Randall find when he searched Hartley's pickup?"

"The fur Hartley had stolen from my trap and three moose legs."

The courtroom roared with laughter. Even the judge had a difficult time to keep from laughing. He said, "I remember that case well."

"Mr. Peasley, explain to the court who shot the moose and put those three legs in the pickup body."

"I did." Again there was more laughter. Ian was smiling too.

"So, you admit you framed Max Hartley. You shot the moose and put it in his pickup."

"Yes—well, I didn't shoot it exactly."

"Well, what did you do? How did you kill it?"

"I set a snare in a moose trail made from a small wire cable. Then I waited. When the moose got tangled in the snare and had stopped thrashing about, I hit it in the head with my axe.

"Trapping is the only income I have. He was stealing my income. I wanted him out of my area."

"Your area, Mr. Peasley? How much land do you own?"

"None."

"You mean you didn't want the competition of another poacher where you poached."

"I have never poached while trapping. Nor have I ever taken another trapper's fur. When I poach, it is to feed myself or if someone else needs food. As I said, Max Hartley was a thief, stealing my income."

"What became of the fourth moose leg?"

"I took it back to my cabin and ate it."

"It's too bad that the statute of limitation has expired, Mr. Peasley. Is there another incident where you took it upon yourself to administer your justice?"

"Yeah, there was another time. It was the summer when the village and the sawmill were taken down."

Ian knew instantly what Parnell was talking about now. Now he would hear the rest of the story about Jimmy Hoggan and Steve Lawrence. He was smiling again. He was actually enjoying this.

"These two outsiders came into the village and decided they were going to shoot a deer that John Corriveau and I had been watching."

"So, what did you do this time?"

"I snared the deer, cut the hind legs off and stripped the saddles, and after dark, I took what was left and propped the head and forward shoulders up to look like a real live deer. Hoggan and Lawrence came along and shot it, thinking it was a real live deer. Ian was there and he arrested them both for night hunting."

Again, the courtroom roared with laughter. Everyone, except Morgan and his attorney. They didn't see the humor in it.

Judge Julian Werner said, "I apologize to the court for laughing. I presided over this case also and often wondered who propped the deer head up. Continue, Mr. Barnes."

"So, you set Hoggan and Lawrence up and you ran off with the meat. What did you say to the warden this time?"

"I had no idea that the warden was around until I heard him holler. He surprised me too. Just good fortune, I guess."

"What did you do with the meat?"

"I gave most of it to the Corriveaus. They were an elderly couple and had run low on meat and John had heart problems."

"Is this only a game to you, Mr. Peasley?"

"No sir, I take poaching very seriously."

More laughter.

"Hoggan and Lawrence were going to poach in your area and you didn't like it, so you took matters into your own hands.

Is that correct Mr. Peasley?"

"Well, if I had told the warden that these two were going to kill the deer I had been watching, I doubt if he would have let me have it. I did what I thought I had to do."

"You seem to play the game well, Mr. Peasley. Are there any more incidents?"

"Well, sort of. But it was different."

"Come now, Mr. Peasley, enlighten us."

"Well, when Warden Randall arrested me with that deer, I had been set up by John Corriveau. He watched as Ian carted me off. Then he was in the clear to bring home the dead moose he had shot the day before. He knew Warden Randall would be away from the village for at least two days. This would give him plenty of time to take care of the moose."

"Did you help shoot the moose?"

"No, in fact, I didn't know anything about the moose until I got out of jail."

"Then what did you do?"

"Well, I walked up the tracks from Smyrna Mills after I was released. I got to Corriveau's camp during the night and I kept them awake all night, screaming like a banshee. John got to swearing and cussing and Stormi, his wife, kicked him out of her bed for good, unless he agreed to attend church for a month and not cuss and not drink with the boys. I thought that, that was just as much punishment as the fifteen days I did in jail for him."

Again, the courtroom roared, Ian, the judge and even Buster and his attorney, this time.

"It seems, Mr. Peasley, you learned the game from a master.

"Your Honor, I think we have heard enough from this witness. No further questions."

"Redirect?"

"No, Your Honor. I'd like to recall Game Warden Ian Randall."

As Ian and Parnell walked by each other, Ian said, "So you were the banshee."

"You're still under oath, Warden Randall."

"What did you do with the deer head and the eagle?"

"After leaving Mr. Morgan at the county jail, I went home and dissected both the head and the eagle and removed a spent bullet from each that I took to the crime lab in Augusta for ballistic comparison to the .22 mag. Remington rifle I had confiscated from Mr. Morgan."

"Is this the report you received?"

"It is."

"And what was the conclusion?"

"That both the deer and the bald eagle were shot with the same rifle, a .22 mag. Remington automatic rifle. The same rifle that I confiscated from Buster Morgan."

"No further questions, Your Honor."

"Defense, do you have any?"

"Only a couple, Your Honor."

"Make them quick, then we'll break for lunch."

"Warden Randall, did Mr. Peasley, at any time, include you with his scheme to frame my client?"

"No."

"How about Max Hartley?"

"No."

"And how about the Hoggan and Lawrence case?"

"No."

"So, he acted alone in all of those events?"

"Yes."

"That's all I have, Your Honor."

"Does the prosecution have anything else?"

"The prosecution rests, Your Honor."

"Does the defense have any witnesses?"

"No, Your Honor."

"Okay, I'll hear closing arguments after lunch."

Barney Small joined Ian and Parnell for lunch at the Elm Tree Restaurant. "You know, Parnell, I always figured you had something to do with that screaming banshee. John told me about it years later, but not about the moose he was sitting on, watching me arrest you."

"I felt bad for doing it to him. I didn't realize he'd get so scared."

"Did you ever confess to him?"

"No. We had become good friends and I didn't want anything to ruin that. Besides, he felt so bad for what he did to me that he gave me his cabin on the knoll and everything in it."

"Why did you do it?" Barney asked.

"Well, I was new at the village. I arrived by train the day before. It was a dirty trick. He took me out in his canoe, knowing Ian would show and find me with the deer. Then he'd be safe to move the moose. I didn't like the fifteen days in jail and I didn't like being used like that. So, I played a dirty trick on him."

Parnell was beginning to like eating in restaurants, as much as he could eat and the county paying. The food was good too. And the waitresses, young and friendly.

Barney couldn't help from thinking what a paradox Ian and Parnell were. Ian was the law. He lived being a game warden every minute of every day. And Parnell was equally enthusiastic about his way of life, his domain. Yet here the two of them were, the best of friends. What was even stranger, he believed that Parnell could, tonight or the next, poach a deer or moose and have no misgivings about doing it and not feel as if he was offending his friend, the game warden, Ian Randall. And no doubt, if Ian were to catch Parnell red-handed, he would not have any misgivings about arresting him or worry that Parnell would be offended. Barney smiled to himself and thought, *All just part of the game.*

* * * *

Judge Julian Werner addressed the prosecution, "Are you ready with your closing arguments?"

"Yes, Your Honor.

"We have shown the court that Mr. Morgan doesn't poach

to feed himself or his family, but that he is nothing more than a cold blooded killer who purposely shoots his victims so they can run off to suffer and die later. He found a weird sense of pleasure bragging to others about what he considered his great exploits. And it was, in fact, his bragging that led to his demise.

"However true it appears to be, Parnell Peasley did not frame Mr. Morgan. He simply put the evidence where the warden was sure to find it. Did Parnell leave telltale signs that anyone would pick up and understand the meaning? No, he left a speck of his own blood on the glove box, knowing that once the warden saw that, he would widen the scope of his search. Mr. Morgan himself didn't see the blood, it was that miniscule, but Parnell knew that Warden Randall, trained for years to see the unobservable, would react to it.

"There was an abundance said about Mr. Peasley framing other victims. Described as only a great game to him. I sooner think that Mr. Peasley was more concerned about justice, seeing the culprits are held accountable for their deeds.

"It has been suggested that the warden, Ian Randall, had framed Mr. Morgan or had taken part in Parnell's elaborate scheme. But Mr. Peasley's own testimony clarifies the issue and exonerates Ian Randall of any wrongdoing.

"We have proven, beyond a reasonable doubt, that Buster Morgan did possess said deer head and bald eagle and that he shot both with the .22 Remington mag. rifle the warden confiscated from Morgan's vehicle. Thank you."

"Defense, are you ready?"

"Yes, Your Honor.

"Your Honor, for two days we have listened to fantastic tales that belong in Sherwood Forest with the Sheriff and Robin Hood. I believe I have proven that what Mr. Peasley did was not so much out of the sense for justice according to law, but for his own sense of justice, because someone poached in his area. His own words.

"Even though Warden Randall didn't put the deer head in

my client's pickup, the evidence and inference obtained has to be as poisonous as if Mr. Peasley was acting under the direction from the warden. He knew what he was doing and he knew what the consequences would be once the warden arrived. Therefore, Mr. Peasley should be held as culpable as if he were a sworn officer. Therefore, making any evidence found by the warden, like fruit from the poison tree. Thank you, Your Honor."

"That was very interesting, Attorney Barnes. Officers are indeed held to a much higher standard of conduct because of the authority that they possess, regardless if they are in uniform or not.

"This has been an unusually interesting case to preside over. While I have found Mr. Peasley's life and stories interesting, I cannot condone your behavior in its entirety. But that doesn't mean when you put the deer head and bald eagle into Mr. Morgan's vehicle that that was illegal. Therefore, I find what Warden Randall discovered pursuant to his search of the vehicle, that the evidence does not fall into 'fruits of the poison tree' category.

"Therefore, I find that all the evidence was both admissible and credible. Mr. Morgan, I find you guilty for having a loaded firearm in your vehicle and I fine you one hundred dollars. Since the deer head and the bald eagle were put into your vehicle as evidence to what you had been doing, I find you not guilty of illegal possession of deer or illegal possession of a bald eagle.

"The prosecution did prove beyond any reasonable doubt that you did in fact shoot the deer and the bald eagle. I find you guilty of killing a deer in closed season and guilty of killing a bald eagle. I fine you five hundred dollars for the deer and three days in jail. For the bald eagle, Mr. Morgan, I fine you six thousand dollars and three hundred and sixty days in jail. Time to be served at the Charleston Correctional Facility. At that time, a payment program will be set up for you by your probation officer, so you won't have to come up with the entire amount after spending almost a year in jail. But let me warn you, Mr.

Morgan, you miss one payment and you'll be back in Charleston.

"I have watched you all through the trial, Mr. Morgan. There were times when your facial expression revealed to me what you were feeling towards Mr. Peasley. You appear to me to be someone who can be very vindictive. After you are released from jail, before you decide to even the score with Mr. Peasley, think about it first. Think about how he did this right under your nose. His ability to find his way through the woods at night and there doesn't seem to be anything that he is afraid of. And then there is his outstanding military record. If you decide to even the score, you will lose. You'll have a year to think about it.

"My recommendation is, Mr. Morgan, that while serving your time at Charleston, get some psychological help, and stay as far away from Mr. Peasley as you can.

"The time you have already spent in jail, waiting for trial, will be credited towards your time at Charleston.

"Good luck to you, Mr. Morgan."

"Ian Randall, I find that you conducted yourself very professionally. Especially concerning the search of Morgan's vehicle. You said you didn't open the door and search, or check the rifle when there was no one around. That took restraint. Some wardens would have and then lied about it.

"You should be commended on your professionalism."

"Mr. Peasley—" he paused. "You are a very interesting and unusual person. I have believed every word you have spoken. You are a righteous person. Misguided at times, perhaps, but righteous and above all, honest.

"I have, as well as everybody in the courtroom, enjoyed your stories. Although, in my position I cannot condone violations of the law. Therefore, it is the judgment of this court that you are guilty of illegal possession of deer. To wit, two legs, and I fine you one hundred dollars. And I'm afraid the statute of limitations has indeed expired on the other two dastardly deeds.

"Mr. Peasley."

Parnell stood up before answering, "Yes, sir."

"How are you getting home?"

"Your Honor, I'll take him," Ian offered.

Just then, the clerk of the courts opened the judge's chamber door and handed him a slip of paper. "Ian, your supervisor, Charles Vernon, has asked that as soon as you can dispense of the courtroom, you are wanted at Rockabema Lake in Moro Plantation. There is an eight-year-old child lost."

Ian left immediately. "Well, Mr. Peasley, I guess you lost your ride."

"If I can get a ride to Smyrna Mills, I can walk the tracks to Howe Brook."

"How far is that, Parnell?" the judge asked.

"Only about eighteen miles. It'll take six hours."

"Nonsense. I'll give you a ride myself. It'll give me a change of scenery

"Bailiff, you'll take charge of the prisoner. Someone from across the street should be over soon to escort Mr. Morgan back. I'll be about five minutes, Mr. Peasley.

"Court adjourned."

* * * *

Parnell paid his fine and waited in the hall for Julian Werner. Five minutes turned into twenty, then thirty before Judge Werner stepped out into the hall. "Sorry to keep you waiting. I had to finish sentencing papers for Morgan."

On the way to Werner's Lincoln Continental car, Werner asked, "I've been meaning to ask, what did you do to your hand?"

"I got it caught in a 330 conibear beaver trap. Cracked two bones in the back of my hand."

"I thought the season was closed on beaver in the summer."

"It is. I have been trapping nuisance beaver for a woods contractor."

The road turned to gravel once they were beyond Harvey Siding. The local woods workers were just coming out from work. Each vehicle slowed and the occupants looked strangely at the Lincoln Continental. They probably were not accustomed to seeing such a fancy car in the woods.

Julian Werner drove up the knoll, right to Parnell's cabin. "Don't you get lonely at times, way in here by yourself?"

"Sometimes, particularly in the winter."

"My grandfather spent a winter in here somewhere, trapping back in the 20s. I don't know where he built his log cabin. It wasn't much of a cabin. Not as big as yours. Listening to him talk, there was barely enough room to stand.

"It was cold that winter and the snow was deep. The only way he could tend his traps was to snowshoe his trails after each snowstorm to keep them packed down. He did all right on beaver, I guess. He made enough money that winter, come spring when he sold his fur, he bought a small farm in Presque Isle. That's where I was raised. He said he got so lonely at times that he made a sign and nailed it above the door. Camp Lonely, he called it."

"I have seen that cabin, Your Honor."

"Parnell, you don't have to call me Your Honor out here. My name is Julian."

"Your grandfather's cabin is in between Hastings and Mack Brooks. Levesque's original road goes close to it. It was small, alright."

Werner extended his hand to shake Parnell's. "Mr. Peasley, it has been an enjoyable experience meeting you, listening to your escapades and talking with you."

Chapter 7

It had been several days since the end of the trial and Parnell had not seen or heard from Ian. But that wasn't unusual. Sometimes months would pass before Ian would make a showing. Ian had found the eight-year-old that night, just before dark.

Apparently, the boy's father had taken him with him looking for Lost Pond. Ian knew that area as well as he did Howe Brook and St. Croix. He knew of an old road that went up along West Hasting Brook, and then branched off towards the west. Ian found the boy on this old road.

Merle Yates showed up at Parnell's one bright, sunny day. The temperature was 90°F in the shade. An unusual day for the early part of September. Parnell didn't have air conditioning in his cabin. Hell, he didn't even own a fan. So he sat on the porch in the cool breeze. Only today there was no breeze and the air was hot. "—heard my boy got almost a year in jail for shooting that eagle. He may have been a blowhard, but he did a good job for me. When he gets out, I hope he'll come back to work for me.

"The newspapers are full of the stories you told in court. Are they true?"

"I won't lie."

"Remind me sometime, never to shoot a deer around you." They both laughed.

"I have more beaver problems if you're interested."

"Where?"

"Long Brook, about a mile beyond the Howe Brook Mountain turn. You can't miss it. Water is over the road. Beaver have two three-foot culverts plugged."

"I'll go up this evening. Maybe the temps will be cooler.

"How many crew do you have working now?"

"We're in three different areas. With five crews each."

"Seems to me, how you're cutting the forest, is too fast."

"These areas are near water, ponds and deadwaters, where paper companies can't spray insecticide for the spruce bud worm. We're to harvest the spruce and fir in these damaged areas before the wood is lost.

"This winter we're going to pile down wood at the siding, here at Howe Brook and put the logs on the northbound train."

* * * *

That evening, Parnell put his traps and gear into the back of his pickup and drove to Long Brook. There was a good six inches of water over the road, softening the roadbed into mud. He had to unplug the culverts first and the only way to do that was to crawl in from the downstream end. The beaver had this culvert plugged about midway through. He had to crawl on his hands and knees.

He started tugging on some branches at the top of the dam, throwing them behind him. Water was now coming over the top and he was soaking wet. Hurrying, he grabbed a piece of deadwood and the whole dam began to give way.

Parnell started crawling backwards, but he wasn't fast enough. The entire dam gave way, sending him out the end of the culvert, like a cannon ball with all the wood and mud swirling in the pool below the culvert; he was having a difficult time trying to stand. After a while, he got to his knees and crawled out of the swirling water and mass of sticks and mud. He was damned if he was going to crawl into the other culvert now.

He waited on the tailgate of his Studebaker for the water above the road to drop enough so he could find the beaver runs. He set all six conibear traps, but no leg hold traps this time.

While he was standing near his pickup, trying to wipe off some of the mud, using his shirt, he heard one of the traps snap.

It was the trap he had set in an older run. The trap had taken the beaver right behind the head. Parnell compressed the springs and released the beaver. He reset the trap and dragged the beaver back to his truck. "Too bad summer fur isn't worth anything."

Before getting covered with beaver swamp mud, Parnell had wanted to make an excursion out the Howe Brook Mountain Road. Earlier he'd heard some machinery running and simply wanted to see what it was.

He decided to tend his traps at Long Brook the next morning. Merle wanted to get rid of the nuisance beaver as soon as possible. He had three more. "There should be one more beaver."

Today he made his excursion to see what the noise was. At the end of the road, there were only two storage sheds, what looked like piping and a portable welding machine. Just then someone came up from one of the many trails leading away from the sheds. "Can I help you?" the man said with a peculiar accent.

"Good morning. Just looking. Curious about the noise, that's all. I'm Parnell Purchase." Purchase seemed more natural than Peasley, and besides, he liked the sound of it.

"Good morning, sir. It's another grand day."

"A bit warm for me. I'm not nosy or anything, but I'm curious as to what you're doing."

"Prospecting for minerals. We just got started drilling two days ago."

After talking with this person for several minutes, Parnell just had to ask, "You aren't from around here, are you?"

"Why, you don't think I have the Maine accent?"

"No, actually far from it. I just can't place it."

"Virginia. I haven't been home for—well, ever since I went to work for Chevron Resources. When one job is done, they send me to another. I was in Allagash before coming here. I hate your blasted black flies."

"What mineral in particular are you looking for?"

"Copper. There is that big deposit west of Ashland at Bald

Mountain in T12-R8 and there's another deposit almost as big in T6-R6 near Picket Mountain, and if this deposit is as big as the company thinks it is, then instead of shipping all the rock to India for processing, there'll be more likely a crusher built in Masardis. This plant would crush the rock only and ship it to India to be smelted."

"Why would the company ship it to India to be processed? Seems to me it would be more cost effective to process it here and then ship it as pure ore. Besides, look at the employment benefit for the area."

"Well, I'm told it would still be cheaper to ship the ore to India to be processed, because their labor is not as expensive. No unions, and very few environmental laws.

"The environmental laws of this state are so rigid; we may not be able to mine any of the sights.

"The ground work and explorations are all complete at Picket Mountain in T6-R6. The next step is to move a huge boring machine in to make an entrance shaft down to solid granite. But the environmental laws are stopping us in our tracks.

"That mine would be all underground and would operate for twenty-five years. The first two and a half years, the company would mine only gold."

"There's that much gold there?"

"Yes, a good vein of the stuff. When Getty Oil was doing explorations there, the engineer said he found oil at two different drill sites. We found evidence of oil in Merrill too. This whole northern part of the state is rich with mineral deposits.

"I don't understand how the environmentalists have gotten such a strangle hold on this state."

"From the outside, would be my guess," Parnell said. "How would this deposit be mined?"

"Probably it would be strip mined. The rock is not the solid granite that's required for underground operations."

"How spread out is the deposit?"

"Our first exploration drilling showed deposits seventy

percent around the mountain. In time I hope to determine how the ore runs and if the vein shoots off in a tangent.

"We also have to map the underground water sources that we find and any arsenic or radon traces."

"If this mountain was strip mined, when the ore was all removed, what would be left? A big hole in the ground? A waste dump? What?"

"The rubble would be bulldozed into the hole and covered over and the entire area would be landscaped and seeded with spruce and fir trees. Admittedly, it would look like hell until then."

"I can't say I'd like hell existing in my backyard, but I understand and can appreciate your struggle with the environmentalists. Mining would surely give the state's struggling economy a boost too."

Parnell drove back to his cabin, deep in thought. The outside world was catching up to him. He had hidden away for so long at Howe Brook that the only way he knew what was happening on the outside was what he read each day in the newspaper delivered by Ansel Snow.

He returned to his home and sat on his porch, sipping brandy, smoking a cigar and pondering new discoveries. How he wished he could turn back the years when the village was full of life. The families who lived here were not rich in monetary means, but they all lived a richly fulfilled life. People were so happy.

He stayed on the porch late into the night. He had lost his appetite. Besides, he was too busy reminiscing to bother to eat. It was after midnight and Parnell was still sitting on the porch. The only noises were those of nature. A great-horned owl behind the cabin, at the top of a dead brown ash tree. Loons on the lake. Crickets in the grass. A lonely coyote howled up the tracks. They were all musical notes to him.

When he awoke early the next morning, he was still sitting on the porch. After breakfast and a pot of black coffee, he was still feeling melancholy and he didn't know why, and this was bothering him. Seeing what life was like on the outside during the Morgan trial, had that subdued him? Was he in a depression?

But it wasn't only his mental state that was affected. For sometime now, long before the trial, his insides were all messed up. Walking didn't agitate him. He could walk all day. It was when sitting still that he felt worse, and was unable to explain beyond that.

The train went through and blew its whistle. His paper had arrived. He decided to take another canoe trip around the lake. He picked up the paper and would read it later. He took his fly rod and trolled a streamer that Ian had used. A warden's worry. It was actually late in the season to be fishing, but Parnell didn't know but he might pick something up trolling over a spring.

He paddled by the mouth to Howe Brook. He saw deer and moose, but no trout. He canoed all the way down to the old roll dam and nothing, not even a lake chub. On his way back, along the west shore, he circled a couple of times out in front of the ledge peninsula; nothing. He was beginning to wonder about the warden's worry streamer. He circled two times by Blackpoint and again, nothing. Nothing at the mouth of Tracy Brook.

He knew of only one more spring hole. That was about mid-way along Emerson Ridge. There, spring water ran on the top of the ground into the lake. There was always open water here in winter. Nothing on the first pass. He waited a few minutes, letting everything calm before paddling through again. This time he set out away from shore another ten feet and kept his paddle in the water. The streamer sunk out of sight in the dark water. Then, just as Parnell was about to bring the canoe around for another pass, the tip of his fly rod doubled over and touched the water.

He picked the rod up and set the hook. The trout jumped out of the water, clearing the surface with its tail, as he thrashed back and forth, trying to free itself. The belly of the brookie was a deep orange color. Parnell knew the meat would be a deep pink color. It wasn't an exceptionally large brook trout, maybe two pounds or better, but it would surely taste good with a boiled potato.

Parnell broke his fly rod down and laid it in the bottom of the canoe. He decided to canoe up Smith Brook as far as the trestle before turning back.

There was a family of mink swimming under the trestle. They were not deterred in the least by Parnell's sudden appearance. He sat and watched them disappear upstream.

Tears filled his eyes as he slowly passed Corriveau's camp. Stormi had sold the camp just before she died. He never met the new owners, maybe because they didn't keep it long before they sold it to someone from New York. And he had never met them either, or even seen anyone at the camp since John and Stormi left years ago.

The uneasiness inside of him was getting worse and he was glad when he got out and pulled the canoe ashore, back at the boat landing. As he walked towards his cabin, the uneasiness started to subside. But as soon as he sat down again in his chair the same feeling returned.

He ate his trout and boiled potato that night, but he wasn't hungry. He ate because he knew the fresh trout would be delicious cooked in salt pork fat. He ate it to satisfy his palate and taste buds. And it was delicious.

The restlessness was back and he was feeling a lot of discomfort on the inside. Just where, he wasn't certain. So, he went for a walk along the tracks toward St. Croix Siding. Darkness had already set in and he was still walking towards the siding.

About a mile before Beaver Brook, he found a new woods road that crossed the tracks towards the river. Only the right of way had been cut. "Probably a winter operation." He walked all the way to St. Croix Siding. The siding was no longer being used as a log yard and the scaler's camp was gone. All that remained now was a string of empty rail cars, parked on a sidetrack, that hadn't seen use in a while. The iron wheels were all coated with rust, as were the rails.

It was after midnight when he returned to his cabin. He turned the lantern out and lay on his bed without taking off his clothes first. He slept well until the southbound train went through and blew its whistle.

That morning, while enjoying a cup of coffee on the porch, he realized what he had to do. He washed up, put on his new casual clothes, put some money in his pocket and drove his Studebaker to the town office in Masardis.

"What can I do for you?" the clerk asked.

"I'd like to license my pickup, please."

"Is this a renewal or a first time registration?"

"New."

"What make and year?"

"It's a 1955 Studebaker."

"Oh my! I don't know if this registry will go back that far. I've never seen a Studebaker before. Oh yes, here it is. I'm surprised."

After many calculations, the clerk said, "That'll be forty dollars."

Parnell paid her in cash. "Thank you, ma'am."

He didn't want to be in Werner's court again for operating an unregistered vehicle. He drove to the medical center in Ashland to see Doctor Hatford.

"What can I do for you, Mr. Purchase?"

"Ah—it's Peasley. And it's a long story." Parnell tried to explain to Doctor Hatford how he felt, but he knew he was being anything but direct.

"Maybe we should start with a thorough physical. When was your last physical?"

"When I was in the Army, just before I resigned my commission. I was twenty-six then."

"Then I take it, you haven't had any vaccinations since leaving the Army?"

"No, I haven't."

"Have you ever been sick in all this time?"

"Sore throat, aching muscles. That's about all."

"Fascinating." Doctor Hatford listened to his heart and took his blood pressure. "There's nothing wrong with your cardiovascular system. I wish my heart was as strong as yours."

He checked his respiratory system and that too was excellent. He checked his spine for a misalignment. That too was fine. His vision was perfect. His joints were a little stiff. "Some arthritis, but nothing you need medication for yet."

He felt at Parnell's neck, "Any soreness?"

"No."

He put pressure on both shoulders, squeezing. "Any soreness?"

"No."

He felt under Parnell's arms and applied pressure. "Any soreness?"

"Yes, some."

Doctor Hatford went over Parnell's entire body, looking for signs of soreness. The last thing to check was his prostate. "That's sore, Doc."

"Your prostate has enlarged. This might be causing the discomfort when you sit. I'll need to draw some blood and I'll send it to the lab in Bangor to have your blood analyzed for PSA and your cholesterol levels. I need you to pee in this cup so I can have it analyzed for sugar."

"How soon will you know about the blood work?"

"You come back a week from today and I'll have your report."

"What exactly is PSA?"

"It's the amount of antigens in your blood. A level of five, for your age, could mean—could mean that you have signs of prostate cancer. These figures are not 100% accurate, but it is a good signal that perhaps a biopsy should be done.

"I really can't tell you anymore, Mr. Peasley, until we get

the results back from your lab work."

It was a long, lonesome ride back to his cabin. He needed something to do, so the next day Parnell began working on his winter supply of firewood.

As long as he kept himself busy, he was fine. But when he stopped for lunch or a break, his mind was back to thinking about what Doctor Hatford had said.

The next morning, Merle Yates showed up at the cabin and had two more beaver complaints. "These are both on the East Branch of Howe Brook. They're flooding the old road that follows up along side the brook. You can't miss the flowage. They're right in the road."

This was becoming a great summer time job. He was busy setting traps at least two or three days a week. He wasn't getting rich, but there was enough money for a grubstake through the winter. He set both conibear and leg hold traps. That evening, after supper, he decided to take a ride out and see. He took his rifle just in case.

At the first flowage there was a large beaver dragging more branches across the road. Parnell kept the motor running and the headlights on. From inside his Studebaker, he pulled his rifle to his shoulder and took a bead on the beaver's head and squeezed the trigger. "There. I'll have fresh beaver to eat now."

He checked the other traps and had one male beaver he had caught in a dam set. At the second flowage he had two small beaver in conibears. Still feeling that odd discomfort on the inside, Parnell skinned the beaver he had shot, after eating supper. He washed out the body cavity and then hung it up in his root cellar. Through the years, he had developed a real liking for fresh beaver meat.

He canned most of the beaver meat. The next day he fried one hind leg. It had a deep, rich flavor. It was a good substitute for venison. He threw the innards out back, along the back trail. There had been a mother fox around that summer.

Later that afternoon, as he sat on his porch, he happened to notice a bald eagle circling over the lake, looking for its evening meal. The bald eagle reminded him of Buster Morgan and he found himself wondering how he was faring in jail. Had he sought any psychological help? How many deer and moose had he shot before he was stopped? "Too many."

* * * *

The day Parnell was dreading had arrived. He put on his new casual clothes again and drove out to Ashland.

"Good morning, Parnell. How have you been feeling?"

"Living with anxiety."

"That's quite understandable." Doctor Hatford touched under each arm. Parnell flinched slightly. "More tender, huh?"

"A little."

"Any discomfort in your groin?" Then he pressed on the inside of each thigh.

"That's a little tender."

"That wasn't there last week. You can get dressed again." While Parnell dressed, Doctor Hatford removed the lab results sheet from Parnell's folder.

When he was finished dressing, he sat in a chair next to Hatford's desk.

Doctor Hatford cleared his throat several times before continuing. "Your lab results aren't good, Parnell. Your cholesterol and sugar are excellent, but your PSA is far too high. It is 8.5. I strongly recommend a biopsy as soon as possible, Parnell."

"What will the biopsy tell you?"

"The biopsy is taken from your prostate and examined under a microscope for malignant cancerous cells."

"Okay, what if the prostate is full of cancer?"

"If it is in the early stages of development then chemotherapy. In more advanced stages, as I'm sure yours is, then the only option is surgical removal."

"What else is there, Doc? I can tell you're keeping something from me."

"The combination of a high PSA, enlarged prostate, soreness under your arms and in your groin indicate cancer of the lymph nodes. This is also treatable with chemotherapy. But you need to get to a specialist as soon as possible."

"That all takes a lot of money, doesn't it, Doctor Hatford?"

"Yes, I'm afraid it will."

"How long do I have if I choose to do nothing?"

"These PSA readings are not conclusive in themselves, but the tenderness in your groin and armpits makes me believe cancer has already spread to your lymphatic system. I can't tell you how long, Parnell. I'm not a specialist. But the sooner you get to a specialist, the better your chances will be.

"There is no way for me to say how long you have, Parnell, without knowing how far advanced it is. If, indeed, you have cancer."

"Why cancer in the prostate? I haven't been sick in over thirty years."

"The prostate is a muscle, and like any other muscle, it needs to be exercised. The older men become, the less the prostate is used. Any muscle, unused, soon loses some of its vitality. It differs with different men. But sooner or later, almost all men will develop cancerous cells in the prostate."

"The only way I can afford to see any specialist would be through my V.A. benefits, if I can still get in at Togus."

"I wouldn't delay, Mr. Peasley."

Chapter 8

The drive back from Ashland was the longest ride Parnell had ever taken. So much was going through his mind. Should he go to Togus or should he say the heck with it? What if he had full-blown cancer now? Would he ever leave Togus? Would he never see Howe Brook again?

He tried to eat something, but he just didn't have the appetite. He ate a couple of mouthfuls and then set his plate aside. Instead, he poured a glass of brandy and sat on his porch, watching a September sunset. By midnight, he was exceedingly tired. The kerosene lantern was turned off and he went back to bed.

The morning was bright; birds were singing, probably getting ready for their flight south. The air was cool and dry. A perfect morning. And for an unknown reason, Parnell was feeling good, mentally. He had decided to make the trip to Togus and see a specialist and find out what they had to say about his condition. But before stopping at Togus, he would go see his mother in Boothbay Harbor. He would leave tomorrow.

Not wanting to leave his home a mess while he was away, he started cleaning. The dishes were done first and put away. Anything that might spoil before he returned was taken to the root cellar. Cobwebs were swept down and the floor swept. Anything that belonged outside was taken to the sheds. The books and magazines were straightened and what wouldn't fit in the bookshelf was piled neatly on the floor beside it. He even washed the windows.

He was excited about seeing his mother, brother and sister

after all these years. What changes would he see? He was genuinely excited about the trip.

There was plenty of firewood piled in the two sheds. At least he wouldn't have to worry about staying warm after he returned. The only question he had: would he be back in time for fall deer season? If not, he guessed it wouldn't hurt if he took another deer out of season, or perhaps a small moose.

By noontime he had everything picked up and put away, cleaned. He made a sandwich and washed it down with a glass of water. Then he poured himself a glass of brandy and sat on his porch. His favorite spot. He wasn't sure what had happened during the night to make him feel so carefree today. He had accepted the fact that he had cancer and he was certain the specialist at Togus could cure him of it. He wasn't worried. Not at all.

Then he remembered—he couldn't understand why—a partial dream he had had last night of John and Stormi Corriveau. Stormi was shouting at him to stop cursing. That's all he could recall.

Ian was driving up his driveway. "I wonder what he wants," Parnell said aloud.

He walked around the cabin to greet him.

"Hello, Ian. Where have you been since the trial?"

"Oh, I had some things, personal things, to take care of."

"What can I do for you today?"

"I came in to spend the afternoon with you. Just talking." Ian unbuckled his gun belt and put it in his car.

Parnell was speechless. "I was sitting on the porch. Would you like to join me?"

Before sitting down, Ian took his uniform shirt off and draped it on the back of his chair. He had just a t-shirt on, but it was a warm September day. "I could use a glass of your brandy, too. A tall glass."

Again, Parnell was speechless. He wasn't sure what Ian was up to, but he wouldn't rush him. Perhaps it was simply another game, but he doubted if that was what Ian had in mind.

Parnell sat down. "That was some trial. That defense lawyer was really beginning to get on my nerves."

"They always do that. If they can get you flustered then they hope you'll make a mistake. If you do, they'll call you a liar and question your entire testimony."

"That seemed like a stiff fine. I mean, three hundred and sixty days in jail, plus a fine?"

"Well, the fine could have gone as high as ten thousand dollars and a year in jail."

"Why didn't he go for a trial by jury? Instead of district court with a judge?"

"Well, shooting an eagle, the DA would have played on the jurors emotions and they would have definitely found him guilty. With only a judge to determine the case it can be fifty-fifty. In this case, the evidence was stacked against him and his lawyer knew it.

"I haven't talked with Merle Yates recently; how are you doing with trapping nuisance beaver?"

"It's a lot easier than winter trapping. No ice to cut and the water is warm. Only—I've learned not to crawl inside of a culvert to clear it of beaver dams." Parnell told Ian about his experience of being shot out the end of a culvert and how he had almost drowned.

"I used to do that, too. But now if I can't unplug a culvert with dynamite, the wood contractor has to."

"I met one of your fellow wardens while I was buying some of those new conibear traps at the hardware store in Ashland. The conibear works fine for nuisance beaver in the summer, but I'm not sure about using them this winter."

"Actually Parnell, the conibear is a lot easier to use than the leg hold trap; and it has already proven to be more productive. Most of the trappers are using them now. How's your hand?"

"I cut the cast off right after the trail. There's a twinge of pain sometimes, but Doctor Hatford said that would be expected."

"What did you think of that warden you met in Ashland, Dan Glidden?"

"Friendly enough sort of fellow. He knew his marrow about trapping."

"He's a tough nut, that one."

"How do you mean? He likes to fight?"

"Remember, two years ago, when I wasn't around here at all during deer season?"

"Yeah."

"Well, the first week of that season, I spent a day working with Dan in and around the Twenty-Mile Brook country. That's some big country, west of Ashland. We had had a good day. We had four loaded gun cases and two twilight hunting cases and we each had shot our limit of partridge. About seven that evening, we started driving out from Third Musquacook Lake and near Squirrel Pond, we encountered a large party of non-resident hunters from Fall River, Massachusetts, camping. They were a friendly lot, perhaps too friendly and that made me suspicious. While I was checking hunting licenses and firearms, I noticed Dan was in deep conversation with two of them.

"We didn't find anything wrong, or illegal, only suspicions, so we left and headed for Ashland. On the way back, Dan asked me if I had seen the telephone-pole-climbing gear that one of them had. I was too busy checking licenses and I hadn't noticed. When Dan asked them, one hunter said sarcastically, 'Oh, Joe likes to hunt high up in the trees.'

"Dan chewed on this a bit and after midnight, he drove back to Squirrel Pond. He concealed his pickup and walked through the woods to their campsite. He made one big mistake, though."

"What was that," Parnell asked.

"He forgot to take along any food or water."

"I don't understand," Parnell said, confused.

"Well, he laid there for three days and three nights, watching them."

"Does that remind you of anyone?" No answer.

"Dan discovered the real purpose of the pole-climbing gear when he observed them hanging two deer up into the tops of tall spruce trees. This of course sparked his attention. But he lay there another night and most of the next day and witnessed one of them trapping. Of course, he didn't have a trapping license. The other two had failed to attach their tags to their deer, and that's why the deer were hanging in the treetops.

"It took determination and perseverance to stay there without food or water. Not to say anything about cold nights."

"You two seem to be much alike when it comes to your job," Parnell commented.

"When you hauled Max Hartley off, did he give you any trouble?"

"Nope. I told him that if he started anything, I'd drop him." Ian began to laugh. "He was mad as all get out! He never did figure out who put those moose legs in his pickup. If he had had an ounce of intelligence though, he should have been able to figure it out. Maybe he did later and he was afraid of you."

"Well, he had it coming. Anybody who would steal another's income isn't worth the time of day."

"You know, Parnell, you should have become a game warden. You and I would have made an awesome team." They both laughed.

"Parnell, why did you prop that deer up in the field? The one Hoggan and Lawrence shot at."

"I didn't like them coming into the village and taking our deer. I figured, if I could take it out from under their nose and embarrass them, then maybe they'd stay out of the village. But damn it, I didn't know you would be there that night. I had just left the field when they shot. You almost caught me too. Only neither of us knew the other was there."

"Wished I had caught you. No offense, you understand. And nothing personal."

"I understand."

"Hoggan and Lawrence never figured it out who got

their deer and propped the head up. You should have seen the expression on their faces when they saw what they had shot." Ian started laughing. "That's what this job has all been about." He laughed some more.

"I want you to explain to me, in more detail than you did in court, about what really happened when I arrested you for that deer."

"John asked me if I wanted to go for a canoe ride around the lake. He wanted to show me the sights. I noticed he kept a watchful eye on shore. All the time, he was looking for you. We kept close to shore all the way around the lake and then we went up Tracy. He had the deer tucked away in the cool moss in a spring near that first little stream on the left. We loaded it into the canoe and he told me to head back to his camp. He'd be along shortly after he dragged another canoe out of the swamp. He had been there the day before and after shooting the deer, he was afraid you might have heard the shot, so he hiked home, circling across Smith Brook.

"He watched us until we were out of sight up the inlet. He waited until dusk, then he canoed home with a moose in his canoe. He knew then where you were and felt safe.

"I had fifteen days to think and spew about him setting me up. Only I didn't know why. I didn't know anything about the moose until later."

Parnell told him about walking up the tracks, after being released from jail, and how the idea of using fishing line and hook stuck in his bedroom window screen was spur of the moment. How he had made the awful sound three different times, "And each time ole John would start spewing and cussing and Stormi giving John hell for cussing.

"You know, that makes the most God awful sound, particularly at night, that you could imagine. Stormi got so upset with him for cussing that she sent him out of her bedroom. So he went out on the porch with his shotgun. This is when I went running through the alders screaming." They were both laughing and tears were streaking down Parnell's cheeks. "And—and he shot at me with that shotgun! I heard the shot going through the branches above my head.

"But the best part of that was Stormi kicking John out of her bed and bedroom. 'If you ever want to sleep in my bed again, John Henri, you'll have to repent. For a whole month, you'll have to go with me to church functions and no drinking with the boys!' That's what really hurt John."

"Did you ever tell him you were the screaming banshee?"

"No, I never had the heart to tell him. He and Stormi had become such good friends. I just couldn't do that to him."

"I pinched Stormi once. It was the year the village was taken down, in the spring. She and John were fishing up Tracy and I waited at the mouth of the brook for them to come out. John had just his limit. They each had their own creels. Stormi was determined that I check her license and fish. She had several short trout and I think it was eight trout over her limit.

"John acted genuinely surprised. He said, 'Stormi! After all these years and I discover I'm married to a poaching wife! If anyone is going to poach, it'll be me.' She was upset and afraid I'd tell people in the village. I had to promise that I wouldn't."

"You know, Ian, neither one ever said anything about that to me."

"I could never have proved it, but I'd bet my life John put some of his trout in her creel. He set her up."

"He may have had to get back at her when she made him attend church. I have really missed the ole reprobate and his schemes."

Ian started laughing then; and the tears were streaking down his cheeks. "He had nothing over on you, Parnell. You have played the game better than anyone I have ever known." They laughed some more.

"I always wanted to catch you, one more time. That confession in court doesn't count. It'll have to be some younger warden now, Parnell."

"What are you talking about, Ian? You sound as if you're conceding, giving up."

"I suppose, in a way, I am conceding. You see, after midnight tonight, I'll no longer be a game warden. I'm retiring. I've had thirty great years. Cost me two wives and two bank accounts. I met a nice woman a year ago, from New Brunswick. She's French and Indian. Beautiful and ten years younger than me. She has a twelve-year-old boy who loves the woods and fishing and he and I get along great. We're getting married shortly after— well, in two weeks.

"I don't want to lose this one and if I don't retire now, I surely will lose her. Playing the game, so to speak, has become an obsession with me."

"I'm happy for you, Ian. I'll miss you, but I'm happy for you. What is her name?"

"Maria Bechard. I'll bring her in so she can meet you. I have already told her all about you, so she wants to meet the person who gave the district attorney illegal deer meat." They both laughed again.

"You should find yourself a good woman, Parnell, to keep you company in here."

"I had one once. We were supposed to be married when I returned from Korea. When I got home, she had another. I sort of lost interest after that."

They were both silent then. Parnell filled their glasses with more brandy and offered Ian a cigar. "Thanks."

"You know not everyone knows my real name is Peasley? I'd like to keep Purchase. Sounds like it has character."

"I don't suppose there'd be any harm in it."

"I'm leaving tomorrow. I think it is time that I went to see my mother. She has probably read the articles in the newspaper about the trial."

"You are coming back, right?"

"Yeah, this is home now."

Then on another note, "Things have sure changed here.

Look at all the roads now. You can drive anywhere you want. And the companies, in my opinion, are taking too much, too fast.

"The other day, I talked with a mining engineer who works for Chevron Resources and he is prospect drilling on Howe Brook Mountain in T8-R3. He said he believes there is a large deposit of copper there. And if that isn't bad enough, Merle Yates was saying last week that he is piling down lumber here at Howe Brook to be slashed and shipped out by train."

"How's that any different, Parnell, from when the mill was operating?"

"None, I guess. It's just that I've become accustomed to being by myself here."

"You need to get out for a while, Parnell. You have shut yourself away from everything too long."

"Perhaps. I would like to eat a lobster. The meat is so sweet and delicious, almost as good as moose meat." They laughed some more.

"It won't be long before we have a legal moose hunt again. There is a coalition today, with petitions asking for a state referendum for a legal hunt. I think it'll happen. Maybe not this year, but certainly in a couple of years.

"I firmly believe we have too many moose as it is. Too many people are being injured in car-moose accidents. And the B&A train from Ashland to Millinocket, if truth be known, probably hits several every week."

"You have probably seen a lot of strange and funny things happen during your career as a warden."

"You know, I could write a book about what I have seen. Of course, I can't write so anyone can read it. My supervisor always marks me down in my annual efficiency evaluation. He says he can't ever read my reports. But honestly, there are a lot of stories there."

Then Ian got to laughing and tears were streaming down his cheeks and he almost upset his brandy glass. "I have to tell you this story. It's the God's honest truth. There was this big Native

American who lived in Oakfield and had a big family. He worked hard, but his family seldom had any extras. I had received several complaints of shots being heard about ten o'clock at night on Sam Drew Mountain. I knew immediately who it was and I also knew if I arrested him, he wouldn't have the money for any fine and his family would go hungry while he sat in jail.

"I thought about it for a couple of days, looking for some way to stop him without showing my hand. I bought red reflectors, that you see on bicycles, and I took the glass reflector off and put a tiny bulb inside and wired it to a battery and attached them to a stick with a switch down at the handle. I tested it one dark night and it was just what I needed.

"This guy liked to hunt dark, foggy nights, so I watched the weather reports and chose my night. I walked in from the other side of Sam Drew during the afternoon, while ole Jim was working. Then I waited. I ate lunch and had a cup of coffee while I sat under an apple tree along a path I knew Jim must be hunting. Sure enough, about 9:45 p.m., I heard him breathing heavy as he walked along the path. I didn't see him until he was about forty feet away. I crouched down behind the apple tree and held the stick out and switched the red eyes on." Ian started laughing again, and he had to pause to dry his eyes. "He took another couple of steps before he saw them. They must have looked quite menacing in the fog. He hollered and threw his rifle and ran back down the path, still hollering. After I stopped laughing, I turned my flashlight on so I could find his rifle. He had a .30-.30 Winchester and two shells.

"You know, for a man as big as Jim was, he could sure run. A week later, I stopped to see him one night, after supper. I gave him his rifle back and said I'd found it on Sam Drew Mountain. He had written his name on the stock, under the butt plate. He thanked me for returning it, but didn't say anything beyond that.

"The complaints stopped and I don't think he ever went out at night again. And he kept the story of those glowing eyes to himself."

"I guess seeing those red eyes glow in the fog like that, maybe I'd stop night hunting too. That must have been a terrible fright for him."

"Yeah, I think it was and I think, eventually, he figured it out, that it was me. He has never spoken to me since, even though, about once a year, I'd give him a road kill moose."

"You may make-out at times, Ian, how this is only a game to you, but you care about people. You didn't have to give Jim a moose every year. You do it because you care. How many other families are there that you make sure have meat?"

"I don't give it to the same ones all the time."

"No, you spread it around, trying to help as many people as you can. Why? Because you care."

Ian wanted to change the topic, to get away from the appraisals of his work, his character. "Have you heard of the Meneola Camps in T9-R4? They'd be north of Beaver Brook."

"Aren't those camps owned by someone from New York?"

"Yes. Did you ever hear the name Walter?"

"Wasn't he the camp watchdog, or boss?"

"That's the one. Did you ever meet Walter?"

"Can't say that I have."

"That's not surprising. Few people have. A few years ago, I was in that way, poking around. Actually, I was looking for a short cut to get into Griswold Siding, when I came across quite a network of elaborate trails. I spent all day walking those trails. And they all led back to the camp. Some had color markers. At the time, I didn't know what they meant, but they had a purpose.

"I went in again, during bird season. I circled around back—actually it was on a Sunday. I spotted two men clearing brush from one of the trails. I followed them back to the camp, staying back far enough so they wouldn't see me. There were six men there now. I was interested in the camps and asked a lot of questions. The answer I received most often was 'I don't know, you'll have to ask Walter.' 'Well, where is Walter?' I'd ask. They'd shrug their shoulders and say 'I don't know.'

"Well, you can just imagine how suspicious that made me. I was determined to meet Walter.

"Remember the fall, two years ago, when we had so much snow early in November?"

"Yeah."

"I got a call the first week of deer season that there was a lost hunter from the Meneola Camps. I hiked in. There was eight inches of new snow and the temperature was −2°F. Walter himself met me at the door. He really existed.

"Apparently, all of their hunting trails were color coded, depending upon degree of ability. George was the friend who was lost and he was a novice. Walter had given him strict orders not to hunt on any trails that were not coded blue. We had eliminated all the novice and intermediate trails, so we all took different advanced trails, looking for his track.

"I went along the South Branch of Blackwater Brook and started following a trail through quite a swampy area. I didn't find his tracks until I had crossed Blackwater and started up a hardwood slope. It was cold and I knew George would be cold. I followed his track for miles. They were not getting any fresher until I crossed the T10-R3 town line. My batteries were dying rapidly. I didn't have enough light to continue following his tracks, so I backtracked my own. The batteries were soon completely gone and I lost a heel on one boot.

"It was four in the morning by the time I got back to the Meneola Camp. We decided to wait for daylight before going out again. The wardens from Fort Fairfield and Caribou were called and they started driving the roads from Chapman. An hour after daylight, they had him. He walked over ten miles that night and he was supposed to have had a heart condition.

"When we had George back at camp, Walter's son had made a dog house out of cardboard and painted George's name on it. There was a six-foot leash attached to the doghouse. When Walter confronted George, he said, 'George, you were told to stay on the novice trails and to stay away from the advanced areas.' Then he asked for George's hunting license and ripped it into several pieces and gave it back to George and said, 'You're all done hunting for this trip. You won't even leave the porch.'

"Before leaving, Walter fed us a three course breakfast and invited me back for Thanksgiving dinner."

"Did you go?"

"Yes, and what a feed they put on!"

"You should come out and have Thanksgiving with Maria and me. This will be the first Thanksgiving that I haven't worked."

"I'd like to. I'll plan on it then. What are you going to do after you retire, tomorrow?"

"I'm going to stay home and finish some projects that I never had time to finish before. Maria is a nurse at the hospital in Houlton and I'm going to have her supper ready for her every evening. I'll take her son fishing and teach him to hunt and trap and how to think like an animal. I'm going to do all the things I haven't taken the time to do for the last thirty years."

They talked and sipped brandy all afternoon. Parnell had forgotten, for the moment, about his cancer and about leaving Howe Brook tomorrow to see his family. That afternoon, his family was right there in his cabin.

"If only John could see us today, Ian. I think he'd disown me."

"I'm not so inclined to agree. After he and Stormi moved out, I stopped twice to see how they were getting along. He and I talked like you and I have this afternoon. They both really missed the village, but I understood Stormi's reluctance to stay."

"There's something, Parnell, that I just have to ask."

"Okay, what's up?"

"During Morgan's trial, when the DA asked what happened to the two legs and you said that he had eaten the last steak…he never asked you to explain and the defense left it alone. Now, tell me the rest of the story."

"It was the day that your supervisor, Charles Vernon, and

the DA came in to talk with me about what I knew about who put the deer head and eagle in Morgan's pickup. I had already admitted that I had put them in his pickup and I didn't fully trust the DA. He seemed too slippery for my satisfaction. I figured, if he ate some of the meat while he was here—well, I was hedging the probability of being charged later. But it didn't work, did it?" They laughed.

"No, you actually proved there was a corpse. The judge had no choice then, than to do what he did. My only regret was that I didn't catch you fair and square. That would have been a grand way to go out on retirement."

Ian stood and stretched and took his empty glass back inside and put it in the sink. Then he put his shirt and gun belt on. He turned to look at Parnell. There was sadness in his eyes and in Parnell's.

Neither one knew what to say next. They stood there for a moment, just looking at each other. Finally, Ian reached out with his right hand to shake Parnell's hand. "It's been fun, Parnell." Then he walked outside and got in his car and drove home.

* * * *

Parnell had a sandwich and a tall glass of water for supper. Then he poured himself a tall, tall glass of brandy, lit a cigar and sat on his porch to watch his last sunset for a while. He was anxious to see his family, but he wanted to be back here for Thanksgiving.

There was a smile on his face as he heard the echo in his head when Ian called him 'friend.' That afternoon had been the most enjoyable time that he could remember, since the village left Howe Brook.

"John's gone and now Ian's gone. Damn, I lost my playmate."

Chapter 9

In the dark, Parnell walked down to the shore of the lake. He stood there, looking and listening. He lit his last cigar. Several loons had gathered just off shore in front of him. They were curious as they watched him, almost as if they knew he was leaving. The biggest loon swam towards Parnell, not at all afraid. It stopped about five feet away and looked directly at Parnell and made a very low squall, just barely audible to Parnell. Then the loon turned and joined the others and the group quietly swam off.

Parnell sat on his overturned canoe. The moon was just up over the horizon. He said aloud, "It's hard to believe how I ever found so much happiness living here alone, Mr. Purchase."

He put his cigar out and lifted his canoe over his shoulders and walked back to his cabin. He locked it in the shed with his Studebaker pickup truck. He locked the shed door and the wood shed. The keys he put on the table inside, along with the magnetic key for the root cellar.

He looked at the wall clock, 2:00 a.m. He went to bed and slept surprisingly well. He awoke when Ansel Snow blew the whistle of the southbound train. He got up, cleaned up and packed his pack basket with his good clothes.

For breakfast he had bread and cheese and washed it down with black coffee. He made sure that there were no dirty dishes or food left inside. He put his rifle in the rack and made sure it was empty.

Through the years, he had acquired quite a bankroll. He now counted out the amount he had saved from his years of trapping. "I'm a rich man. I have twenty-one thousand, four hundred dollars." He rolled the bills up and stuffed the roll in his pocket. He pulled the curtains over each window and emptied the water bucket. He shouldered his pack and closed and locked the door.

He walked down to the tracks, never looking back at his home. As he walked the tracks, he passed where each building had been when the village was still there. He saw each building in his mind. He cried as he walked by Corriveau's camp. Still, he didn't look back.

He paused for a moment on the trestle across Smith Brook and looked downstream. He paused again at Weeksboro Siding, trying to find the fireplace where Ian had built a fire the night they had slept there.

Every step along the eighteen miles to Smyrna Mills held fond memories. At Shorey Siding, he had to stop and rest. His legs were lame and his back hurt. He ate some cheese and bread and drank some water. He had to stop and rest two more times before he got to Dudley Siding. "I must be getting old. There was a time when I'd walk this without stopping."

From Dudley Siding, on to Smyrna Mills, Parnell had to stop and rest more frequently. He began to wonder if he could make it without sleeping out that night. He ate the last of his cheese and bread and drank some more water.

He was below White Lake. He knew he would make it now. There was truck traffic ahead; lights. He breathed a sigh of relief. Nine hours later, he walked into Whitey's Market. He would board a Cyr bus for Boothbay Harbor.

The woman at the counter asked, "Good evening, can I help you?"

"Yes. Can I take the bus from here to Boothbay Harbor?"

"You sure can. You'll change buses in Augusta."

"One, one-way ticket please."

"You aren't coming back, Mr. Purchase?"

"I'm going to visit my family. I don't know how long I'll be

255

there. I do have to be back for Thanksgiving, though. How did you know who I am?"

"Everybody knows who you are now, Mr. Purchase, since the Morgan Trial. Your picture was in every newspaper in the state."

"Do you have someplace I could sit down, please? That walk from Howe Brook really tired me out."

"You walked from Howe Brook?" Linda asked.

"Yes, I've walked it many times through the years. Only it had never taken me so long as it did today."

"Follow me, Mr. Purchase. You can wait in my office. The chair isn't much, but at least you can sit down. By the way, I'm Linda White."

"Pleased to meet you, ma'am. I guess you already know who I am."

"Did you really feed the DA illegal deer meat?" she asked.

"It seemed a good thing to do at the time. But it ended up costing me a hundred dollars."

"And all those stories in the newspaper about you seeding evidence for Ian to find—are those stories true?"

"Yeah."

"And you stuck up that deer head after you had taken the hind legs—that's true also? You actually did that?"

"Guilty."

"How did you shoot the deer without the warden hearing your shot, but he heard the other fella's?"

"I didn't shoot it. I caught it in a snare." She started laughing. Parnell smiled.

"What's the big road just beyond here?"

"Oh, you mean I-95?"

"You mean the turnpike comes up here now?"

Linda started laughing again. "Excuse me for laughing. Only people from the southern part of the state call I-95 a turnpike. Around here, we simply call it 95, or the Interstate. It runs to the New Brunswick border in Houlton."

"So, it's actually Interstate 95?"

"Yes."

"I'm afraid there is a lot of changes to see."

"Would you like some coffee and something to eat?"

"Oh, that would be fine."

"I'll take a roast beef sandwich out of the freezer and pop it in the microwave."

"In the what?"

"A microwave oven. Come with me and I'll show you." Linda took his hand and held it as they walked back into the store. She took a sandwich out of the freezer and showed it to Parnell, and then she put it in the microwave oven and turned it on. In two minutes, she removed it. It was steaming hot.

"Well, I'll be to go to hell." He put his hand inside the microwave oven. "There isn't any heat. How did it get so hot?"

"Radio waves, vibrating at high frequency causes the food to heat up and cook."

"I wouldn't have believed it, if I hadn't seen it with my own eyes."

Linda took Parnell back to her office and she went after a cup of coffee. "Here, I didn't know what you have in it."

"Black is fine."

"My mother's maiden name was Howe."

"Any connection to Howe Brook?" Parnell asked.

"Her grandfather was a trapper in that country years ago. We never knew if Howe Brook was named after him or not."

"What's your maiden name?"

"Friel."

"Your family owns the mill in Smyrna Mills?"

"My father, Vinal, and his brothers."

"And Friel woods camp at Frost and Adams Ridge?"

"The same."

"Looks as if you made it out just in time. It's raining now."

Suddenly, Parnell was feeling very tired. He wanted to stretch out and sleep, but that would have to wait until he was on the bus. Linda noticed how tired he was becoming, too. "Why don't you wait for the bus right here, Mr. Purchase? I should get back to work. I'll come get you when your bus arrives."

"Thank you." He sat back in the chair and soon his chin was resting comfortably on his chest.

At 8:00 p.m., the bus for Augusta arrived and Linda awoke Parnell. "Mr. Purchase, your bus is here. You can board now."

"Oh, thank you." She walked with him to the bus and carried his pack basket for him.

"You have a good trip, Mr. Purchase. And come back."

"Thank you again. I hope to be back before Thanksgiving." He found an empty seat and sat next to a window and put his pack in the aisle seat. Then he went to sleep.

* * * *

There were many stops along the way, and Parnell slept through them all. And no one moved his pack or disturbed him. The bus finally came to a stop at the Augusta terminal at 12:45 a.m. Parnell changed buses to a Coastal Transit bus. There were stops at Gardiner and Wiscasset only, before arriving at the terminal in Boothbay Harbor.

He couldn't just knock on his mother's front door in the middle of the night, so he found a comfortable chair, at the terminal and waited for morning. He was soon asleep.

The bus terminal came alive with morning commuters at 5:30 a.m., and Parnell soon found himself in a throng of busy people. No one paid any particular attention to him; even dressed as he was with a pack basket for a suitcase. He was hungry and found a lunch counter at the opposite end of the terminal. He ordered eggs and bacon, and a pancake with real maple syrup.

He still had one thing to do before going to see his mother. Outside of the terminal, he hailed a taxi. "Where to, old timer?" a young, fresh guy inquired.

"The nearest barber shop, please." The town had grown and changed too much, he didn't recognize anything. At the barbershop, Parnell asked, "Will you wait for me, while I get a cut and shave?"

"Sure, but it'll cost you while I wait."

"Without a doubt," Parnell replied.

With a close haircut and the beard gone, Parnell looked at himself in the mirror and this time he saw Parnell Peasley. He paid the barber and gave the taxi driver the address to his mother's house. Even here, nothing looked familiar. The trees were taller, the streets were wider, and the houses were painted with brighter colored paint, not the drab colors he remembered.

The taxi stopped at last in front of his mother's house. He paid the driver and just sat there a minute, wondering if he should drive on or finish the trip. "Well mister, you going to get out, or not?"

That made up his mind for him and he opened the door and stepped out. His mother was standing in the front window, watching as her son walked up the driveway. It was an awkward few moments, as his mother came outside and they stood, face to face. Then all the old hurt feelings left and they hugged and Parnell kissed his mother's forehead.

Mrs. Peasley was crying. She had thought Parnell was dead somewhere, until she had read about the Morgan Trial in the newspaper. But still there wasn't any way she could contact him. She had to wait, and now, here he was. She noticed a huge change in Parnell. Not so much his outer appearances, but he commanded an inner peace and a quiet sort of self-assurance. She could better understand now, all the articles she had read in the newspapers, about what he had confessed to doing.

While Parnell took a shower, the first he had had since he boarded the train in Bangor for Howe Brook Village, Mrs. Peasley called her daughter and Parnell's brother, Richard. Becky was especially happy to see her brother. Richard wasn't as friendly, but he kept their meeting cordial.

At the supper table that evening, Parnell announced to his entire family, "Tomorrow, I have to go to Togus, to the VA

Hospital. Doctor Hatford in Ashland says I have a cancer and that I should see a cancer specialist as soon as possible." To change the subject, he said, "This weekend, I want to have a family get together and a lobster and clam bake. It'll be my treat. Richard, do you know where you can buy some good clams and lobsters?"

"I'll take care of it, and I'll help chip in also."

"Thanks, Richard, but that won't be necessary. Besides, I'm tired of eating moose and deer meat for nearly thirty years." Everyone laughed.

Mrs. Peasley also noticed how easily Parnell commanded authority now and delegated to others. Oh, how she had missed her eldest son.

* * * *

In the morning, Parnell took the bus to Augusta and then hired a taxi to take him to the VA Hospital at Togus.

Much to Parnell's surprise, Doctor Hatford had already called ahead and advised Doctor Schmidt that Parnell would be coming to see him and all the admission forms had been filled out in advance. All Parnell had to do was sign them.

"Doctor Hatford has forwarded your medical history, Parnell. I need to draw some blood and have a complete urinalysis done. While the lab does that, I'll give you a thorough examination.

"Since your last visit with Doctor Hatford, have you noticed any more soreness that you have had? Do you get more tired easier?"

"My groin is more tender as are my armpits and there's something in the middle of my back. It feels like I've been kicked and I was exhausted when I walked out of Howe Brook. I didn't know if I would be able to make it."

"How far was the walk?"

"Eighteen miles."

"Well, no wonder you were tired. How long did it take you?"

"I was over nine hours walking. It usually only took me about six hours."

Doctor Schmidt looked at Parnell's back. There was quite a noticeable lump on his spine, midway on his back. "I'll do a biopsy of this, your groin area and each armpit. The lab will work up the samples during the night and we'll have the results in the morning. I would like you to stay in the hospital overnight, Mr. Peasley, so we can work up another PSA culture, first thing in the morning. Then you can have breakfast."

Doctor Schmidt had never been one to mince words. He believed his patients deserved to be told the truth as soon as he knew it. "Mr. Peasley, from my observations, I would surmise that you have had prostate cancer for some time and it has spread from your prostate, to your lymphatic system. There are lymph nodes in the groin area, armpits, throat, back, intestines and many other areas. The soreness you are experiencing is because these lymph nodes are now cancerous and that lump on your back is a tumor.

"We'll know more tomorrow morning, when we have the lab results back. I'm sorry to have to tell you this, Mr. Peasley, but I believe I should be direct with you."

"Thank you, Doctor Schmidt, I appreciate that."

"Just relax, I'll get my assistant and we can do the biopsies."

* * * *

Doctor Schmidt had finally finished sticking him with needles. The only procedure that was at all painful was the eight different needles stuck into his prostate.

"What type of therapy will you recommend?"

"That'll all depend with the lab results. We will talk about that tomorrow.

"Once you have a room, you are free to go anywhere on the VA grounds. I would rather, for right now, that you don't go beyond the grounds. There is an excellent restaurant downstairs and you can have anything you like. Oh, one more point, Mr.

Peasley, no more eighteen mile hikes."

"Okay, Doc, tomorrow then."

One of Doctor Schmidt's clerical assistants was assigned to assist Parnell during his stay at the hospital. "Mr. Peasley, my name is Daloy. I'll be your guide and assist you with anything that you might require. Right now, I'll show you to your room."

Daloy escorted Parnell down the length of a long corridor to a corner room with two windows. "Would it be okay if I opened these?" Parnell asked.

"If you want. Maybe you'd like to lie down and rest for a while, Mr. Peasley, before we explore anymore?" she asked.

"Please, call me Parnell. For a long time, my name was Purchase and frankly, I'm having a difficult time getting used to Peasley again." Then he had to explain why the change and how it had accidentally happened.

"Okay, Parnell. I'll be back in one hour."

"Okay." Daloy left, but she didn't close his door. From past experiences with other patients who were waiting on bad news, she knew that closed doors could signal finality, a final closure.

Parnell stretched out on the bed. It was more comfortable than his. He refused to think about his problem. There would be time for that, but not right now. He wasn't sleepy, but the bed was sure comfortable. He rolled over onto his side so he could see the outside.

He was still watching outside when Daloy returned an hour later. When she touched his shoulder, he jumped. "Oh, I didn't hear you come in."

"Were you sleeping, Parnell?"

"No, just daydreaming."

"Are you ready for lunch and to do some exploring?"

"Yes, I'm hungry and Doctor Schmidt said I could eat anything I wanted."

They took the elevator downstairs. Parnell had long forgotten about elevators. The restaurant was huge and only a few people were seated. Parnell checked the menu. "Good, they serve lobster. I grew up in a fishing village and I haven't tasted lobster meat for nearly thirty years now. Would you like lobster too, Daloy?"

"Oh, I can't afford that," she said.

Parnell said, "No problem. This is my treat. It isn't everyday that I get to have lunch with such a pleasurable young lady."

"Okay," and she smiled a million dollar smile at Parnell.

"How would you like those cooked, sir?" the waitress asked.

"Broiled and basted with butter."

* * * *

When lunch was finished, Daloy walked with Parnell, window-shopping along the basement walkway. There were many shops and hair salons and one in particular that caught Parnell's attention: a legal affairs office. "I need to go in here, Daloy."

"Okay, I'll be back in a little bit to see how you are doing."

She returned and Parnell was waiting in the lobby for her. "You ready this soon?"

"Yeah, let's go for a walk. All these people are starting to wear on my nerves."

The grounds outside were like a park. There were many trails to walk, and every so often, park benches to sit and rest. The sky was blue, with only a few clouds left. There was a cool breeze coming from the north. *The surface of St. Croix Lake would be rough with a north breeze,* he was thinking. There were other patients out for a stroll, some in wheelchairs.

"I take it there aren't any wild animals running loose around here?"

"Not by design, but occasionally, there will be a moose saunter through. Last fall we even had a bear."

They strolled along a trail that took them around the perimeter of the complex. It had been a nice walk, but now Parnell was tired and he needed to lie down for a while. "I have to leave now, Parnell. You'll be served dinner in here tonight."

Before she left, Daloy showed Parnell how to use the remote control, so he could watch television.

"Wow, there sure have been a lot of technology changes."

"Yes, Parnell, there have." They both laughed.

After eating supper, Parnell wanted to go for a walk around the grounds again, but he wasn't sure if he was feeling up to it. He knew what the problem was and refused to think about it. Instead, he turned the TV on and flicked through the channels until he found a movie: *North to Alaska*, starring John Wayne. He had only ever seen one other John Wayne picture and he liked the actor.

The movie was good, except he couldn't understand why it was so cluttered with commercials. The next movie was a western, again starring John Wayne. He undressed and got into bed and hoped the movie would put him to sleep.

The western came to an end at midnight and Parnell was still very much awake. He didn't know if he could take another John Wayne movie, so he dressed and went outside for fresh air. He was feeling better than he had after supper. So, he decided to go for a short walk. The moon was only half full, but he had prowled in the dark before. The air was warm and crickets chirped everywhere, and there were literally thousands of lightening bugs. He found a grove of pine trees atop a slight knoll. There was a park bench there, but Parnell preferred the soft blanket of pine needles on the ground. He sat with his back against a huge pine tree and listened to the city sounds in the distance. The fresh air and the scent of the pine trees made him sleepy. He yawned and stretched out on the ground, in a natural indentation.

* * * *

The next morning, a big truck blowing its air horn, out on Route 17, awakened Parnell. He awoke thinking Ansel had just delivered his newspaper and had blown the whistle of the southbound train. He opened his eyes thinking he was home, at Howe Brook.

Daloy met him as he was walking through the side entrance. "Oh, Mr. Peasley, you had us all worried. We didn't know if something had happened to you, or if you decided to leave. Where have you been?"

"I couldn't sleep inside last night, so I went out under the pine trees."

"More like home, Parnell?"

"A little."

Parnell went back to his room to shower and shave. After breakfast, Daloy walked with him to Doctor Schmidt's office. "I'll be right here, Parnell, when you have finished."

"Thank you, Daloy."

"Come in, Mr. Peasley, sit down."

"I can hear it in your voice, Doctor. It isn't good is it?"

"No, I'm afraid not. A week ago, your PSA level was 8.5. A week later it has increased to 10. All of the biopsy results indicate advanced cancer, and growing very rapidly."

"Now what? Do we treat it or cut it out?"

"I could surgically remove the tumor on your spine, remove your prostate and cut away the cancerous cells in your legs and armpits, then put you through radiation treatments and chemotherapy; but all that is going to do is prolong the inevitable, for only a short time.

"Personally, I don't think you would survive all the operations, considering how much tissue we would have to remove. If you did survive, then you would still have to endure the radiation and chemo treatments.

"I take no pleasure with telling you this, Mr. Peasley, but if I were you, I would get my things in order and make the best of the time I had left."

"How much time, Doc, if I do nothing?"

"Two months, at most."

"I don't want to die here, Doctor Schmidt. I'll die in my cabin at Howe Brook."

"I can understand how you are feeling, Mr. Peasley. There'll come a time when you'll have to come back here. The pain and discomfort will become too severe and then we'll have to administer morphine intravenously.

"I don't paint a pretty picture, I know, Mr. Peasley. But I believe I should be honest with you."

"What do I do between now and when you have to administer morphine intravenously?"

"I'll give you several prescriptions. One will be for morphine to be taken for severe pain."

* * * *

Parnell took the bus back to Boothbay Harbor. How he hated the idea of dying here and not in his own home, but he understood what Doctor Schmidt was saying about the pain towards the end.

Before going right to his mother's house, he stopped first at the savings bank where he had deposited twenty-seven hundred dollars, twenty-eight years ago. "Yes, Mr. Peasley, we were wondering if you would ever come in. Your account has certainly increased. A total of seven thousand, one hundred, eighty-three dollars and seventy-six cents."

"Thank you."

* * * *

That evening, after supper, when Parnell was alone with his mother, he gave her twenty-five thousand dollars, all in cash. "It's okay, Mom. This is all the money I have saved from trapping. I won't have any more use for it."

Then he told his mom that he had only two months to live.

Chapter 10

Ian left Parnell sitting on his porch and drove home. There was a tightness in his throat; knowing someone like Parnell had made the thirty years mean something. But as he drove, he was troubled by the thought of giving up the game. But, if he didn't, his marriage to Maria wouldn't last any longer than his other marriages.

After supper, he telephoned Maria and then he poured himself a brandy and sat out on his porch. Twilight was waning and in the distance, towards the east, he could just make out the sound of the southbound train as the engines backed off, powering down as it approached the downgrade at Shorey Siding.

He went to bed and woke up at exactly midnight. The thought went through his mind, *I'm no longer a game warden.* He lay awake all the rest of that awful night. *Have I made a mistake?* Even if he had made a mistake, there was no turning back now. He had signed his retirement papers, making his decision official. He was now and forever, Ian Randall.

* * * *

A week following his retirement, he and Maria were married, at his house. Maria and her son, Eric, had already moved in. For their honeymoon, Maria wanted to take him back to visit her parents in Kedgwich, New Brunswick. They spent several days with her folks. She was excited about showing Ian where she had grown up.

When they left her folks, they toured New Brunswick and Nova Scotia. Many times while on their trip, Ian would suddenly find himself thinking about Parnell and his sense of justice. He enjoyed telling Maria about him. "I asked him to have Thanksgiving dinner with us. I hope that's alright?"

Ian took his new stepson bird hunting, and they both really enjoyed each other's company. Eric—he worshipped Ian. All the kids at school talked about the ex-game warden. And most had stories to tell about when Ian had their dad for one thing or another. Eric wanted to grow up to be just like his step-dad. Ian loved the attention Eric was giving him. Maybe retirement wasn't going to be so bad after all.

Ian and Eric stopped one day to see Parnell, but his cabin was locked and the curtains were drawn. "Maybe he is still visiting his family in Boothbay Harbor."

Trapping season had come and Ian taught Eric how to trap and how not to get his fingers caught between the jaws. The price for fur had dropped, but Ian still enjoyed teaching Eric.

As much as Ian enjoyed Maria and Eric's company, there were times when he truly missed being out there, prowling the woods, chasing poachers. His new wife and stepson had become his crutch towards a new life. Without them, he would soon have become depressed.

The first morning of the open deer season, Ian took Eric hunting along East Hasting Brook, where he had fallen into the crevasse and had broken his leg. They saw tails, but nothing to shoot at.

At noon, Maria had just finished making lunch when a FedEx van drove into the driveway. "Ian, there's a FedEx delivery van out here." Ian came upstairs from the basement and met the driver at the door. The driver was holding a small package.

"Are you Ian Randall?" the driver asked.

"Yes, I'm Ian."

"I have a special delivery for you. Would you sign this delivery conformation, please?" The driver handed Ian the clipboard and pointed to a 'X.' "Here."

"Thank you." The driver handed Ian the package and left.

"What is it, Ian? Did you order something?"

"No, I can't remember ordering anything."

"Who is it from?"

"The delivery confirmation says 'Legal Affairs Veteran's Administration, Togus, Maine.'"

"Are you a veteran, Ian?"

"No."

"I wonder what they want with you. Are you going to open it, or just stare at it?" Maria asked.

Ian opened the package and removed a very pretty blue urn. The lid was taped closed. Still, Ian had no idea what he was holding. Maria removed the sealed envelope from the box. "Maybe this will explain, Ian." She gave him the envelope and she held the urn.

He opened the sealed envelope and removed another official looking envelope. On the outside, in bold lettering: 'The Last Will and Testament of Parnell Purchase.'

Ian started to cry and laugh at the same time. He said, "Took that name to the grave with him." Maria didn't understand what Ian had said, but from the sadness on his face, she decided not to ask just yet.

Ian opened the envelope and unfolded the pages contained therein:

Dear Ian,

If you are reading this letter then you must know that I have died. The doctor at Togus discovered I had cancer throughout my body. Too advanced to do anything about it. I am happy that I came to see my family and say hello and goodbye to my mother. There is no reason to feel sorry for me or sad. I have lived a good life. I lived it according to my needs not someone else's. My only regret in life is when the village left Howe Brook. A part of me died then also. The urn you now hold contains my ashes. I have only this one last request. That you put my ashes in the water at the mouth of Tracy Brook. This is where I placed John's ashes when he died.

I hope you are enjoying your retirement and your new life with Maria. If you give her as much attention as you did poachers, you two will have a long and happy life together.

As the end was coming near, I had a visit from John Corriveau. He was looking young and strong. He said that when I was ready, he knew where we could find a nice young moose (huh, huh). This may have only been a dream but at the time I thought he was here with me in this room.

As you read this we are probably together again and enjoying a feed of moose meat.

You and John were the best friends I ever had. John gave me the cabin on the knoll after I was released from jail. I think he felt really bad about the trick he played on me. Maybe now I can tell him about the banshee.

Getting back to the cabin Ian. It is yours and everything in all the buildings. The key should accompany this letter. There is still plenty of food in the root cellar. No fresh meat; the DA ate the last of that. There are several canning jars filled with different kinds of meat. I won't tell you what they are, you'll have to figure that out for yourself. But don't go telling anybody what they are. I wouldn't want people thinking that I left my cabin to a poacher.

When you arrested me twenty-eight years ago for the deer in my canoe, I instantly liked you. The manner in which you conducted your authority. If I showed any anger, it was not directed towards you. From that encounter with you and throughout my existence at Howe Brook I have nurtured a growing admiration and respect for you and call you friend.

Words are coming hard for me now and my eyes are clouding with tears.

It has –been a Great Game.

Your friend,
Parnell Purchase

About the Author

Mr. Probert retired from the Maine Warden Service in 1997 and began to write historical novels about the history in the areas where he patrolled as a game warden, with his own experiences as a game warden as those of the wardens in his books.

When you work at something that you enjoy, then it never becomes just a job. For Probert, it was more fun than playing baseball. But that doesn't mean that everything was easy because it certainly was not—like having to summons a friend to court or having to pull a friend's daughter's lifeless body into a boat.

Mr. Probert now has twenty-five books in print and the *Whiskey Jack* series is his favorite series, but *Ekani's Journey* is the single favorite.